The Adventures of Watts and Sherlock

The R.X. Problem
Of Jackals and Crusaders

Sherlock Returns

Sherlock Returns

–The Adventures of Watts and Sherlock–
Book Three

By Katie Magnusson

Chapters

The Murder of Adrian Rolands

Sixteen months ago, my best friend tackled Miriam Sangrave through a top story window. Everything he owned was left to me. I wanted it to be a hoax, for him to have faked his death somehow, but I couldn't make myself believe it. I wanted to hope he would come back, but the sight of him going through the window was burned into my mind.

I did what I've always done, and kept myself busy. Ghost still lived above me, in the attic. I wasn't going to kick her out, and to be honest I liked knowing there was someone else around, even if I hardly ever saw her. I visited the Irregulars from time to time, checking in to make sure they were doing ok and occasionally patching them up or supplying basic medicines as autumn and winter set in.

Winter is a busy season for rogue medics. Frostbite is just as unpleasant now as ever, there's a new flu virus every month, and we still don't have a cure for the common cold. Half the time I end up prescribing holistic 'home remedies' rather than meds.

As spring came around, my workload lightened, and I started trying to get back into some semblance of a social life. It didn't work very well. Most of my free time was spent reading medical journals and trying to get Ghost to eat something. She's worse than Sherlock, which is frightening.

One day, I opened the door to Sherlock's bedroom for

the first time since he'd died. I knew I'd been putting it off for far too long. There was a layer of dust on everything. What had started as an attempt to clean out memories turned into an exploration of the man I knew so well, but knew so little about. The small tobacco patch set up by his window had died, though I discovered a small room accessible through his closet that had bunches of tobacco leaves hanging in it. The closet itself held clothes of a wide variety of styles, along with his collection of suits, most black, a few greys, navy, and one white. The collection of vests was more colorful, with reds, oranges, greens, and even a purple.

All his other clothes were kept in the dresser, and the chest at the foot of his narrow bed held his disguise kits and props. An empty teacup sat in its saucer on the small table by the bedside, left there forgotten in the thrill of a case. The top of the dresser held his cuff links, pocket-watch, comb and brush, an inkwell and two fountain pens, and a small case holding a straight razor.

I was marveling at how anyone could shave with an oddly shaped knife when I noticed his violin tucked safely away in the corner of the room. Strains of strange music flew through my memory as I opened the case. I lightly ran my fingers along the varnished wood, and shivered.

Slowly, I closed the case and left the room, closing the door behind me. I went out that night, got utterly wasted, and woke up with a splitting headache in a hotel room I didn't remember checking into.

Nights out were approached with much more caution after that. I went out regularly, back into my old routine of 'work hard, play hard.' If I kept myself busy, I didn't have to think about the dull ache I felt whenever I was home. If I could stay away, I wouldn't have to clean out that damn bedroom. I could keep putting it off to when I had some time at home, and then just keep never being home.

It was ridiculous, of course. I knew it was, I knew it was irrational and harmful, that I was just causing myself more grief by not facing it. But then, I've never been very good at dealing with grief. He once joked he'd let me know within a year if he faked his death. I'd been hoping, somewhere deep in me, that he'd been serious, that maybe... well. As the weather turned cold again, I finally stopped hoping, and started packing.

It took a while. One day, Ghost came down and started to help me as I packed his things into boxes. I was thankful for the help, though a bit embarrassed. The boxes remained in his room, to Ghost's unspoken disapproval. It wasn't as if I was using the room, so there was no point in renting storage. She liked her set up in the attic, I wasn't going to ruin it with a bunch of boxes, and I wasn't ready to sell anything. I got it put away. That was good enough for now.

Work picked back up with the winter season. I had plenty of patients to occupy my time, and I was finally getting on with life, or so I thought. Ghost informed me I was wrong.

"You should get out more."

I glanced up at her as I hung up my coat and hat. She'd just come down from the attic as I'd come home from making my rounds. "That's funny coming from you."

"I go out. I just don't leave my room."

"Exactly."

She crossed her arms, sweatshirt baggy on her thin frame, "Doc, I've been to clubs that you would swear up, down and backwards are just as real as anything 'real.' You work, drink, and maybe sleep with the person drinking next to you. At least my social life involves learning names."

I glared at her. "Names like Ghost?"

She rolled her eyes, "It's been over a year, *Watts.* You've got a room full of boxed up memories you won't ever get rid of until you make a damn friend."

"Please, tell me how I need to just move on," I fumed, "it's not like I heard that every single time someone in my family died. 'Give it time,' 'you'll adjust,' and every other sentimental line people who don't know what to say rattle off just to save themselves the discomfort of saying nothing. I'm aware of what I'm *supposed* to do. I don't give a damn."

Ghost looked at me a long moment, and swore. She sat down where she stood. "Dammit, Doc. I'm trying to help."

"I know," I sighed. "I know. I thought he'd come back, or at least let me know he was alive…" I cleared my throat, banishing its tightness with practiced ease, "I'll make you a deal. I'll go out tonight if you come with me and eat something."

"What does me eating have to do with anything?"

"You're slowly killing yourself, that's what. Virtual clubs don't serve food, and you hardly ever eat what I cook. You survive on nutrient-packs and the minimum amount of water required to live."

"Don't worry about me."

"It's my job."

She frowned, but shrugged. "Sure. Why not?"

We found a quiet place on the edge of the Corporate Sector. It was done up in retro 'diner' feel, with a small dance floor added. After the first couple drinks I managed to stop glancing at my silent phone, and after the first several bites Ghost seemed to be enjoying her food.

"How long had you lived together?" she asked out of the blue.

I blinked. "A while." How long had it been? "Maybe a year and a half, I guess." I shook my head. "Seems like longer."

She shrugged. "You haven't talked about him. Just curious."

I grinned, just a little. "And what about you? How long have you been running?"

"A while," she smirked.

I chuckled. "Alright."

We didn't talk much, but we didn't need to. Then the evening turned from pleasant to interesting.

The flash of police lights caught my attention as we exited the diner. I heard Ghost sigh a little as I made my way down the street toward them, but she followed along without saying anything. The police cars were parked by a housing building, cops gathered outside the main door with the bored attentiveness that said they were waiting for the crime scene unit to show up. I gently pushed my way through the small crowd of curious onlookers that had gathered.

"What happened?" I asked.

"Got a call. Can't say more than that," the cop nearest me replied.

I nodded, knowing better than to argue. The best way to

keep details of any police matters from the press was to say as little as possible for as long as possible. I stuck around in the hopes of gleaning a little more, my curiosity piqued. Ghost sighed again.

"You don't have to stay."

"Neither do you," she countered with a small grin, "and I'd rather stick around than walk home alone."

"You could drive," I suggested, but she shook her head.

"It's shiny, Doc."

I gave it no more thought, though I appreciated her staying. I honestly don't know why I stayed. I hadn't actively sought out crime scenes since losing Sherlock. For some reason, after a night of relaxation, I found myself walking directly toward police lights, as if I were simply following him again.

It was this feeling that made me blink in surprise when Red walked out of the building. She was surprised to see me too, understandably. We hadn't spoken much in the past year, our jobs no longer in line with each other.

She gestured that the policemen on guard should let me in. I cast an apologetic look at Ghost, who shrugged as if to say it didn't matter. She was still grinning. I smiled in thanks and quickly followed Red inside the building and up the stairs.

"How've you been?" Red asked.

"Keeping busy. You?"

"The same. Thought you might care to take a look, seeing as how you're here anyway. It's something in his line." It was obvious who she was talking about.

"Is it murder, then?"

She nodded. "Name's Adrian Rolands. Neighbors

describe him as quiet, kept to himself a lot, but always polite. No criminal record whatsoever, not even a parking fine."

We stopped at a room on the third story. Red opened the door to reveal the sparsely furnished sitting room of a small apartment, containing a couch in front of a tv and a table behind that. Across the table sprawled the form of a dead man, a bullet through his head. He had been shot from behind as he sat at the table, falling forward. Underneath him was his computer. He'd been dead for a few days.

"So, he was working on something when he was shot from behind," I said. "Either he was forced to do something on the computer, or he knew his murderer and simply had his back to them."

Red filled in the blanks, "No one in the building reported seeing or hearing anything suspicious. The only reason we were called in tonight's because the landlord wanted to collect an overdue rent and noticed the smell as he pounded on the door. The door would have automatically locked when the killer left."

"Isn't there a security camera in the building?"

"Yep, but that's what makes things a little more complicated."

She pointed to the window. In it was a bullet hole. I stared at Red. "You aren't seriously suggesting he was shot through the window? The shooter would have had to be firing from the building across the street!"

"That building's recently abandoned, so it's possible. There's glass bits on the floor by the window, so something came through. The lab boys are going to see if the angle matches. You're welcome to stick around if you want."

I hesitated. "As much as I'd like to, I can't. Will you keep me informed?"

"Absolutely."

I hurried back down the stairs, found Ghost, and led her away from the crowd. "You can't drive, can you?"

She responded by sticking her tongue out at me.

I grinned. "Sorry. I should have realized the only reason why you were sticking around is that you didn't want to walk home, alone or not."

"You aren't quite as quick as your friend, but you catch on."

"Thanks," I drawled sarcastically as I found a public car.

"I would have stayed anyway. Even if I could drive, I mean."

"Really?"

She nodded. "Your first time back at a crime scene. Wanted to make sure you were ok."

I considered her for a long moment before starting the car. "Thanks."

"For what?"

"Worrying."

She shrugged. "Just returning the favor."

I started driving. "He would have found that interesting. The crime scene, I mean." I described it to her and the two of us spent the ride home speculating wildly about possible scenarios. Sherlock would have been disappointed and amused by our lack of objectivity as the ideas became more cinematic and less logical, but it was fun.

Red was as good as her word, calling me the next day.

They'd narrowed down the time of death to early evening three days ago. The weapon was likely a higher caliber handgun, and the hole in the window corresponded with the location of the wound. The victim had been going over betting figures, and seemed to be in some debt. Whoever the killer was, they were a crack shot to be able to hit him in the head through a window from a building across the street.

"Why didn't anyone report a gunshot?" I asked.

"Must have used a silencer," Red replied. "Nobody reported it at the time, but residents recalled hearing a loud sound a few days ago, though none were willing to describe it as a gunshot. We're still searching for a motive - his gambling debt seems the best lead right now."

"Let me know when you find something."

"Sure thing."

"And Red, thanks. It's... good, to try and help like this again."

"From what I hear, you've been doing more than a fair share of help to people away from crime scenes, but I know what you mean. And don't mention it."

I hung up, my sigh stifled by an idea hitting me. "Ghost!" I called up the attic stairs.

"I'm already looking for stuff on Adrian Rolands!"

I smiled. "Thank you!"

"Did you know he's married?"

I ran up the steps to find her lying on the loveseat, feet dangling over the side, her equipment on a small table in front of her. She was jacked in, eyes open but seeing something other than the attic room she'd made her home.

"What do you mean he's married?"

"Few years ago, he got married. Must not have gone well, because shortly afterward the joint bank accounts separate, and his name is off the lease of their place. But he never got a divorce. They separated, but they're still legally married."

"What's her name?"

"Sabia Monahan."

"Red should know about this."

"If the police background check doesn't turn this up, then they need more help than we can give," Ghost muttered.

I chuckled. "Good point. I guess we're pretty useless right now."

"Pff, speak for yourself. I'm always useful. That usefulness just isn't always taken advantage of."

"I stand corrected. I shall leave you to your independent investigations and return to my useful practice of healing the sick."

The police did indeed know about Sabia Monahan, and not just because she was married to the victim. She was on the security footage, entering and leaving the building the night of the murder. Red invited me to come along to the large apartment in the Corporate Sector for the interview.

Sabia Monahan was a slender, all around average looking woman. She was mildly shaken but not terribly upset over the death of her estranged husband. When asked why they hadn't divorced, she said Adrian hadn't wanted it, and as she hadn't had any desire to remarry she didn't push the issue. Apparently, the police could add either "hopeless romantic" or "egotistical bastard" to the list of things they knew about the victim, depending on how you interpreted his desire to stay married.

"Ms. Monahan, our records show that you own a handgun of the same caliber as the bullet that killed Mr. Rolands," Red said.

She blinked in surprise. "Am I a suspect?"

"Could you tell us what you were doing in the evening, three days ago?" Red asked in her most genteel voice.

"Three days ago? I went to see Adrian after work, and then went to the shooting range. I'm something of a regular, you can ask around."

"Do you own a silencer?"

"No. But you already knew that, unless you were expecting me to tell you I obtained one illegally."

"Never hurts to ask. All the same, we'd like to test your gun, if you don't mind."

Her brow rose, but she shrugged as she retrieved it. "Sure."

Red took the gun, "Why were you visiting Mr. Rolands?"

"He asked me to come, but wouldn't say why. Turned out he wanted to ask for money to help with his gambling debt. I said no, we argued briefly, I left."

"I see. Thank you for your cooperation, Ms. Monahan."

"Sabia, please," she showed us out.

"Well, that would have been too easy," I muttered.

Red chuckled. "Yeah, she might be lying, but she gave over her gun."

"It probably won't match. She could have borrowed one,

especially if she's a regular at a shooting range."

"True. The other possibility is that someone came to collect on Rolands's debts and decided to eliminate any possibility of a next-time."

"But then why shoot him from across the street? If they came to collect, then shouldn't his credit cards be missing? At least there should be a posthumous withdrawal from a bank account."

Red sighed, "If Monahan shot her ex, then I don't know how we'll prove it. There weren't any distinct footprints in the building across the street where the killer would have stood. I hate to say it, Doctor, but we can't solve them all."

To say that I was unsatisfied would be an understatement. That night I couldn't get any sleep; my mind refused to just shut up and be still. That no motive had been found kept gnawing at me, and the more I thought about it the more I was convinced that something had been missed. How the hell did Sherlock do this? He would have gone to every place every possibility took him, without question. I had no desire to come home as beat up as Sherlock often did, but doing nothing and going nowhere was driving me crazy.

Then again. There was one place I could investigate without fear of getting myself killed, even though I was certain it would lead to a dead end. Still, it was better than doing nothing.

I went into the shooting range the next day, wondering what the hell I was doing. I was so distracted, I ran into a brightly dressed man who was coming out. After mumbled apologies, I registered at the front desk, borrowed some goggles and earmuffs, and found a free stand. I figured it was the easiest way to get people to warm up to me, and it was refreshing to aim my pistol at a non-living target. I was a bit out of practice, and started enjoying myself. I was also attracting attention.

"You're very good," a man with an instructor's badge around his neck said from behind me as I came out from the shooting stand. "I don't think I've seen you here before."

"First time here," I said, "A lady I know recommended it. Sabia?"

"Yes, I know Sabia. She's a regular. Friend of yours?"

I shrugged, "More acquaintances. Friends of friends. I've never seen her shoot, but I heard she was good."

"Yes, she's quite excellent, actually. I taught her."

I tried not to look as happily surprised as I felt. "Oh! When does she usually come by?"

"Every other day, if not every day, in the evening after she gets off work."

Lucky I was there in the early afternoon. "I'll have to keep that in mind."

The instructor nodded with a quick smile, "Be seeing you around then." He walked off to speak to another customer.

I went to the front desk to return the gear. "Thanks so much - um, I don't suppose you rent out silencers, do you?"

The man behind the desk looked at me curiously. "We have a couple available for members who wish to try them, but of course they remain on the premises."

"Of course. I was just curious. Ah, does Sabia Monahan come here?"

"Sorry?"

"Sabia Monahan. She's a friend of mine. Do you know her?"

"Yes, I remember that name."

"I don't suppose her husband ever drops by here?"

"Her husband?" he was surprised.

"Isn't she married?"

"She doesn't wear a ring and..."

"...and?"

He was flustered. "It's none of my business. Have a good day."

I didn't want to push my luck, so I left, wondering why Sabia Monahan being married would be shocking.

I went back to her apartment building to ask around. As is often the case in the Corporate Sector, very few people knew anything about her. Neighbors tend to mind their own business, engaging in only the minimum social interaction necessary to be cordial. Of course, in Non-C people keep a covert eye on their neighbors out of a general concern for personal safety. Cordiality gets set aside for a healthy dose of practical wariness.

I'd given up and was headed out the building when an older woman was coming in.

"I don't recognize you," she said with some sugar-coated suspicion.

"Friend of Sabia Monahan's," I said, "the lady in room 435. Average height, brunette? Gets home late, carries a gun?"

The gun did it. "Oh! Her. Yes. I don't know people's room numbers, but I keep track of everyone that comes in and out of the building. I live next to the front door, you see."

"Do you really?" Thank god for busybodies. "It's kind

of surprising that she would carry a weapon openly."

"Oh, she doesn't," she leaned forward conspiratorially, "I know about it because she was here the other night with a gentleman and they were talking about shooting as they waited for the elevator. He comes home with her often, sometimes they talk about guns, sometimes it's more… personal."

"A gentleman."

Nodding with a grin, she amended, "I suppose that's what you'd call him. He was well-behaved at least. I think one time I saw him with a badge of some sort around his neck." I described Sabia's instructor from the shooting range. The busybody nodded, "That sounds like him."

Interesting. "He comes by often?"

"Oh yes." She eyed me up and down, appraisingly. "You're not another one, are you?"

I laughed. "Ah, no."

"Well, you're better than the brightly dressed fellow, that's for certain. Though I suppose I'm jumping to conclusions thinking –"

"Brightly dressed fellow?" My mind instantly turned to the man I'd run into at the shooting range.

"Short black beard, bright purple jacket. Came around asking for her last night. I told him what I've just told you."

"Huh. Thanks." That Sabia was seeing her instructor was pretty clear, but that was far from proof of her murdering her husband. This brightly dressed man, though. Who was he? Someone trying to collect on Adrian Rolands's debt?

I thought a return to the crime scene might spark an idea. Naturally, I wouldn't be able to go back into the apartment without a police escort, but that wasn't my goal anyway. The apartment had been thoroughly searched, and I was sure any chance I might have had at noticing something had already passed. Instead, I wanted to see the place where the murderer must have stood when they did the deed. Feeling a trifle foolish, I attempted to emulate Sherlock's care in observing everything around me as I climbed the steps of the abandoned building. It had been left unguarded and access was easy. As I walked up the stairs, I noticed a homeless man taking shelter from the chill winds and for a brief moment I felt a little guilty about being here instead of going around to patients, even if I didn't have any appointments that day.

I found a room with a view of Adrian Rolands's apartment. The room's window had been smashed out long ago, probably in a fit of bored vandalism. Drawing my own pistol, I tried to line up the shot. I found an approximate area for where the shooter would have stood. Now that I could see for myself where the killer had been standing, I had no idea how, or even if, the information was helpful.

With a heavy sigh, I glanced around the room, turning up the zoom level of my cyberoptic in the vain hope that I would stumble across some trace of someone being here. To my great surprise, I did find something useful, though not at all what I had been looking for. I called Red.

"Hey Red, I'm in the building across the street from Adrian Rolands. Could you bring your lab boys back over here?"

"Why?"

I smiled. "Because I'm looking at a bullet in the wall behind where the killer would have stood."

Red arrived quickly, a very young and very indignant crime scene investigator in tow. When he realized what he'd missed, he looked at me with mild suspicion. I smiled back at him.

"You assumed the shot came through the window, so you only looked to see where the killer would have stood and didn't give the back wall as much attention as it deserved."

"And you saw the bullet in the dark with a passing glance," he grumbled as he removed the bullet from the wall.

I shrugged. "Cyberoptics help." He scoffed, but I could tell the use of technology had softened the blow to his pride. He was several years younger than me, and clearly from closer to Corporate sector, if not in Corporate sector. He had a lot to learn.

"Well, Dr. Watts," Red said with a small grin, "You have succeeded in making this case even stranger than before. Thanks."

I shook my finger at her, "Now, Detective, that's not true. It is the most mundane case that is most difficult to solve. The more extraordinary the case, the easier to unravel... or something like that."

"A little rusty in your reading?"

"Didn't have much reason to pick up the stories again. Frankly, didn't want to."

Red nodded sagely. "Well, you've done him proud. If that bullet matches up with the one we retrieved from Rolands, then the murderer was in the room with the victim, and fired a shot out the window to make it seem like he was killed from across the street."

"So, you're looking for a shot with a steady hand and

impeccable aim with a particular dislike of Adrian Rolands, who was in the room with him that night."

"Ms. Sabia Monahan fits, except that her gun isn't the murder weapon."

I grinned. "She got it from a friend."

There was no way to prove my theory of course, but that didn't stop me from returning to the shooting range later that evening. I timed it perfectly; Sabia was getting a few very intimate pointers on her stance from her instructor. I waited until the instructor left before casually approaching, giving her plenty of time to see me coming.

"Are you looking for me?" she asked, meeting me halfway.

"Yes. I wanted to know why you did it."

"Did what?"

"You must have used a silencer, which means you went there intending to shoot him, so it couldn't have been a crime of passion."

"I don't have to listen to this."

I gently grabbed her arm as she turned away, "Hold on, I'm not the police."

"But you were with the cop who talked to me."

"I know her, I tag along, but I'm not an officer. I'm a doctor. I couldn't arrest you even if I could prove it, and I'm honestly curious to know why."

"I'm not saying anything else to you unless you eject that optic."

I blinked. "Eject it?"

"You could be recording me for all I know. I don't have

any reason to trust you."

She had a point, and I had no argument for it. I turned my cyberoptic off and ejected the eye, holding it carefully in a handkerchief. To my immense satisfaction, she recoiled a little at the sight of a metal-plated hole in my skull, but finally told me what I wanted to know.

"I wanted a divorce. He didn't, even though he was getting no benefit from being legally married, just keeping me from marrying someone else."

"So, when he called you wanting money, you mentioned divorce, and he said something that pushed you over the edge?"

"I went knowing he would ask for money. This was an old routine by now, Doctor. I went, with the forms notifying him I had filed for divorce. He was insulting enough, and I was tired enough that when he blew me off, I shot him."

"But you went there with your boyfriend's gun. You knew you were going to shoot him."

"I grabbed his gun by accident."

"And the silencer?" She didn't say anything. "Ah. You knew he could, and would, draw the process out for as long as possible and didn't want to wait. So you took your boyfriend's gun and silencer, deciding to kill your husband if he refused to simply agree to the terms. You shot him in the back of the head, then in a moment of inspiration shot through the window to make it seem like he'd been shot from across the street. You're an excellent marksman, you could line up the shot with the wound in the back of his skull."

More silence.

"Does the boyfriend know?"

"He probably suspected something, but he didn't say anything."

"How'd you get the glass debris all over the floor?"

"Crushed one of his drinking glasses, scattered the dust, carried the remains out with me in my purse."

"Can I put my eye back now?"

"If we're done talking."

I smirked as I replaced it, giving her a small bow. "Thank you for your time, Ms. Monahan."

As I turned away, I caught a flash of color going through the door. I hurried after it, leaving the shooting range and finding Red outside talking to a brightly dressed man casually leaning against the wall.

His short coat was pastel violet, while his pants were black with a silver stripe. A gold scarf was tied around his neck, and his black hair was shaggy and wild, unlike his perfectly groomed beard. To complete this insane picture were a pair of black gloves and shoes.

"A pleasure to see you again, Detective," he was saying, "now excuse me, but I have some pressing business."

"Not so fast," Red stepped in front of him, hands on her hips, "what are you doing hanging about here?"

"Here? A customer wondered what happened to Adrian Rolands. He was a rather familiar face in a certain gambling house, suddenly gone. There was some concern about him skipping out on his growing debts."

"Uh huh. So why are you spying on him?" Red gestured with a nod towards me.

The strange man shook his head, "I was spying on the

lady. Reporting her husband's death is all well and good, but for the sake of completeness I wanted to know if she killed him. Now I know," he inclined his head towards me, "thank you very much."

"Who is this guy?" I asked.

"Calls himself Sebastian. He sells information on anything to anyone willing to pay, though the first time I heard of him was last Christmas when he came in to claim a bounty on an arsonist wanted in five cities."

Sebastian shrugged. "Business was slow."

"You gift-wrapped him."

"'Twas the season. And he looked so pretty in a bow."

I chuckled. "You must be insane."

Sebastian grinned, a touch maniacally. "I'm not as mad as all that. Now, if you don't mind, I really must be going. Ta." And he was gone.

"Well, then," I muttered, "that was strange."

"Yeah. So, did you get what you needed?"

"Sabia Monahan killed Adrian Rolands because he wouldn't give her a divorce."

"Can you prove it?"

I pulled out a small, old fashioned tape recorder from my pocket. "Yep."

Red laughed. "I seem to remember seeing that little gadget from somewhere."

I smiled. "Worked for Sherlock then, figured it might work for me now."

"Well done, Doctor," Red shook my hand as I handed over the tape, "It was nice working with you."

"Thanks, Red."

I headed up to the attic as soon as I got home. I wanted to ask Ghost what she knew about brightly dressed crazy information dealers, but she was deep in cyberspace and unresponsive. I sighed and left her to it, making myself a drink before lying down on the sofa. What a strange day.

It had been great looking into a case like that, but so weird without Sherlock. I still missed him, but I thought I might be able to start moving on now. Oddly enough, helping Red had enabled me to come to terms with the loss of my friend. More to terms with it than I was before, at least. Emotionally exhausted, I drifted off to visions of skyscrapers and waterfalls.

I woke to the sound of someone knocking. With a yawn and a muttered curse, I tried to clear my head as I checked the security camera. Sebastian stood outside my door.

I opened it just enough to look out at him. "Yes?"

"Sorry to disturb you, but I'm… on business. May I come in?"

"Why are you here? Specifically?"

He shrugged, holding up his left arm. Blood soaked the cuff of his glove. "Rumor has it you're one of the best medics in the City, Doc."

"No one actually says that."

"Really? I wonder how I heard it, then."

I rubbed between my eyes to fend off the headache I knew would be coming. "How was it injured?"

"Old. Keeps opening," he removed his coat. A trail of blood ran down the sleeve of his shirt. I pushed the sleeve up to reveal a large cut, only recently healed, more recently re-opened, and very infected. "Been cleaning it out, but -"

"You apparently aren't doing an adequate job." I rolled my eyes, cursing my conscience. "Come inside. Sit at the kitchen table and don't touch anything."

He smirked and nodded. I grabbed my things, cleaned out the wound out and bandaged it properly. It would scar, but he had a number of those already.

"You get into a lot of knife fights?" I asked as I worked.

"Something like that. I do try to stay away from violence when I can. Healthier that way."

"Ha, sure, and near impossible, I bet."

"True," he looked around as we spoke. "Nice place. Just you?"

"And the ghost in the attic."

He chuckled. "Never took up with anyone else, eh? After the detective fellow died, I mean. This is where he lived, right?"

"Yes he did, and no I didn't," I said with a scowl. "Why haven't you had a medic look at this before now?"

"Haven't found a competent one I can trust."

"Butchers with sewing needles," I muttered, smiling a little at the memory.

He blinked. "You took the words right out of my mouth."

I glanced at him, something not sitting right. "You're all fixed up."

"Thank you." My strange patient rolled his bloody sleeve back down, standing as he glanced around the room once more. "You haven't changed a thing in the past year."

"How the hell would you know…" I trailed off as his eyes met mine. They were grey, and so very sorry. I leaped out of my chair, stumbling backwards, my heart pounding as he removed his other glove. The light shone off his brass hand, and suddenly I couldn't breathe. "Sherlock."

He nodded once. "Hello, Watts."

I rushed to him, took his face in my hands and kissed him full on the lips. Then my fist collided with the side of his face.

"What the hell!? You're supposed to be dead!" He didn't say anything as he slowly got up off the floor. "I can't believe you did this. The goddamn Great Hiatus! Really?!"

"Sixteen months is hardly three years—"

"That's not the point! I thought you were dead!"

"I know, and I am sorry—"

"Will! That's how you did it, that's how you faked the body. Jackals would be able to find a dead body no problem, and scavenge together a brass hand to go with it. Destroy the face so that it can't be recognized, trust that I'll be too distraught to test the damn thing, and perfect!"

"I thought it would be prudent to see what the City's reaction to Sangrave's death would be, before announcing my own survival. I hadn't planned on so long an absence, but the opportunity was… too good to pass up."

"Too good to pass up." I swore. "Would you have walked away if I hadn't brought you inside?"

"I would have returned."

"When, in another sixteen months? Maybe stretch it to the full three years?"

He winced. "Watts, please—"

"Why didn't you tell me?"

"If you believed I was dead, so would the rest of the City.

I couldn't risk tempting you to some indiscretion which would betray my secret."

"You could have told me later! You could have faked your death for a week and then let me know what you were doing! Do you have any idea what sort of Hell you put me through? What this past year's been like?"

"I had no idea that you would be so affected—"

"Stop quoting the damn books at me!" I shouted, slamming the table.

He blinked, stunned. "I didn't realize I was." He took a breath and tried to start over. "James—"

"It's Watts."

He took a step forward, a world of hurt on his face for a moment, but then it was gone. He stayed where he was, his voice matter-of-fact. "Watts. I know that there is nothing I can say that will excuse my action and I will not try to, but you must let me speak."

"Why?"

"It would be impossible for me to beg for forgiveness while silent."

I scoffed, "You think that's an option?"

"No." He was serious. After a moment, he continued, "Nonetheless, I must try."

I leaned against the kitchen counter, arms folded. "Ok."

"It had of course occurred to me that my death would be the perfect opportunity to lie low for a time. I fully intended to tell you I was alive after a little while. What hadn't occurred to me was how tantalizing the very possibility of infiltrating so many aspects of the underworld would be. My new life consumed me. To be brutally honest, I lost track of time. I lost track of myself.

"I swear to you, my friend, I did not realize what I had done," he met my skeptical gaze with earnestness. "I didn't know you would suffer so much, I refused to accept the possibility. I was not myself this past year, and I am ashamed to say I very easily could have stayed buried behind a mask for another year longer. Seeing you made me realize just how much my foolish ambition had cost, the damage I had done…" he trailed off, looking down. I'd patched him up so many times, been by his side as he lay in bed unable to move, but I'd never seen him so vulnerable as in that moment.

"Forgive me." His voice was quiet as he ventured a cautious glance up at me, "Please. I don't deserve it, but if you ever…" he looked away again, struggling to find a word. Then he sighed, standing straight and tall with his hands behind his back, some of that familiar detachment returning as his eyes met mine again. "If you permit it, I would like to come home. Even if you hate me."

I considered him for a long moment. "You forgot about me."

I may as well have slapped him. "No! I could never forget you, but I could have nothing to do with you. I was someone else, I couldn't let myself think of you, no matter how much I wanted to, no matter how — clearly, I am an idiot, but I couldn't let Sebastian meet you until it was forced upon me in the form of a frustratingly determined red-headed police detective." He smiled, just a bit, at my involuntary laugh. "Seeing you again… I had to come tonight, not just for the injury, but to see you. It was blatantly clear to me from the moment I came inside that I wouldn't be able to walk back out that door."

"What if I say no?"

He paled, but steeled himself. I flinched to see all his emotional walls go up. "Then I will leave."

"Where?"

"Does it matter?"

I couldn't answer right away. If I didn't want anything to do with him, then it didn't matter where he went. But it did matter. I was far from forgiving him, but he was alive. He was alive, and he was home, and damn it I didn't want him to leave.

He tensed as I approached, and gasped in uncomfortable surprise as I hugged him. "If you ever do anything like this again, I'll really kill you."

He held me tight with a relieved sigh, "That is perfectly fair."

We stood in silence for a moment. A shocked "Holy hell!" echoed from the attic stairs.

Sherlock half-grinned, looking up as we let go of each other. "Good evening, Miss Ghost."

Ghost smiled, in spite of herself. "You survived."

"Yes."

"Shiny. Watts forgive you?"

"I would not say that, yet."

"Maybe one day," I said. "Your things are packed up in boxes, but still here. Hadn't got around to getting rid of them yet."

"He means it took him a year to pack them in the first

place, and couldn't bring himself to get them out," Ghost corrected, ignoring my glare.

Sherlock glanced at me with surprise, and acknowledged her words with a pained nod. "I see. Thank you."

I shrugged, and gestured to his door. "Welcome back."

With a miniscule smile, he made his way to his room. He hesitated a moment, his hand on the doorknob, before entering the home he hadn't seen in over a year.

I turned to Ghost. "Drink?"

"Just this once. And that's just to make sure you don't down the whole bottle."

"I wouldn't do that."

"After seeing Sherlock return from the dead? Like hell you wouldn't."

An hour, and only two glasses, later, I slowly opened the door to Sherlock's room. He'd completely transformed back to his old self, at least externally. Now he held his violin reverently, gently tuning the unique extension of himself and his emotions he'd been so long without. He didn't even notice me. I gently closed the door and left him to it. As the first hesitant strains came from behind the door, I couldn't stop myself from smiling.

The Almandine Drive Affair

I'd been content to leave things be that night, but morning found me wondering if my relief at having him back alive overrode my desire to beat the hell out of him. He was also acutely aware that I hadn't forgiven him, and was on his best behavior. The result was a morning of awkward tension, as if we were new housemates all over again.

So, I made coffee, asked what he wanted for breakfast (nothing at the moment, thank you,) and watched from the kitchen table as he built a roaring fire, sat in his chair, and smoked a pipe. Judging by the look on his face, it was a spiritual experience.

"I take it criminal information dealers don't smoke?"

"Not like this."

I cleaned up and got dressed for work. He was at his desk when I came out, preparing his index of scrapbooks.

He answered my questioning glance, "I don't want to risk forgetting a single piece of information I gained as Sebastian."

"Makes sense. Be back tonight."

Work helped. Still, I didn't really have that many appointments, and the ones I had were mostly follow-ups and simple complaints, so it was only late afternoon by the time I finished. I briefly debated staying away longer, then told myself to stop being an idiot and just go home.

I came in as Sherlock was getting ready to leave. "Watts.

I didn't expect you until later."

I shrugged. "Didn't take as long as I thought. Where are you going?"

"I was going to take a walk to the police station. I imagine Red will want to know I survived, and I thought a personal visit would be better than a phone call."

"Sherlock. It's below freezing."

"Not by much," he said as he donned his gloves and top hat. "It's not as though I've never walked through the cold before."

I looked him over, the top hat catching my attention. He was in full Victorian garb, a winter overcoat covering his suit. He looked like a character from *A Christmas Carol*. I smiled. "You're going like that."

"How else would I go?" The question was deadpan, but a familiar half-grin flashed with the humor in his eyes.

I chuckled as I went to my room. "Wait right there, let me put my gear away, and then I'll drive you."

"You don't have to—"

"I'm not letting you walk there. Besides," I added as we left, "you think I'm going to pass up the chance to see Red's face?"

"You're looking forward to the dressing down she's going to give me, aren't you?"

"Oh, absolutely."

It was worth going just for the looks on all the cops' faces as we walked in. Brief periods of silence followed in Sherlock's wake, quickly covered by whispered mutterings, "I thought he was dead?"

Red was at her desk, filling out paperwork. She glanced up at the approaching figure, and did a double take. She slowly stood up as he stopped before her desk, nonchalantly leaning on his walking stick, and removed his hat.

"Good evening, Red."

A broad smile spread across her face, "You son of a bitch."

If he hadn't been sure how to take her greeting, doubt was extinguished by her sudden bear hug, followed by a quick, firm shake of his shoulders. "You are an absolute idiot, do you know that?! Do you have any idea the sort of trouble you caused? Of all the impulsive, irresponsible, slapdash, idiotically cinematic, and unnecessarily dramatic stunts to pull! I should have you arrested for sheer chicanery!"

He managed to summon some coherent thought, "I don't believe that's a formal charge."

"Then I'll make one up! God knows there's plenty to choose from where you're concerned! Well don't just stand there, sit down!" She glared at the assembled crowd, "Don't you people have jobs?" Everyone scattered. Sherlock and I sat. "What the hell have you been up to?"

"Sebastian."

"You were..." her jaw dropped as she sank into her chair. "That was *you*?! Bounty hunting and information selling and..." He simply nodded. Her face fell into her hand. "I feel like such an idiot."

"You, and everyone else apparently, thought I was dead. You had no cause to be suspicious."

"Gracious of you," she scoffed, folding her arms as she

leaned back. "Watts chew you out yet?"

"Yes."

"Good. I presume you had a hell of a lawyer ensure you weren't breaking many laws with your fake death?"

"Naturally."

"So how'd you do it?"

"Clever use of contacts and great physical exertion."

She rolled her eyes and chuckled. "Fine, then. Have I told you you're an idiot yet?"

"Along with irresponsible, impulsive, and unnecessarily dramatic."

She smiled. "Good. Gotta hand it to you, though, you sure know how to make an entrance." He inclined his head with a small smile. "I suppose I'll have to see about getting the liaison thing reinstated."

"I never quite liked the idea of the police keeping track of me."

Red shrugged, "I don't like my superiors breathing down my neck every time you do something stupid, but it means I'm the one who gets to deal with you, so it's usually worth it."

Sherlock was confused. "Working with me is worth the excessive inconvenience?"

Red shook her head, a fond expression on her face. "It's good to see you, Sherlock. I'd chat more, but if I don't get this report written up by the time I leave today, it'll be my hide."

He smiled, modestly. "I'm sure we'll be in touch."

As we stood, she said, "Come to Christmas dinner."

Sherlock froze and stared at her, a small look of panic on his face. "I beg your pardon?"

"You. Are invited. To Christmas dinner. With my family."

He blinked. "Dear god, it's December."

"We'd love to," I answered for him. He shot me a quick glare, but it didn't have any heart in it. He sighed, and nodded.

"Good," Red grinned, "I'll see you before then, I'm sure. Have a good night, gents, and Watts? Don't be too hard on him, he's only human. An ass, no mistake, but still only human."

I couldn't help but smile. Sherlock was carefully neutral as he placed his hat back on his head. "I'll try to keep that in mind," I said.

We returned home in silence, but the air was a little lighter than before. Sherlock went back to his index, working through the night. We didn't say much.

In the morning, I found him in the middle of the living room, sword in hand. His original had been destroyed by a cyborg. I'd bought him a replacement, almost an exact replica of the first, but he hadn't had much opportunity to use it before 'dying.' Now, he examined every inch with great care, brow furrowed.

"Something wrong?" I asked.

When he finally answered, his voice was unusually quiet. "My first sword was given to me by my instructor, my second by my friend. It's an odd comparison. They are nearly identical blades, yet the simple knowledge of who they are from and why they were given make them entirely different."

"Have you told the Irregulars?" I asked.

He blinked, startled. "What?"

"Do the Irregulars know you're alive yet?"

"I hadn't told them." He was a bit ashamed by this.

I shrugged, "We'll go see them right now."

"Are they…?"

"They're all still there, all alive and well, and they'll be happy to see you."

We arrived at the Hideout, as the Irregulars call it, in the afternoon. Music played softly from within, and we could hear muffled voices. Wendy answered my knock, opening the door wide to let me in. "Doc! This is a surprise…" she trailed off as Sherlock entered behind me. I stood to the side to give the half dozen Irregulars present a good look at their employer returned from the dead. Sherlock met each bewildered gaze, a small smile on his face.

With a cry of alarmed excitement, each and every one of them leaped to their feet and nearly tackled him in a massive group hug. Sherlock staggered, stunned.

"You're alive!" they all shouted, blended with chimes of "I knew it" and relieved cheers.

Laughing in spite of himself, Sherlock gently pried them off, "My goodness, such a greeting. Let me look at you all." This had been the last thing he'd expected. With a quick cough to clear the emotion from his voice, Sherlock once again the general before his troops. As he performed his inspection, he tried in vain to hide his smile. "You all seem physically fit at least," he glanced at me for confirmation.

I nodded, "Yeah, though they'd be better if they'd come to me for follow ups every time one of them breaks something."

They rolled their eyes. I had long ago given up any hope

of the Irregulars coming for regular check-ups, but, damn it, the least they could do was follow doctor's orders.

Sherlock grinned. "Ah. And is all well here?" he asked them. They nodded vigorously.

"We're fine. A little short on funds," Wendy smiled, "but we've been getting by."

"Good. I apologize for my sudden departure, but—"

"You fell through a window," all six said in unison.

Sherlock blinked. "Well. Yes."

"I knew Will was up to something," Michael said, smugly. "I didn't believe you were dead for a minute."

"Yes, you did," everyone around him scolded.

He shrugged, unabashed. "You were gone a long time."

Sherlock nodded, "I was. Now," he sat down on the floor where he stood, gesturing for the Irregulars to do the same, "tell me everything I've missed."

We spent the rest of the day with the Irregulars, catching up on their lives and the gossip on the street that Sherlock hadn't heard about – the stuff not directly related to the criminal world. The other half of the Irregulars slowly trickled in as the day went on, and each one had a similar reaction as before. And, like before, the sudden emotional display was quickly followed by customary professionalism... as professional as any of the Irregulars ever gets, at least.

It was evening by the time we left. Sherlock was still reeling from the experience as I drove us home. "Thank you for keeping an eye on them," he said.

"Of course. You ok?"

"This homecoming has been much more emotional than

I expected."

I smirked. "I bet." It started to snow. "Probably be a white Christmas."

Sherlock sighed.

"What do you have against Christmas?"

"Nothing at all, it's the social requirement I find ridiculous."

"Last time you got away with a simple season's greetings, but this year I intend to really get into the season."

"Enjoy."

"Oh, no," I grinned as I pulled up to 122 Break Street, "I'm taking full advantage of your guilt and hauling you along with me tomorrow."

The look on his face might have been terror.

His streak of penitentiary behavior came to a screeching halt the next morning over coffee.

"No."

"Oh, come on. You've seen worse war zones than the Corporate Sector in December."

"That is debatable. If you desire to force your way through seas of unhappy shoppers seeking ridiculously expensive gifts for loved ones and acquaintances that will only be used once and promptly forgotten about, be my guest."

"Coward," I challenged.

Sherlock raised an impassive eyebrow. "If that is the best baiting you can do, Watts, I am sorely disappointed in you."

I shrugged, "Fine. Stay at home. I shall brave the storm of consumerism by myself, and enjoy it." I donned my winter coat and hat, calling upstairs, "Ghost! Want to come shopping?"

"You're kidding!"

"Just thought I'd ask!" I laughed.

"I'd rather get fried in cyberspace than stampeded in a mall!" she called back, making Sherlock chuckle.

"You know," I said to him, "it'll be worse the closer to Christmas it gets."

"Precisely why I intend to stay in this house until New Year's Day."

I shook my head, "You'll go crazy without a case. The few news sites that have reported rumors of your return have still just been rumors. The cops know you're back, sure, but the rest of the City still thinks you're little more than an urban legend. What better way to definitively announce your return to life than by walking through the Corporate Sector?"

Rubbing between his eyes, Sherlock sighed. "Damn it, Watts, I hate this time of year."

"I know. Come on, I'm an old pro at this. It'll be fun."

He stood, shaking his head, "You have a disturbing definition of 'fun.'"

I had fun, at least. The Corporate Sector was in a full array of kitsch, streetlights and rooftops covered in white and blue lights, a decorated tree in every hotel and square, and holiday music playing from every storefront. Everyone bustled around carrying bags of brightly wrapped packages. I smoothly led my fortunately dexterous friend through the throngs of people as I window shopped, trying to get ideas for a small gift for Red and Ghost this year. I like the spectacle of the season. Either you throw yourself into it and go with the flow, or you just get stressed out by it all.

I also enjoyed the reactions Sherlock's presence caused. He was in full Victorian dress, top hat included, his brass hand shining, and everywhere we went someone would stop and stare for a moment. He even stopped a brawl from happening, simply by getting in the middle and scolding them, an event a media-man was quick to record. He enjoyed the attention, but hated the setting.

Still, he was a decent sport about the whole thing, suffering in silence… for a while. I did my best not to roll my eyes or laugh as I listened to him rant on the way home, unable to contain his disgust and frustration any longer.

"Why is that song even played? It has nothing to do with Christmas whatsoever."

"It's not supposed to be about Christmas, it's a traditional—"

"No, it is from a musical written in 1959 about an Austrian family just before World War II," Sherlock's rapid-fire retort made me blink in surprise, "It has nothing to do with any holiday, be it Christmas or Hanukkah or Solstice or…" he floundered, "Pancha Ganapati."

"Or what?"

"Hindu celebration of Ganesh."

"Who?"

"Never mind."

"Why do you even know that?"

"My point is," he continued, "the song is completely unrelated to the season, and simply adds to the annoying sentimentality of every shopping center in the City."

Cautiously, I ventured, "But the wintertime imagery—"

"A single mention of snowflakes and mittens does not constitute wintertime imagery!"

Grinning wider, I followed the detective into our home. Sherlock went straight to his pipe, tossing his coat and hat to his chair.

"And I suppose the season somehow avoids all this in the Colonies," I smirked.

"The lack of volume of superfluous goods diminishes the materialism somewhat, yes. Though I do concede that much of the season is sentimental drivel. The entire holiday is nothing but a materialistic, consumerist headache."

"Point taken, Scrooge."

He winced, "You have no idea how much it pains me that you only know that reference through media."

"Actually, I read the book."

"Really?"

"Ages ago," I admitted, ignoring his amazement, "but I read it. And liked it."

"Hm. Then you should recognize that Ebenezer Scrooge had no qualms about the materialism of Christmas – if anything he would have been happy to make a profit off it if he could. He hated the 'goodwill toward men' part, until his spiritual intervention. And it is the distinct lack of any sincere effort toward goodwill that disgusts me about modern Christmas."

I shrugged. "I still think you're overreacting."

"Hmph."

His mood did not improve as the month went on. Ghost's unexpected love of punk rock carols didn't help. When she switched over to trans-Asian pop, I thought Sherlock might possibly throw her out.

"Could be worse," I reminded him.

He started to roll his eyes, then reconsidered. "True. However, what infuriates me is not so much her choice in music," his voice rose so that she would hear him, "but the fact that she is purposefully *not using headphones!*"

I doubled over laughing as Ghost turned it up. Sherlock glared at me, but only for a moment before an honest smile filled his face. A truce was met, though Sherlock still remained firmly against any attempt at "getting into the spirit" of the season.

Then the Almandine Drive was stolen.

Now, normally, the news of the only prototype of a highly valuable and potentially revolutionary device being stolen would make Sherlock extremely happy. When no clue to its whereabouts could be found, Sherlock was positively thrilled. He eagerly awaited the details of the case, the promise of a challenge energizing him.

And then the challenge was gone. The news sites all reported that the Almandine Drive had been found, and the police were currently searching for the thief. The stolen property had been returned, and the prototype's debut was being rescheduled for the new year, with heightened security.

"Ah, well," he said to me at the breakfast table, "even the police must have a stroke of luck sometimes."

"That's awfully generous of you," I drawled.

"Luck is what it is," he huffed, "though to be honest, the City Police cannot even take the credit. Corporate Security chased the thief through the sector until he escaped to the Non-

Corporate sector and out of their jurisdiction. He dropped the drive in the chase." Sherlock drummed his fingers on the table, suddenly thoughtful.

"Something wrong?"

"I'm not sure," he gave a small self-deprecating smile, "Perhaps when a man has special knowledge and special powers like my own it rather encourages him to seek a complex explanation when a simpler one is at hand."

I nearly choked on my coffee. "Special powers?"

Sherlock waved his hand dismissively, "A Victorian turn of phrase, you know perfectly well what I mean."

Someone knocked on the door. Sherlock's brow rose as I showed in a man in a long synthetic leather coat, the left arm ripped at the shoulder to show off his chrome cyberarm, his blue mohawk spiked.

"I confess," Sherlock said, "I never thought I would ever see you outside that… shop. This is quite the surprise."

Rip of "Rip's Spare Parts" was distinctly uncomfortable. "Yeah. I ain't in the habit of visiting clients. Heard the rumor you were back. Here on business. Sort of."

Sherlock's surprise shifted to incredulity. "You have my complete attention."

"Well. See, it's not really a big case or anything. Just a small thing…"

"Rip, your presence in my home was shocking enough, but seeing you anything less than confident is simply incredible."

The mild jab did the trick. "It's like this, right? I was closing up shop last night and see a guy getting hassled by some gangers. Easy picking, this guy, typical Non-C worker type, in a rush, has a toy in his hand. Probably spent most of his last paycheck getting a gift for a kid. Anyway, these three surround him and give him a hard time, he gets willing to put up a fight when they take the toy. I don't want any sort of trouble happening on my doorstep, so I show my deathstrikes and run them all off. All four of them spook and the toy gets dropped. Well, most days I'd hawk it or toss it, but this time…"

"You thought you would try to find the owner and return it," Sherlock clearly couldn't believe what he was hearing.

"It's Christmas," Rip stated, a little defensively, but perfectly serious.

It took Sherlock a few moments to snap out of his astonishment. "Yes. It is. Ah, do you have the toy?"

Rip brought it out of an inner coat pocket. It was one of the many retro lines of little kid's toys that had been released this year; a stuffed white bear in a Santa Claus suit that played music.

"I don't suppose anything that might identify the owner was also left behind?" the detective half grinned.

Rip shrugged, "There's this." From another pocket he pulled a soft green cap. "Couldn't really tell anything about the guy. Only got a look at his backside when he was running off. Don't expect you to find him, but thought it worth a shot." With that, the body-bank owner left us.

"So," I crossed my arms and leaned against the table, "how about that goodwill?"

Sherlock chuckled. "That was certainly one of the more surreal experiences I've ever had." He picked up the cap, a small reflective smile on his face before focusing and assuming a hawkish gaze as he examined it. "Watts, would you be so kind as to retrieve my lens from my desk?"

I grabbed his magnifying glass, but as I held it out to him he held out the hat to me.

"What can you deduce?" he asked with a grin.

I cocked an eyebrow, put his lens down on the table, took the hat and turned on my cyberoptic's magnification. "Well, there's a logo on the front that I don't recognize. Whoever's hat this is, he has brown hair, recently had a haircut, and smothers his hair with gel. There's cleanly trimmed hair stuck to the inside. There's a lot of dust around the lining…"

"He works on a construction site," Sherlock supplied, "the logo belongs to a construction company, and the accumulation of dust supports the idea that he works on site. Anything else?"

"Um…" I turned the hat over a few times, feeling like I was missing something. With a sigh, I relinquished the hat. "What did I miss?"

"Actually, you did very well," Sherlock said. "The only point of interest you missed was the fact that the man has a strong sense of self-respect."

"How can you tell that?"

"This hat is in excellent condition. Someone who goes to such lengths to take care of a hat clearly has a deep sense of pride in himself, no matter the occupation."

"What if it's just his only hat and he wants to get as much out of it as he can?"

"Ah, but he was willing to fight over a toy rather than

run, as would have been the sensible but more cowardly thing to do."

I shrugged, "That's plausible."

He chuckled with a wry grin. "I'm glad you agree." He got up and placed the toy and cap on a shelf by his desk, "Unfortunately, the best I can do is have the Irregulars spread the word around the construction sites that an item has been found outside Rip's shop and that the owner can claim it here. Ben should be right for the job, he occasionally works at the sites."

"Even though he's sixteen," I muttered.

"He is big for his age, easily passing for a few years older, and he is typically paid to run errands rather than work with the machinery directly. I don't particularly like the idea, but I don't particularly like most of my Irregulars' occupations when they aren't working for me." He was quiet for a moment, then shook his head, "I'll tell them later today. For now, I would like to take advantage of a quiet moment to do some reading, before Miss Ghost wakes up and subjects my ears to another round of holiday torture."

Sherlock informed the Irregulars as he'd said he would, staying out longer than necessary to escape Ghost's music. I noticed that she didn't play it as incessantly when Sherlock wasn't home. I didn't comment. When he finally returned that evening, Ghost was deeply entrenched in the Net and the house was silent, resulting in supper with a much more amiable companion.

Two days later, Red dropped by to re-invite us to

Christmas dinner. "I wanted to make sure you were really coming," she said. "Thought it prudent, considering you're… you." At Sherlock's hesitance, she laughed, "Just come over, why not? My wife's a good cook, my daughter would love to meet you, and it would be a welcome back gesture from me."

Sherlock sighed. "Very well. If you're sure Mrs. Murphy won't mind."

"She'd be offended if you refused."

With a gesture of defeat, Sherlock said, "In that case, we will most certainly be there. Oh, do sit down, Red, stay awhile. Let me offer you some holiday cheer." He went to the mantelpiece and poured three small glasses of scotch.

Red was stunned. "Thanks. Don't mind if I do," she sat by me on the sofa, taking the glass and savoring her first sip. "Wow. Been ages since I've had the real stuff."

Sherlock's brow rose at Red's obvious appreciation before settling into his chair with his pipe. "Stroke of luck with the Almandine Drive."

Red smirked. "Aha, this was all an elaborate ruse to get information."

Sherlock smiled. "No. My apologies, the invitation was genuine. My attempt at small talk, however, is going to be somewhat skewed."

Red nodded, chuckling, "That figures. And you're right, it was incredibly lucky, which is how I knew it was going to bite Corporate Security on the ass, something I take a bit of satisfaction in, I can't deny."

I choked back a laugh as Sherlock's surprise morphed into eagerness. Something had gone wrong with the Drive, something the press didn't know about yet. Red was loving it.

"What happened?" Sherlock asked.

"Well, while the police are getting criticized for not having found the thief yet, Corporate Security returned the retrieved drive to the company, who promptly tested it for damage and discovered it was a fake."

"A fake!"

"What makes it even better is that CorpSec let up on the chase after the guy because he had dropped it. If they hadn't let up, he wouldn't have made it across the sector border."

"What was his escape route? How did he manage to steal the Almandine Drive in the first place?"

Red savored her next sip a little longer than was probably necessary. "He's an employee of the company. He was working to set everything up for the big debut display, and just walked off with it."

Sherlock and I blinked. "He walked off with it?" I repeated, incredulous.

"The thing's smaller than your thumb," Red pointed out, "easy to palm. Everyone was busy with the setup, the Corporate Security were bored, he waited for a moment no one was looking, swiped it, and nonchalantly walked off. He didn't get very far before someone noticed, and the chase was on."

Sherlock went to his desk and brought out a map of the Corporate Sector. "His route," he repeated as he spread out the map, "do you know how he got out of the sector?"

Red shook her head as she looked over his shoulder, pointing. "The display was being set up over here, but he exited the sector here. Security mentioned that they chased him down

Market Avenue, then onto 13th Street and from there through this alley to Border Park, where they lost him. We started the search for him at the park, and moved out from there. Haven't found any trace of him," she chuckled humorlessly, "and now that the drive's a fake, cops are getting all the grief instead of the Corporate Security idiots that let him get away. Not that I can really complain, it's not my case."

"Not your case?" I asked.

"Not my department, remember?" They returned to their seats, "And they haven't seen fit to reinstate my position as official Lestrade yet."

Sherlock choked on his scotch.

"If you're dying for a case though, there's always the usual anger-driven manslaughters, petty thefts, and mugging gone wrong," Red sipped at her glass and muttered, "and a Santa obsessed maniac."

"A what?" we exclaimed.

"Maybe not Santa. Maybe he has a thing for bears."

My jaw dropped as Sherlock's brow furrowed. "Red. Are you suggesting that the police are spending valuable time and resources looking for a man who is stealing toys like the one on that shelf?" he pointed.

Red glanced over at the shelf with the toy Rip had found. "Yes! Why do you have one?"

"An acquaintance brought it. Why on earth is this a matter for the police?"

"Well, it is theft of property, no matter how petty or silly," Red spoke deliberately, like she was calming down a small child, which made Sherlock bristle. "And worse, whoever it is has gone to great lengths to get at these things. A number of people have reported being attacked by an unidentifiable man who seemed primarily interested in getting at those toys, and he's broken into multiple private residences in the past two days, each time posing as an electrician or building safety inspector."

"What makes him unidentifiable?" I asked.

"Witnesses never get a good look at him, he's either wearing a hat pulled low or false facial hair or is moving too fast."

Sherlock scoffed, "These witnesses are not blind, surely they must have seen something, no matter how trivial it may seem."

Red rolled her eyes at Sherlock's acidity. "The witnesses inside buildings all reported a man of similar height in a uniform, but that's all. No one ever pays attention to workmen. The ones who were attacked said he was five feet eight, give or take a few inches, with a long dark winter coat and a wide brimmed hat. If you can find him based on that, I will personally see to it you get a medal."

Sherlock gave a short laugh. "Very well, I'll stop criticizing you."

"No, you won't. Wouldn't want you to, really. Just keep the criticism to stuff actually worth criticizing."

Sherlock sighed. "I'm afraid I can't help myself, I'm... restless."

Red nodded, "I figured."

"So, nothing connects all these robberies?" I asked.

"All the victims bought their toys from the same store, but that's it. As it's one of only two stores with any stock left, it's not surprising."

"Which store?" Sherlock asked.

"It's on the corner of Market and 13th… oh." Red put her glass down and her head in her hands. "Oh, no way. No. Way." She glared at the grinning consulting detective. "This is your fault."

"My fault?"

"I blame you for the sudden and bizarre ways my life plays out like a mystery novel."

Sherlock smiled, broadly, "I'm afraid I have nothing to do with that, not intentionally at least. Cheer up, Red, at least you know who the thief is, and where the drive is hidden."

"The Almandine Drive thief is the same guy that's stealing bears?" I exclaimed.

Red sighed, and tossed back the remains of her scotch. "Yep," she coughed, "looks like it. Which means he probably hid it in one, which means someone's going to have to track down a hell of a lot of toys, a few days before Christmas no less."

"Maybe not," Sherlock shrugged, "we don't know how much time had passed before the thief returned to the store in an attempt to retrieve his item, or how many toys were sold."

"You going to be there in the morning?"

"Oh, Red," Sherlock smiled, "I wouldn't miss it for the world."

The toy shop had a constantly shifting hologram of all the hot toys of the year playing across the roof, while the windows were filled with their featured deals lit up in red and green lighting. White and red dressed sales associates had just barely finished arranging the displays when we walked through the door. We were the first in the shop, but shortly behind us started a trickle of early-morning shoppers.

"Can I help you find something today?" a pretty young man with a dusting of white glitter eyeshadow asked us.

"No, but you can help me a great deal by answering a few questions," Sherlock was all business, the detective in full force. He'd gone with a modern suit and overcoat this time, hoping to avoid unnecessary attention, but his manners were still as commanding as ever. Red smirked. She was with us in an unofficial capacity, at least for now, primarily to enjoy the show.

'Zeph,' as the nametag identified the glittery sales associate, was taken aback but maintained his smile and nodded. "What questions?"

"Were there any strange visitors to the shop recently?"

"No."

"Are you certain?"

"Yes… well, I mean, there was a guy in our storeroom, but Lani caught him and threatened to call Security. He got out of here real fast after that."

"The storeroom?"

"Yeah, looking at all our Santa Bear inventory. I just heard about it, I didn't get into work 'til later."

"Where is Lani?"

"She works the afternoon shift today, she'll be in at one o'clock."

Sherlock sighed. "Of course. We'll be back."

"I've got to get going," Red said as we exited the shop, "I can be back here this afternoon, but I suspect you're more than capable of handling this without my help."

Sherlock half grinned. "I will keep you informed. Ah, Red, one question before you go. Do you have any idea why the thief, being in possession of a decoy, did not simply swap the drive rather than run with it?"

"The display dock was specifically designed to match the drive's contours. The decoy didn't fit properly. Both Security and the Company figured the surface had been damaged when it hit the ground, and kept it quiet until they could determine if its functionality had suffered as well. That's when they found out it was a fake."

"I see. And the name of the thief?"

"Don't know."

"You said he was working to set up the display, surely Security must have a record."

"They have a list of people cleared by the company to be there. All of those people have been accounted for. This guy got in with a fake badge."

Sherlock nodded once. "Thank you."

"Since the investigation is on hold," I started to suggest as Red left, but Sherlock cut me off.

"If you wish to remain in this artificial construction of vacuous transient pleasure, I won't stop you," he declared as he started walking.

I hurried after him, "Ouch. That was particularly harsh, even for you."

"To be fair, that description applies to the Corporate Sector in general, not just during the holidays."

I cocked my head, concerned. "You've never talked that

way about it before."

"I'm in a foul mood," he grumbled, "It is cold, it is early, the sector's ridiculous smoking ban prohibits me the comfort of a cigarette, and I am…"

"Chomping at the bit?" I supplied.

He grinned a little. "Yes. Though 'champ' is the verb."

"Champ?"

"Champ; to bite or chew noisily. This meaning is now obsolete in vernacular speech, the word being replaced by 'chomp', also a verb of the same meaning, though chomped things are often eaten while champed things are not."

"You know you sound like a textbook when you do that?"

"So you've said."

"Are you heading to the park?"

"If one can call it that."

"Think you'll find anything?"

"Not at all, but I have to do something until this afternoon."

Border Park is a square strip of green towards the edge of Corporate Sector, accented with some artificial trees to provide a small bit of shade to the occasional shoppers taking a break or having an impromptu picnic with their take-out lunches. When it was first put in place, there was a small playground for children, but Corporate Sector families apparently disliked the park's proximity to the border, and Non-C families disliked the park's location inside Corporate Sector, each for different reasons, or perhaps different perspectives on the same reason. Either way, the playground was removed, replaced with a fancy bird bath and a rock garden. Now the whole park was covered with a thin layer of snow. The footprints of a man running were still visible, showing how little the park was visited, especially in the winter.

"The prints disappear as soon as he reaches the street on the other side," Sherlock stated, "giving us no indication of his hiding place. Without knowing his identity…" he stopped, eyes widening. "Watts, I am an idiot."

He ran back the way we came before I could say anything. I chased after him, plowing through crowds, narrowly dodging cars, until he ran through the doors of the Corporate Security Headquarters. I slid to a halt outside, debated going in after him, cursed a few times, and followed.

The young officer behind the front desk was staring at him, amazed. "I - I'm sorry," he stuttered, "ah, but I can't—"

"For heaven's sake, just tell whoever was in charge of security for the Almandine Drive to get down here, or send me up to them."

"But… um, ok, hang on a sec," the officer quickly dialed a code, waited a moment, and reported, "Mr. Cole will be right with you."

The man who came out of the elevator a moment later hadn't even changed from his clothes into the black and white Security gear. He was a few years younger than us and looked more annoyed than people usually do when Sherlock summons them. He also seemed vaguely familiar.

"Ah," I could hear Sherlock's hopes sinking as he spoke. "How's your little girl?"

"She's great. So's the wife. Gonna tell me anything

new?"

"I wasn't, given the unfavorable reaction it provided last time, however if you like—"

"What are you doing here?"

It finally clicked. The officer in charge of security for the Almandine Drive was the same one who questioned us after Sangrave had her henchman shot through a window. We hadn't exactly hit it off.

"I simply wanted to ask why you haven't given the security camera footage of the Almandine Drive theft to the police."

"Who says we didn't?"

"If you had, they would have identified the man."

"Just because the press haven't reported it, it doesn't mean the police don't know it."

Sherlock raised a skeptical brow. "You are suggesting that the police are in possession of all information required to find this man, and yet haven't?"

"Looks like it."

"And this isn't simply an attempt at throwing all the media attention and blame on the City Police and away from the glaring fault of a Corporate Sector Security so lax in their duty that they let a man with a fake I.D on site and then let him walk away, halting the chase when they thought they had the goods and not caring about the fate of the thief?"

"You need to leave," Cole glared.

"Of course, if it wasn't a case of Security incompetence, then that means a Security officer was in on the theft—"

"I said you need to leave. Now. I'm not going to ask

again."

Sherlock held up his hand in mock surrender. "We're going. He can fill in all the details when we find him."

"If the Police can't find him, why do you think you can?"

"Oh, sir," Sherlock smiled, "what is finding a simple thief to a man who has come back from the dead? Merry Christmas." With a bow and a flourish, we walked out.

I held back my laugh until we were on the street, "That was the most egotistical statement you've ever made."

He cleared his throat with a miniscule shrug, "Yes, well. I find I am warming up to this little problem. There is nothing quite so stimulating as a case where everything goes against you."

"This is going to be your big comeback, isn't it?"

"Hm? Oh. I suppose."

"You're such a diva."

"Ha! Does that make you an adoring fan?"

I punched his arm, "I'm the manager that makes sure you don't get into trouble."

Chuckling, he steered me towards the edge of the Sector, "Come, there is a place down this way that serves decent coffee. We can pass the time while we wait for 'Lani' to arrive at work."

Sherlock cursed under his breath.

"I see her, she's in the corner by the gaming cards."

"Gaming cards?"

"Cards with codes printed on them for downloads. Monsters, weapons, tools, depends on the genre."

"Watts, just tell me what she looks like."

"Short chestnut hair pulled back in small braids, thin girl?"

"I see her. You saw her nametag with your cyberoptic?"

"Of course."

"There is certainly something to be said for cybernetics." We began our slow progress through the crowded store. "I begin to suspect Red's business elsewhere today had more to do with a desire to stay away from stores in the afternoon," Sherlock mumbled.

"You just now thought of this?"

"You're right, I'm far too trusting. I should always consider ulterior motives in others, especially during this time of year."

"I can't tell if that was sarcasm or not."

He half-grinned, and said nothing. We'd reached Lani. "Before you ask," he interrupted her cheerful greeting, "no, we don't want to see anything, and we do not want help finding anything, we just want to ask you some questions about the man in your storeroom the other day. We're working with the police."

Lani blinked, surprised, but resumed her pleasantly helpful smile. "What do you want to know?"

"When did you see him?"

"I don't remember exactly, we've been so busy... a few days ago, week max."

"Describe what happened, in as much detail as possible."

"I went back into the storeroom to restock our Santa Bear display, and there was a man going through them. I threatened to call Security, and he ran out of the store."

"Details," Sherlock patiently repeated, "I need details.

What specifically was he doing?"

"Just… going through them," Lani was flustered, "looking at their coats and tossing them to the floor."

"How tall was he?"

"He was bent over the stock boxes, I'm not sure. He had dark curly hair, though, and wore a rough winter coat."

"Is there a window in the storeroom?"

"No. Why would there be?"

"Can anyone enter the storeroom?"

Lani shifted uncomfortably. "This time of year, yeah. We leave the storeroom door unlocked because we're always going in and out and it's a pain to have to wait for the scanner to register permission every time, even though we aren't really supposed to."

"I see. He snuck in through the crowd and slipped through the unlocked storeroom door. Has it been this busy all week?" he gestured to the crowd around us.

"Pretty much."

"Has anyone mentioned seeing Corporate Sector Security run by recently?"

"Yeah, a few of them nearly ran over some of our customers a while back coming down Market. Then they came back and went down 13th."

"Would it be possible for me to see a list of all the purchases of one of those bears in the last week, with dates and names of purchasers?"

"We aren't really supposed to give out—"

"I realize it is a bit unusual, but we are working with the police and it would be very helpful." Seeing her hesitation, he produced a thin wallet from his inner breast pocket, "If you need to see identification—"

"Oh, no, don't worry about it," she protested, mildly embarrassed, "Just the last week?"

"Yes."

"Ok, hang on a sec."

As we waited for her to come back, I asked him, "You don't actually have police identification, do you?"

"Of course not."

"You were expecting her to be embarrassed by second-guessing a cop."

"I thought it likely. Corporate Sector residents have very little dealings with the actual City Police force. If it hadn't worked, that wallet holds a false I.D."

I sighed.

Lani returned with a tablet in hand. "I can pull up the report for that item type and send it to you. Email?"

I gave her my address. "I'll forward a copy to Detective Murphy," I said as an aside to Sherlock. The more official this sounded, the better.

"Alright," Lani was still uncertain, but now more anxious to get us out than anything else. "Anything else I can help you with?"

Sherlock tipped his hat, "Thank you very much for your time, miss."

We made as quick a departure as the crowds would allow. "Thank you, Watts."

"For what?"

"For saving me the embarrassment of explaining why I

don't have any place for her to send a file to."

I smiled, shaking my head. "You have got to get some sort of account one of these days. At least email."

"I prefer speaking to people. Besides, typical computer interfaces and I don't work well together."

"You're weirdly paranoid about certain technologies."

"I'm wary, and I honestly don't see the point in a great many 'essential' things. Why not just call a person on the phone? Write down a note?"

"How'd you contact people while you were Sebastian?"

"Word of mouth and messages left at hotel desks. It added to the eccentric charm of the character."

"It made people think you're crazy."

He smirked. "Were they wrong?"

I smiled. "I still haven't figured that out, yet."

"Miss Ghost!" Sherlock called as we arrived home, "I have a job for you!" he sprinted up the stairs as I forwarded the file to Ghost. He came down shortly, and went for his pipe. "Ghost will run the names of the people who have bought those bears in the past week and find their addresses. Then she will find out which of them the thief has already attempted to rob."

"I get the feeling I've been replaced as internet researcher," I joked as I hung up our coats and started making a late lunch.

"My dear fellow, no insult was intended," he said with a small grin, smoke wreathing around his head, "she is simply the more efficient choice. If I'm going to live with a runner over my head, I may as well take advantage of the fact."

"I'm not complaining. Are you going to eat today?"

"Ask me again after I've finished this pipe."

"And after Ghost gives you the results."

"Exactly."

I soon heard the sound of the printer going. The list it printed off was fairly long, but Ghost had already noted the homes that had been broken into and people who had reported being attacked.

Sherlock read over it a few times, and smiled, "Excellent. The attacks on people are somewhat random, likely depending on who he saw with a bear on the street, but the houses!" He leaped up and rushed to the phone. Two cryptic calls later, he was chuckling to himself and quivering with energy. "If all goes well tonight, Watts, it will indeed be a very merry Christmas."

And so it was that I found myself hiding in the immaculately overgrown artificial shrubbery behind the private residence of Ms. Sarai Wescott. It was one in the morning, and it was snowing. Sherlock had ordered us to keep all sound and movement to an absolute minimum, so I couldn't even complain or ask why we were there. Red was with us and maintained her watch with a professional, if tired, air. Sherlock was perfectly still, his eyes fixed on the house like a bird of prey about to dive.

I was thinking about breaking another heat pack when a shadow moved across the small lawn. Red was instantly alert and focused, while Sherlock leaned forward in predatory anticipation. The shadow was working at a window, and after an agonizing silence we heard a faint click as it opened. The thief climbed inside, and we waited.

A faint light glowed within the house. "He's checking

the bear instead of simply stealing it," Sherlock said in a low voice.

"We'll still get him for breaking and entering, even if he doesn't take anything," Red replied, "Let's move in."

But there wasn't time. The thief was already climbing back out the window. As soon as his feet hit the ground, Sherlock pounced.

With a running leap, Sherlock was on the man's back, knocking him against the house and to the ground. Red and I rushed after him, arriving just as Sherlock was thrown off. I planted my left foot squarely in the small of the thief's back, the firm pressure of my cyberleg on his spine keeping him in place while Red cuffed him.

Forcibly standing him up, we discovered a perfectly average looking man of five foot eight or so, with dark curly hair and worn, dark clothes and coat. His snarl soon faded to a resigned grin, no less menacing for its decreased intensity.

His face was suddenly illuminated by all the lights in the house coming on.

"Caught him, did you?" said a grey-haired woman as she appeared at the window in her night robe.

"Yes, thank you. Ms. Wescott, I presume?" Sherlock asked.

"Yes, and you must be the detective I spoke to. It was exactly as you said, there was a repairman today from the security company. I didn't let the bear out of my sight. He turned off my security system, didn't he?"

"Yes. It's fortunate you still use old fashioned locks on your front door. Thank you for your assistance."

"Well, I couldn't just let him take my granddaughter's present, now could I? Would you three like to come in? You're covered in snow."

"Thanks for the offer, Ms. Wescott," Red replied, "but we've got to get this guy into custody. Happy Holidays."

We led our prisoner back out to the street where Red's personal car was waiting. "Less conspicuous than a cop car," she said, "not as secure of course, but it'll get the job done. Especially with Watts in the back with his gun on the prisoner," she grinned.

"The prisoner" rolled his eyes.

As we reached the police station, I couldn't wait any more. "Ok, Sherlock, how the hell did you know he was going to break into that house tonight?"

Sherlock grinned slightly and began his explanation, "When the Almandine Drive was stolen, the thief ducked into a toy store in an attempt to evade Corporate Security by taking advantage of the crowds. He made his way into the storeroom, likely looking for a way out, and found none. Realizing there was a good chance he would be caught, he decided to temporarily hide the Drive. When he expected to return to it is impossible to say, but what is certain is that he underestimated the popularity of those bears."

"He hid it in a bear, took off, was spotted by Security and decided to drop his decoy to escape," I summarized.

"Precisely. He then circled back into the Corporate Sector later, and snuck back into the shop's storeroom to search for the Drive, but the bear had already been sold. He was discovered and forced to leave, but he obtained a list of everyone who had bought a bear between the time he hid the Drive and the time he discovered it gone."

"How'd he get the list?"

"As he has broken into multiple buildings through the simple utilization of disguises, he could have returned to the store or perhaps he got his information online if he is skilled enough. No matter how he got the report, the houses that have been broken into have all been in the exact order of sales."

"And Wescott was next on the list."

Sherlock nodded, "I warned her that if anyone came to the house she should take care to keep the toy bear in her sight at all times. It took some convincing, but she listened, and followed instructions. The easiest point of entry for the theft would be that rear window, hence our hiding in the shrubbery behind the house. He was unable to take the bear during the day, and so he turned off the security system in the guise of fixing it, and came back tonight."

Red sighed. "But this still leaves us without an Almandine Drive."

Sherlock nodded. "True. But at least you now have a list of people who might have it."

With a short laugh, Red turned to the thief, "You had to hide it in a toy, didn't you? On Christmas!" When the only answer she got was a smirk, Red turned back to us, "I'll fill you in on anything we find out."

Sherlock inclined his head, "I look forward to it. Good luck."

Sherlock was in a suspiciously good mood the next day.

I couldn't imagine why; the case had been something of a disappointment. The thief was caught, but the Almandine Drive was still missing, and the resolution was… well, boring.

I said as much to him after lunch. He gave me one of his infuriatingly all-knowing grins. "You're right of course," he said, "it was not nearly the case I had hoped it would be, but it still maintained a small quality of satisfaction in the end."

"How?"

"Well, I did find the Almandine Drive, after all."

"What? No, you didn't."

"Didn't I?"

I stared at him. "You found it?!"

"Dear me, Watts, I think the incessant cacophony of the season may have caused you to lose your hearing."

"Where the hell did you find it! When?"

He grinned again, this time wickedly mischievous. "Guess."

Dumbstruck, I didn't even notice someone was at the door. Sherlock answered, showing in a man with short brown hair in worn clothes.

"Ah, my name's Dean Haining, I'm here to see Sherlock," he said.

"I am he," Sherlock shook his hand briefly, "and this is my friend and colleague Dr. Watts," he gestured in my direction as he went toward his desk, "and this, I believe, is your hat and bear."

I blinked. I'd completely forgotten about the bear and hat Rip had brought us.

"Yes, it is," Mr. Haining said, "I was certain they were

lost for good. I was attacked by a gang while walking home, and when a man with deathstrikes rushed in, I panicked with everyone else and took off. I wasn't too worried about the hat, but the bear was supposed to be a present for my daughter. I was pretty damn surprised when I heard at the site that someone had found it and wanted to give it back. I work construction, you see."

Sherlock nodded. "Well, I'm glad word got to you in time for Christmas. It is a popular toy."

"Yeah. I'm lucky I found this one. Got it for half off."

"Oh?"

"It's defective. The coat covers it, but there's a tear in the tummy. Figured I could stitch it up when I got home, and my little girl would never notice. The man at the shop agreed to sell it to me for half-off."

"That's lucky. Which shop?"

"Games and Gifts, in the Corporate Sector, corner of Market and 13th. Thank you again, you've made my girl very happy. Merry Christmas."

I muttered a stunned but polite 'Merry Christmas' and turned to Sherlock. His tiny smile was a little too smug. "No way," I accused, "this has to be a joke."

Chuckling to himself, he grabbed his coat and hat. "I called Red early this morning and told her the police shouldn't bother interrogating people about their bears. She demanded answers of course, but I told her I had the case well in hand, and would give her results tomorrow. Now, it is Christmas Eve, and I have some last-minute preparations to attend to."

I started to protest, but he was already gone.

I didn't see him much for the rest of the day. Christmas Eve or not, it passed like any other day for me. I had an emergency call from a patient, Ghost remained upstairs as usual, and I tried to keep myself occupied while home.

Then late that night, Sherlock asked me to go with him on an important mission. He'd been preparing for it all evening. With no idea of what we were doing, I agreed. He handed me a sack full of presents and we did our best impersonation of Santa Claus. I've never had so much fun breaking and entering homes. The Irregulars were in for a wonderful surprise.

"And all this time I thought you hated Christmas," I commented as we came home.

Sherlock shook his head, a sympathetic smile on his face. "No, my friend. I hate what the City does to Christmas. There is a difference."

Staying out late to play Santa meant sleeping in Christmas Day, but we were up with plenty of time to get ready to go to the Murphy family's late afternoon dinner. Their address was just inside the Corporate Sector, no doubt to keep their daughter as safe as possible on their budget. The door was answered by the very girl herself.

"Hi!" she said, brown eyes beaming up at us. She had Red's hair, in short curls, and wore a green dress with a candy cane pin. "You're Sherlock," she declared, "and you're Dr. Watts!" she said to me before suddenly becoming very proper and opening the door wide, "Please come in!"

Sherlock smiled pleasantly at the eight-year-old. "Thank you. Our fame precedes us, Watts," he said as we stepped inside, removing his top hat. "You must be Miss Mary."

She nodded, barely containing her excitement. "My moms said you were coming. Do you like our tree?"

We looked to the side. A bright fuchsia pine tree decked out in silver and handmade decorations and bright lights stood in the corner. Sherlock cocked an eyebrow, smiling. "You chose it," he said to Mary. She nodded, proudly. "I have a feeling it suits you very well."

"You can say that again," Red laughed as she came in, sleeves rolled up. "Sorry I couldn't greet you right away, helping in the kitchen. Let me take your coats and hats, have a seat. Can I get you anything? Coffee? Stronger?"

"Stronger," we said in unison.

The apartment was a two bedroom with a large dining and kitchen area and a small living room. It was nice, family pictures hung everywhere along with the holiday holly and garlands and snowflakes. Mary hovered nearby after we sat, uncertain of what she should do.

Sherlock made it easy for her. "Please join us, Mary. We've heard precious little about you."

She eagerly sat at our feet, something Sherlock had not expected. "I've heard *everything* about you."

"Oh?"

"You're the detective that works with Mama Red a lot. You solve a lot of crimes and do a lot of good stuff."

Sherlock smiled. "And what about yourself, miss?"

She giggled. "Why'd you call me Miss?"

"It's polite."

"Then how come no one else says it?" she asked with a

touch of a child's omniscient sass.

"No one else thinks it's important. I am a bit old-fashioned."

"I could tell," she nodded before suddenly blushing, "I mean—"

"That's quite alright," Sherlock was amused. He'd purposefully worn his best Victorian suit, complete with a crimson waistcoat and his golden pocket-watch. "I know what you mean. Now, then, you were going to tell us about yourself."

After seeing him so often with the Irregulars, it really shouldn't surprise me that he's good with kids, but it does. He asked Mary questions about her school, what she liked to do for fun, and not once did it ever sound like he was talking down to her or treating her like a child. Mary, for her part, proved to be a very intelligent girl with a voracious reading habit who also enjoyed playing sports when she wasn't commanding armies online.

That last bit gave Sherlock pause at first. Then he started tentatively quizzing her on military strategy.

Red had been poking her head in from the kitchen since we arrived, but hadn't wanted to interrupt. When dinner was ready, she came in just in time to hear Sherlock coaching her daughter in battle tactics. "What in the world are you teaching her?" she demanded with a grin.

"Actually, very little," Sherlock replied from his position next to Mary on the floor. He'd been demonstrating battlefield troop movements with ornaments. "She's already figured out much of the basics through trial and error in her games. She merely lacks the experience and refinement of historical background to draw upon."

"That's not a bad thing," I reassured her in a low voice, "he's giving you a compliment."

Red shook her head, smiling. "Ok. Well, dinner's ready, so everyone at the table."

The entire meal, Red was obviously restraining herself from interrogating Sherlock, but a glance at her wife would shift the conversation to something completely different, usually about Mary, or Maddie's work as a veterinarian, though Mary demanded stories of Sherlock's work as well. I was happy to oblige.

Then as Maddie cleared away the dessert dishes, Sherlock asked, "How went the interrogation of the thief?"

"Terribly!" Red shouted, earning her a reprimand from her wife.

"Maureen Murphy, you promised you wouldn't talk about work at the table."

"The meal's over!" she protested.

"You're still sitting at the table," Maddie calmly pointed out.

"Then we'll move!"

"It's my fault," Sherlock graciously stated, "I brought it up. I know something she doesn't."

"What else is new?" Maddie muttered with a small grin. "Mary, help me clean up please."

"Gee, thanks," Red said. Once her family was out of the room, she gave Sherlock her best no-nonsense glare. "Do you have any idea how ridiculous this whole thing is? I had to go to my superiors and tell them to put an investigation on hold, just because a Victorian Era madman said so. I had to convince them that not only was it a good idea to restart the liaison program, but to do it immediately, and that you knew where the damn Drive was! If I don't walk in tomorrow with the Almandine Drive in my hand, I'm going to be fired."

Sherlock was taken aback. "Red, I apologize. I was enjoying myself too much, perhaps. I assure you, I never—"

"Yeah, I know," Red waved away his apology, "you were just being you. Have to make everything a big production, don't you?"

He half-grinned, "Not quite everything." Sherlock drew a small gift-wrapped box from an inner pocket, and set it down in front of Red. "A token of the season."

Red stared at it. "Is that what I think it is?"

"Likely."

"Of course it's giftwrapped," she muttered under her breath as she picked it up. Sherlock grinned. Inside was a small, deep red rectangle, nearly paper thin and half the size of her thumb. Red gave a short laugh. "Alright, where was it?"

"It was close at hand the entire time," Sherlock said with as much nonchalance as possible. "Last night I was brooding over the case—"

"Sulking," I muttered.

He ignored me, "—as I was, admittedly, disappointed by the way it had turned out, when I recalled that an acquaintance of ours had recently brought us a bear just like the ones the Drive was hidden in. In a moment of pure impulsiveness, I picked it up and examined it. When I discovered the tear under the coat, I realized what I held. I carefully extracted the Drive, and went to bed."

Red blinked. "So, if you'd just looked at your bear—"

"The entire matter would have been solved in less than three minutes, yes. I have thoroughly berated myself for the gross oversight already, I assure you."

"Good," Red smiled.

"Is that the thing you were so worried about?" Maddie asked as she came in with a tray of coffee, Mary close behind.

"Yep," Red said, "luckily."

Maddie smirked. "Luck? You mean you doubted Sherlock would figure it out?"

Sherlock smiled. "As a friend of mine recently said, I'm only human. I often benefit from a bit of luck now and then."

"Sometimes more than others," I said.

"Indeed. Ah, thank you, Mary," Sherlock said as she brought him a cup of coffee.

"Did you and Mama Red catch a thief?"

"We did. I was just about to ask your mother how the interrogation went."

Red rolled her eyes. "He won't talk, so all we've got is what we already knew."

"You could investigate why Security didn't lift a finger," Maddie grumbled.

"That's easy, honey," Red scoffed, "they're Security. What do they care about police work?"

"I wonder," Sherlock muttered.

I folded my arms, "You just got back from the dead, don't start looking for a new archvillain."

Sherlock laughed. "I'm not trying to, Watts. You may

not believe me, but I would rather not worry about people trying to kill me for at least a few months."

"I'll drink to that," Red lifted her mug.

And we did.

The Story with the Snake

Sherlock insisted Red get all the credit for the Almandine Drive ("Call it a Christmas present,") I think because he was embarrassed by the solution. Still, Red made sure to mention him anytime a reporter asked. Her joke about being the 'official Lestrade' somehow got picked up by the press, who dubbed it her actual title. She was not thrilled at first, but came around to the idea once she got her fellow cops to stop laughing.

With the confirmation that he was really back, the Internet erupted. Rumors flew all over about how he faked his death, and people started showing up at our door just to see him 'do the trick.' Sherlock had to post a warning that people cease and desist, or else be trespassed, or worse. There were a few genuine clients, of course, but nothing challenging. Even with all the attention, Sherlock was bored. Then, on a clear winter's morning, a young woman from the Corporate Sector came to see the detective.

Her name was Tina Eckans, and she was afraid for her life. She wasn't at all hysterical, but simply put her case forward to Sherlock as he sat across from her in his chair, smoke from his pipe creating a haze around his head.

"I do not have any concrete evidence, but I am convinced nonetheless," she explained. "There is a sense of dread over the house. My brother thinks I'm being paranoid, but I know that I have not imagined the sounds of something in my room at night. There's a whistling, and the sound of something moving past my ear, but by the time I turn the light on there's nothing there."

His gaze was intent upon her, almost burning through the thin clouds of smoke. "A whistling."

She nodded. "I can't go to the police—"

"They would never believe you without more evidence of danger," Sherlock finished with a dismissive gesture, "but you hope that I will at least entertain the possibility. Can you be more specific as to why you feel you are in danger? Is it simply these sounds at night?" When she didn't answer, he sighed, "Miss Eckans—"

"Tina."

"— you are obviously from the Corporate Sector, and are very wealthy. That particular shade of ice blue with which you have colored your curls is very vogue this week. Top quality clothing combined with a private car waiting for you outside, with a chauffeur no less, screams money. I've had wealthy clients before, but never for a vague feeling. Why come to me when it would be easy to hire a guard?"

"Our security is top notch, and fully automated. Having a stranger in the house would cause more anxiety than anything else, and be unnecessary."

"If you have such confidence in your security, then you must fear a threat from within the house. Who lives with you?"

"My brother. Our father was recently admitted to a special care facility. Mental issues."

"Which of you stands to inherit?"

She blinked, processing what he was implying. "Kris wouldn't kill me!"

"Then whom do you suspect?"

"I don't know. I thought it was our servants; there are two, and the whistling only happened when they work nights. So, I gave them a few days off." She shifted uncomfortably, "The whistling happened again last night."

"Then your servants aren't the cause, which leaves your brother."

"Kris wouldn't kill me."

"You're close, you and your brother?"

She hesitated. "Not particularly. If he killed me, he'd lose his share of the inheritance."

The corner of Sherlock's mouth twisted up in a miniscule smirk. "How reassuring. What exactly do you want from me, Miss Eckans?"

"I want you to come to my home and see if you… see… anything. I want some peace of mind, and no one is willing to believe that maybe I'm not imagining things."

Sherlock considered her a long moment, a slow exhale of smoke making her cough a little. With a miniscule shrug, Sherlock stood. "Very well."

"You'll help?"

"I will try. Dr. Watts and I — oh, I'm sorry Watts, I presume..."

I smiled, "This afternoon I have patients to see, but I'd be free this evening."

"Excellent. Miss Eckans, if you would be so good as to give us your address, we will see you this evening and hopefully set your mind at ease."

"Thank you," she stood with a sigh, "I'm very grateful that you're at least willing to try."

"A whistling, huh?" I asked after she was gone.

Sherlock nodded as he pulled a volume from his bookshelf. "Yes. We must be careful in this, Watts."

"What do you think's going on?"

"I think that I am not the only person in the City who's read Conan Doyle anymore. The whistling sound in a dark bedroom reminds me of "The Speckled Band.""

"The story with the snake?" He nodded. "So, then it's a trap?"

"Possibly. Or, this all might simply be coincidence. Miss Eckans might be truly afraid, her intuition warning her of a very real danger. I cannot sit idly by and ignore that possibility. We will find out which it is this evening."

The address she gave us was private residence in the middle of the Corporate Sector, two stories of modern architecture in varying shades of white. Tina opened the door and breathed a sigh of relief. "I'm so glad you're here," she showed us in, "Kris does not approve, but… oh, here, let me take your things."

As she put away our coats and hats, we glanced at our surroundings. It was done up to look like we were standing in an old historical country house, completely at odds with the exterior, all brown woods and wicker chairs and squares of oriental rugs along the floors. There was an ornamental fireplace, though here the illusion was shattered by the lack of any heat from the otherwise convincing flames. All the decor of days gone by, without the loss of any modern comfort.

Tina returned with a fashionably dressed man behind

her. "I must apologize for the inconvenience," he said right away, "my sister is -"

"Concerned," Sherlock finished, "and it's no trouble at all to set her fears to rest. If there is nothing here, then we have had a pleasant outing, and if there is something for her to be afraid of, then all the better that we discover it as soon as possible."

The brother, Kris, seemed like he was about to protest, but deflated. "True, I suppose." He and his sister were a study in contrasts. While Tina had short, ice blue curls and vibrant blue eyes, Kris kept his wavy hair dark and tousled, his dark eyes nearly hidden underneath. Tina favored pale colored layered blouses and skirts, Kris wore a suit of dark green in various textures. They shared the same pale skin and full lips, but if I hadn't been told they were related, I never would have guessed.

Tina was very pleased with her brother's silence. "Should I show you around?" she asked us.

"Yes, thank you," Sherlock nodded.

Sherlock's eyes constantly scanned up and down as we walked, taking in every detail of the house. He did not seem much impressed, nor did he seem alarmed. I think Tina was becoming disheartened by his lack of interest, until we got to the bedrooms.

"There are three bedrooms. Kris has the largest, the one our father used to have before he moved. I have the second largest, with the third next door acting as a guest room."

"The largest room going to the oldest sibling?" I asked.

Kris chuckled. "I'm younger, but I grabbed it first and Tina didn't object."

Tina shrugged, "All of my things were already in my room and I didn't want to bother moving around. This is my room," she opened the door.

It was homely, but of a nice size. A brown chest of drawers stood in one corner, a narrow white bed in another, and a dressing-table on the left-hand side of the window. These items, plus a small chair, made up all the furniture in the room, save for a square of carpet in the center. The floorboards and the paneling of the walls were brown oak.

Sherlock stood in a corner and gazed around, "This room is remarkably void of modern accessories."

Tina smiled. "Only because they aren't turned on."

She picked up a small remote from her dressing table and activated the hidden panel in the wall, revealing an entertainment screen. "There are speakers wired into the walls. There's an intercom to access the help, turned on by pulling on that rope by the bed." She turned off the entertainment system, the walls swallowing it again.

Sherlock half-grinned, as unimpressed as ever, but possibly more amused. "I see. You will excuse me for a few minutes while I satisfy myself as to this floor." He threw himself down on his face with his lens in his hand, and crawled quickly backwards and forwards, examining minutely the cracks between the boards. Then he did the same with the room's woodwork paneling.

Tina and Kris looked on as if they watched the antics of a madman. "Well, you wanted him to investigate," I murmured to Tina, "And you get what you asked for."

"I did, but he's just…"

"Strange, yeah. It looks a little weird, but he knows what he's doing."

Finally, Sherlock walked over to the bed and spent some time staring at it, and running his eyes up and down the wall. "Strange," muttered Sherlock, "What is the purpose of that ventilator just over the bed? It does not communicate with the outside air."

"It's purely decorative," Tina smiled.

"Indeed, it would have to be… Who had it installed?"

"No one. It's always been there."

"Always? Well, then perhaps it is nothing after all. Could we proceed to the guest room?"

The guest room was the same size as Tina's room, and plainly furnished. A bed, an armchair, a plain chair against the wall, a round table, and a single decorative bookshelf full of knick-knacks were all it contained.

"I assume it has all the hidden comforts of modern man as well?" Sherlock asked as he slowly walked around the room.

"Oh yes, it used to be Kris's room, so the entertainment system is top quality. Even has a safe hidden in the wall."

"A safe?" I asked. "For what?"

"Valuables, of course," grinned Kris. He opened a panel, revealing a safe with a fingerprint scanner. "I don't use it any more of course, but it's still here if guests want that extra bit of security."

"How does it open?"

Kris demonstrated, revealing the empty inside. "Guests can reset the scanner to their print for 24 hours."

"Why did you use it in the first place?" Sherlock asked.

"I kept my backup drive of all my important business documents there, as well as a few very valuable personal items."

"But why?"

"Oh, Kris doesn't trust anyone," Tina laughed, "Not even his own sister, and definitely not the help. He had another safe installed in Father's room to make up for this one. Ha, and he calls me paranoid."

"Being careful with valuables is not the same as fearing shadows," Kris muttered.

"Indeed, it is not," Sherlock quietly stated, lost in his thoughts for a moment before turning to our hostess. "Miss Eckans, I'm afraid I simply must have more data."

Tina frowned a moment before she was struck with sudden inspiration. "Would you like to spend the night?" The offer was surprising, to say the least. "If it's not inconvenient," Tina continued. "As I said before, the help have a few days off, but if you could be here during the night, maybe you'll find something."

"We are very much accustomed to fending for ourselves," Sherlock nearly grinned, "I'm sure we will manage."

"This is ridiculous," Kris started to groan, but his sister cut him off.

"I want them to stay, Kris. It's just one night. If there's nothing, then I'll shut up about the whole matter."

Kris sighed, and gestured helplessly. "Fine. They're welcome to stay."

I watched Sherlock pace the guest room from where I sat in the bed. "I don't like it, Watts. I don't like it at all."

"Don't like what?" I yawned.

"This whole place. That ventilator, in particular. It doesn't make sense, why bother sending the girl to me with a story clearly intended to make me think of "The Speckled Band," and then put me in the room with the ventilator adjoining hers?"

"Remind me why the ventilator was a bad thing?"

"The villain was murdering his stepdaughters to claim their inheritance. His method was to send a poisonous snake through the ventilator, in the hope of the snake one night biting them. I thought at first that her brother must be the cause, but apart from tormenting her, I see no connection between whistling from another room and life-threatening danger. There's no connection between their rooms. He could simply enter her bedroom I suppose, but why bother with the suspense? Not to mention he'd lose the inheritance. No, unless Miss Eckans is going to try to murder me with a snake tonight, a laughable scenario, I don't see any point in this."

"Maybe it's just a paranoid woman and a weird coincidence."

He sighed. "It is… possible… that the setting has spurred my imagination into running away with me."

"The fact that you haven't smoked since we arrived probably doesn't help," I muttered.

"I am not suffering withdrawal," he protested with deadly calm.

I held my hands up in surrender. "Look, it's late. We're both tired. I'm going to sleep. Wake me as soon as you figure out how this trap is supposed to work."

He half grinned, and shut off the light. I heard him sit in a chair, his fingertips drumming the chair's arm.

I sighed. "You're going to sit there thinking all night, aren't you?"

"Probably."

At least his fingers stopped. "Goodnight, Sherlock."

"Goodnight, Watts."

Tina Eckans was dead in the morning.

Kris found her when she didn't come out for breakfast. He immediately called Corporate Sector Security while I examined the body and Sherlock called the police.

"I was so preoccupied with the notion of a trap, I neglected the very real possibility of danger to my client," Sherlock scolded himself as he stood beside me. "I should have been by her door the whole night."

I shook my head, carefully checking her for any sign of violence. "If this hadn't happened last night, it'd just happen later when we weren't here."

"But in preventing it, I would have at least determined the nature of the danger." He remained expressionless, but angry guilt lurked behind his eyes. To him, this was one more coat of innocent blood on his hands.

"You don't know that for certain," I tried to reassure him, and froze. "Sherlock, look at her leg."

Sherlock knelt down by the bed. "A bite," he muttered, astonished. He dashed out and went straight to Kris's bedroom. "It didn't come through the ventilator, but I'll be damned if it's not hidden in the safe."

Kris's safe also had a fingerprint scanner, and there was no fingerprint sample immediately at hand.

"What are you doing in here?" Kris asked as he came in.

"Mr. Eckans, would you be kind enough to open this safe?" Sherlock asked.

"What? What's going on?"

"What is going on is that your sister has been murdered, killed by a venomous snake in the night, both literally and figuratively."

Kris's eyes widened. "What?!"

"Open the safe, Mr. Eckans."

"The safe... You suspect me?"

"You were the only other person here last night."

"That's ridiculous!"

"Then there is no reason for you not to open the safe."

A pounding on the door drew Kris away, with Sherlock and I close behind him. It was Corporate Security.

"My sister's been killed," Kris was telling the two officers, "arrest these men!"

My jaw dropped. Sherlock's face hardened. "I see."

"What exactly is going on?" one of the officers asked.

"My sister was delusional, paranoid, feared for her life, and had this so-called detective come to our home. Now she's dead, and no one else was here last night."

"This is ridiculous!" I protested.

"That's enough," the officer ordered. He pointed at Sherlock. "You. You're Sherlock." At Sherlock's nod, he said, "You and your friend have a seat." To Kris he asked, "Have the police been called?" Kris nodded. "Then you have a seat too.

Murder scene, we wait for them."

It wasn't a long wait. A benefit of having your own police representative is that when we call to report a murder, we get quick and personal results. Neither Corporate Security or Kris seemed particularly pleased when Red walked through the door, Detective Carson and a forensic team behind her.

"How was being dead?" Carson let slip as he walked through. We hadn't seen him since before Sherlock died, and his help had been invaluable to disrupting Sangrave's plans.

Sherlock permitted himself a slight grin. "Exhausting."

"Detective Carson will oversee the forensics team while we talk," Red stated, gesturing that everyone should stay seated, except for Corporate Security who stood to the side and waited, neither happy nor making a visible fuss about being shunted out of the picture for the moment.

"Now then, the victim is your sister?" Red asked Kris, who nodded. "Were you the one who found the body?"

"Yes. She was late getting out of bed, which never happens. I went to check on her, found her in her bed, tried to wake her and..." he trailed off with a wince and a shrug.

"Any signs of violence?" Red asked us.

"None," I said.

"Apart from the snakebite on her right thigh," Sherlock quietly added.

One of the Corporate guards stifled a scoff. Red frowned. "Am I correct in assuming she was a client?" she asked Sherlock.

Sherlock nodded. "She was afraid for her life."

"From?"

"She didn't know. That's why she hired me, to find and stop any danger there might be."

"She was paranoid," Kris muttered.

"Apparently not," Sherlock and Red said in unison.

Kris sighed, "The fact that someone killed her doesn't mean that there was always someone out to get her."

Red could sense there was something lurking behind that comment, but right then Detective Carson rushed up to her.

"You better come see this," he said.

I was confused as they went down the hall toward the guest room. Sherlock merely raised an entirely unsurprised brow. "What's going on?" I whispered to him.

His reply was a low sigh, "I believe I mentioned two snakes earlier, one figurative and one literal. Detective Carson has found the literal one."

I stared at him as I realized what was going on. "But why?"

"Miss Eckans said he'd be cut off if he killed her," Sherlock quietly stated, grim. "All he has to do is prove it wasn't him."

I glanced at Kris, and saw him grin.

I'd never seen Red look as serious as when she returned. "Mr. Eckans, did you know you there was a snake in the guest room safe?"

Kris's eyebrows shot up in alarm. "Of course not. It was empty yesterday."

Red said nothing for a moment. "All three of you are coming to the station with me." To the Corporate guards she said, "You won't be needed."

"Sounds like a scheme from a story," one of them muttered as we went past.

"It is," said Kris, "and it's from one of *his*," he gestured at Sherlock, who ignored him.

"Save it," Red ordered again as we got into her car and headed to the police station to start the long wait in an interrogation room.

"Detective Jackson. Lovely to see you again," Sherlock stated with a minimal amount of sarcasm.

"Where's Red?" I asked.

The blond prize-fighter of a detective sat down across the table from us. "Not coming. I get to ask the questions, mainly because the Chief heard about this little case and thought Red was too personally involved. Took him a little while to find someone on the force he could trust not to be partial to you."

Sherlock gave a short, almost bitter laugh, "Did you volunteer?"

"No, but I was happy to do it when asked," Jackson wrinkled his nose, "Do you have to smoke those things?"

Sherlock grinned as he blew a ring of smoke into the air, the cigarette dangling loosely from his fingers. "Have to? Not strictly speaking. As there was no instruction not to, I thought I would take the opportunity."

"Put it out. Bad enough habit, at least you could have the decency to use scented ones."

"We have very different definitions of 'decent,' you and I. The synthetic substance in those scented atrocities misses the point of smoking entirely," he complied, grinding the end into the tabletop.

"What point - never mind, I don't actually care. What were you doing at the Eckans residence?"

"Miss Eckans was my client. She was convinced her life was in danger. I thought there would be no harm done in looking into her concerns. We visited in the evening and decided to stay the night."

"Who did she think was out to get her?"

"She wasn't certain."

"You took the case on a vague feeling? Must've been a dull week."

"She specifically mentioned a detail from a story. I was suspicious. We went expecting a trap. When none appeared, I put her feelings down to paranoia, and explained the details as coincidence."

"But she wasn't paranoid."

"Apparently not." Sherlock was pensive, eyes fixed on his interrogator. I couldn't shake the impression of a predator that finds itself cornered by a bigger one, judging his chances of survival in the fight. It was an expression I'd never seen on my friend before. It worried me.

"The toxins found in the victim's body are consistent with those found in the venom of the snake found in the guest room safe," Jackson continued, "a safe which, Mr. Eckans insists, was empty before you arrived."

"The guest room safe was empty when we arrived," Sherlock confirmed, "but there is also a safe in Kris Eckans's room, which we did not see the inside of, and which he would have had time to retrieve something from, depositing it in the unlocked guest room safe." Sherlock's eyes narrowed at Jackson's lack of expression. "But the story that the viper in the next room has been telling is that I must have smuggled in a snake and hid it in the safe after sending it through the ventilator to bite his sister in an attempt to frame him for the crime."

"Yep. Even cites a story to prove his point. A couple Corporate Sector Security guards reported to the press their theories, which the press ran with." With a smirk, Jackson brought up a news site on his phone. "Here's my favorite headline: Sherlock Suspected in Storybook Murder. 'Sources in Corporate Sector Security have recently brought to our attention a bizarre murder in a residential building in Corporate Sector'… redundant, but they're all about sensational sounding… uh, anyway, it goes on, talks about why you were there, the brother's declaration of suspicion so on, ends with this lovely gem.

'While the City Police will no doubt want to ignore it, the fact is that the case mirrors a story featuring the very character their favorite private detective pretends to be. After a lull in such thrilling cases as the downfall of Miriam Sangrave, has Sherlock resorted to inventing his own cases to solve? Has this been his secret all the time? Exactly how trustworthy is a man who is willing and able to fake his own death for a year, with no explanation to his whereabouts? It is interesting to note that Detective Maureen 'Red' Murphy, official police liaison to the popular detective, was first to the scene. Will the City Police dare put their darling behind bars if necessary?"

"That's absolutely ridiculous," I scoffed. "No one could believe—"

"It's highly rated. The comments are about fifty-fifty for

and against, but it's getting shared, a lot, which means by now the whole City knows about it." Jackson didn't even bother hiding how much he enjoyed that idea. Then he surprised me. He sighed and looked my friend in the eye, "Which is why this situation is a pain in the ass."

Sherlock blinked. "You don't simply mean the pressure it puts on me."

"Pff, like I give a damn about your reputation. This is hell for the police, because letting you go looks like we're in league with you."

Sherlock's guard slowly lowered. "You hate to admit it, but you believe I am innocent."

"Of course you're innocent. There was a saucer of milk in the safe. What sort of idiot gives a snake a saucer of milk?"

"There was once a common myth that snakes drank milk, which is probably how the saucer ended up in Doyle's story... the author of the Holmes books," Sherlock further explained, earning him rolled eyes from Detective Jackson. "Of course, since it's in the book, wouldn't that lend further credence to the idea that I have finally 'snapped?'"

"I'm sure that's how Security and the press are going to play it," Jackson huffed, "but as much as I dislike you, I have to admit that you're way too smart to do something so ridiculously obvious." As a morbid afterthought, he added, "If you ever decide to murder someone, there won't be any obvious links to anything remotely related to you."

Sherlock gave a short laugh. "I shall take that as a compliment, Detective Jackson. It is comforting to know you at least acknowledge my intellect, even if you take issue with how

I choose to use it."

I raised my hand before Jackson could comment, "One thing I have to ask. How the hell are we supposed to have smuggled a venomous snake into the house? We didn't bring anything with us."

"In your leg, Doc," Jackson grinned.

My jaw dropped. "My *leg?!*"

"Yep. Which makes you an accomplice."

"But you don't have any evidence to hold us here."

"Yet if at least one of us is not kept in custody," Sherlock drawled, "the media firestorm will make things very uncomfortable for the police throughout the City."

"You got it. Which is why I'm asking you to stay put in a lovely holding cell till we get this sorted out," Jackson turned to me, "and I'd like it if you stayed, too. Accomplice and all."

"You're enjoying this, even though you know we're innocent, aren't you?" I asked.

He nodded. "Unfortunately, we can't hold Eckans. Detective Carson should be finished at the crime scene by now, hopefully he's turned up something useful."

We were kept updated on developments in the case, whether or not it was information we were supposed to have access to. Nothing out of the ordinary had been discovered, other than the snake. A specialist had been consulted, and he verified that the snake found in the guest room was a species originally from India, just like in the story. Typically, the bite was not very painful, and Tina could conceivably have slept through it. Neurotoxins would have paralyzed her, leading to respiratory failure over several hours, leaving her dead in the morning.

"At this rate, I'll go mad after all if I simply sit here and do nothing," Sherlock muttered. "Watts, you are cutting your stay short. I need you to go home and do some research for me."

"Ghost!" I called as soon as I got home, "We've got work to do!"

"You're back! Thought you were in jail."

I climbed the stairs to the attic, "We were never actually arrested, just — wait, how'd you hear about that?"

"Hot gossip right now," she shrugged, jacked in and laid back on the loveseat, feet hanging off the end. "Something about a snake and Sherlock going off the deep end."

"He was set up. The Holmes stories are being used against him."

"What do you want me to do?"

"Run a search of all exotic animal owners, collectors, zoos, everyone in the region, and see if you find any reported thefts or sales of snakes."

"Legitimate breeders first, illegal ones later."

"You got it. I'm going to make a phone call."

I went back downstairs and called the Irregulars. Wendy answered, listened to what had happened and then surprised me. "If it's snakes you want, Twist is your girl."

"Really?" Twist had been recruited by Captain, who found her working at a club. She still danced and did her contortionist routine, but now it was on the street outside cafes and fully clothed. To the best of my knowledge, she had never danced with snakes.

"Not me," Twist said with an audible roll of her eyes as

Wendy gave her the phone, "there was a girl I worked with at the club that used snakes in her routine. She had a boa constrictor and a cobra without fangs."

"Do you know where she got the snakes?"

"Someone called Najas? I'm not sure, it's been years."

"That's fine. It's another possibility to look into. Thanks, Twist." I hung up and called to Ghost, "Add someone called Najas to your list!"

"Najas? That's it?"

"All I got so far."

"Right. Ok then."

I ignored her blatant skepticism and joined her upstairs again. "How's it going?"

"I just started, Doc. You said you wanted a search of the region." She grinned at my sigh. "Just be patient, we'll clear your boyfriend."

I rolled my eyes. "He's not my boyfriend."

"I watched you grieve for over a year, don't feed me that bull."

"We aren't sleeping together!"

"What the hell does that have to do with anything?"

"He left," I said, before I even realized I'd thought it.

"Yeah. He's an idiot sometimes." After a moment she added, "In his defense, he did jump out a window to save your life."

"As part of a plan to fake his death."

"Once a person starts falling, there's not a lot of time to do something about it. He lived, but I bet it was sheer dumb luck. Hell, him going out the window might not have been the original plan, anyway."

I stared at her. I remembered what he'd said just before tackling Sangrave, comparing their conflict to a chess game; "I've never considered myself king."

"No thefts of snakes reported in the region. I've compiled all the legal sales records into a file."

"Any of them to Kris Eckans?" I asked, ignoring the weird discomfort in my chest.

She was quiet a moment as she searched. "Nope. If he bought a poisonous snake, it was under the table from a private collector or off the black market."

"Anything on Najas?"

"Yeah, actually. Good tip, that. Hannah Najas was a private collector who was arrested last year for breeding and selling illegally. She specialized in venomous snakes, and also dealt in constrictors, lizards, and the occasional alligator."

"Alligators? Aren't those almost extinct?"

"Hence 'occasional.'"

"Aha. Lovely."

"What sort of snake was it again?"

"Something called a krait."

"Ok. I've got a list of her customers. Eckans isn't on it of course, but it might still be a starting point for a search."

"Other customers might know who else is selling."

"That's the idea."

"Names?"

"Her most recent krait customers in the City were Mitchell Jerdon and Russell Dabois."

"… Russell Dabois."

"You know him?"

I sighed. "Old boyfriend."

Russell had moved up in the world since I saw him last — literally. His apartment was on one of the upper floors of his hospital's residential building. I'd known him in med-school and couldn't for the life of me remember what his specialization ended up being, but apparently it paid well.

"Ha! I'll be damned, I haven't seen you in ages!" he exclaimed as he let me in. "You haven't changed. Well, the cyberoptic's new."

"So's your height," I countered, "I seem to remember you being a few inches shorter."

He chuckled and shrugged, brown eyes actually shining. That was new too. The rest of him, down to the boyish build, strong chin and casual black and green suit was completely the same.

"I heard you were on the other side of the Border, now."

I kept myself casual and friendly, but cut to the chase. "I heard you collect snakes, now."

He was surprised, but grinned, "Well, I won't deny it," he leaned in conspiratorially, "but most people prefer not to know their surgeon keeps deadly reptiles."

I smirked, "I can imagine. Are they all venomous, then?"

"Not all. Why do you ask?"

"I'm looking for a specific species. Indian origin."

"Ah. I have a few Indian species. Would you like to see them?"

I smiled winningly, "I'd love to."

He took me to a small room filled with glass cages made to mimic every climate. Each one held a snake. "This is my collection," he said proudly, "The Indian species are over here. You'll recognize the cobras of course. I've multiple species of vipers and kraits as well. What were you looking for?"

"Krait."

He gestured theatrically to a cluster of cages, Latin names flowing in velvet tones. "*Fasciatus, caeruleus,* and *ceylonicus*. Though technically I suppose that one is originally from Sri Lanka rather than India. There is also *sindanus*, though his distant ancestors were Pakistani."

I stared. I hadn't actually seen the snake found in the safe, and when the specialist findings had been reported the scientific name wasn't mentioned. All I knew was that it had been a krait. And now I was looking at four of them. Well, two of them. I felt like it would have been specified had it been from someplace other than India.

I pointed to the two possibilities, "What are their common names?"

He smiled, not quite condescendingly, "The banded krait and the common krait. Why the interest? I don't recall you ever being fond of reptiles."

"To be perfectly honest, my interest is… academic. I'm doing research for a friend."

"What brought you to me?"

"Long story."

All his charm was turned on like a switch. "Then this is just a… gift for a friend?" he slid a little closer.

"You could say that."

"Must be a good friend."

"No. I'm unattached."

He grinned. "But you do have a friend who is in a bit of trouble with reptiles." I sighed, face in my palm. Russell laughed, "So you and the detective are not… involved. And here you are, 'doing research' while he is in jail."

"He's not in jail, he's staying in custody voluntarily until this gets sorted out. I was hoping you could tell me who else in the City is collecting kraits and dealing them," I was tired of the charade, but I swallowed my pride and smiled. "And no, we're not involved. When did you ever know me to have a serious relationship?"

"Well, there was Kitty—"

"A single exception to the rule. I learned my lesson."

"Good to hear. Of course, you must realize I'm a little reluctant to give out information about fellow collectors and dealers who may have, ah, less than reputable reputations."

An array of curses flitted through my head. I moved in close, just barely touching him, "What'll it take to convince you?"

Russell Dabois got his common krait from Hannah Najas, but apparently the eggs she'd hatched and sold came from a man called Souta Suta who supposedly had ties to the Yakuza. By the time I'd tracked him down, I was tired and sick to my stomach of flirtatious bullshit. I probably came on a little stronger than I needed too.

I kicked down his door, gun in hand. "My name is Watts. I work for Sherlock. Have you sold any snakes recently?"

I was conscious of few private guards behind me with their guns drawn, but didn't care. I'd already knocked a few unconscious and would have a multitude of bruises of my own the next day. Mr. Suta slowly stood.

"Please sit," he gestured to the chair in front of his desk. I did so, gun still in hand but not pointed at him. He gestured that his guards go relax, and sat down again. "You work for Sherlock. As this is the case, you must certainly know of my aid to certain illegal organizations. Why would I tell you anything?"

"Frankly, I don't give a damn what your connections are. I just want to know if you've ever sold a common krait to this man," I showed him a picture of Kris Eckans, anticipating him using an alias.

Suta thought a moment. "He did not buy it. The snake was old, I intended to get a new one, I owed him a small favor for an investment he made. I gave him the snake, free of charge."

"Which means there would be no connection to him."

"Not directly."

"I don't suppose you'd be willing to swear that he got the snake from you?"

He grinned. "You know who framed your friend. Get him to put together the evidence he needs. He's so good at that."

"Thanks for your help," I sighed.

"A pleasure. It is rare that my guards get any exercise, they are clearly getting soft. Give my regards to Sherlock."

I left, stopping by a bar for a stiff drink before heading back to the station.

I saw Detectives Jackson and Carson talking as I walked in. "Oh, you're back," Jackson muttered.

Carson was a little more concerned, "Find anything?"

"Not as much as I'd hoped," I shrugged, "Sherlock still where I left him?"

They both nodded. "You ok?" Carson asked, "You look like you've got a black eye."

"Yeah, fine. Didn't have a chance to put anything on it. I'll explain later," I mumbled as I made my way back to Sherlock's holding cell. He was sitting on the floor with his back against the wall, eyes closed, ankles crossed, fingertips together. I sat down next to him, wincing at the sore stiffness I could already feel in every muscle of my body.

"Watts."

"How'd you know?"

"The smell of synthahol eliminated the possibility of you being one of our friendly police detectives, at least on duty, and there is no one else who would enter and sit so close without announcing themselves first."

I shook my head with a humorless laugh. "Well, it was for medicinal purposes."

He opened his eyes and looked at me. His brow rose. "Pray tell, what sort of research resulted in a bar fight?"

"It wasn't a bar fight. I was fighting guards to try to get to a black-market animal dealer. Got a drink afterward. He says hi, by the way. Suta."

Sherlock's eyes widened. "You met with Souta Suta?"

"Less 'met' and more 'kicked his door down and demanded answers.'" He blinked, then his brow furrowed as he tried to figure out if I was joking or not. "Literally," I added.

He opened his mouth to say something, stopped, and

shifted to sit cross legged, facing me. "I think perhaps you should start from the beginning."

I told him everything that had happened from Ghost's research all the way up to me going to a bar for a well-deserved drink. He was impassive the entire time, simply focused on my every word. When I finished, his reaction was less than encouraging.

"So, we have confirmed what we already knew, but have no physical proof that it is true."

I stared at him a moment before closing my eyes and leaning my head back against the wall with a sigh. "Pretty much. Now, if you'll excuse me, I'm going to pretend today never happened."

I felt his thin hand on my shoulder, "The day has not been a complete waste," he said, "You have given me an idea for a plan of action."

"As long as I don't have to flirt with anyone," I muttered.

"You would rather fight a team of guards than flirt?" he mocked astonishment, "Watts, are you feeling well?"

I chuckled. "Depends on the team of guards and who I was flirting with. No more old boyfriends, please." I glanced at him with a sideways grin, "Well. Depends on the boyfriend."

"Oh good, your hedonism is still intact," he sighed. "For a moment, I was worried."

"Ha, hardly hedonism. I just like to have fun. I'd forgotten how absolutely boring Russell was. That hasn't changed any, despite the snake collection. I'm sore and black and blue all over, but the fight was…"

"Catharsis."

"That's the word." I paused. "Why am I telling you this?"

He grinned slightly. "I don't know."

"Just letting me ramble on?"

"That implies that you are speaking aimlessly, which is clearly not true. You have stuck to your topic. You simply don't know why you're talking about it." He scoffed lightly, "Don't look at me like I might be mad, Watts, I've been getting plenty of that since I woke up this morning."

I smiled. "Sorry."

He cocked his head. "Was there something else you wanted to talk about?"

I shrugged. "It's unrelated, we can talk about it later." He pursed his lips. My smile broadened. "I promise it can wait. It's not something I want to talk about in a police station."

He grinned with a small silent laugh. "Very well."

"So, what brilliant plan have you come up with since I got here?"

"Oh yes, you're definitely back to your old self. The sarcasm is a clear giveaway." I rolled my eyes. He continued, his professional attitude oddly juxtaposed with his casual position on the floor. "Before I can enact any sort of plan, I need to know one very important piece of information."

"What's that?"

"Whether or not Mr. Eckans has ever purchased any antivenom."

"Antivenom."

"He does not keep snakes. If he knew he would be handling a deadly snake he had no previous experience with, surely he would want to keep antivenom somewhere in the house on the chance that he may get bit."

"But the police didn't find any."

"They weren't looking for any, either."

I called Ghost and told her what we needed. Detective Carson walked in shortly after I hung up. "Thought you'd want to see this," he said, and led us out to where a bunch of officers were gathered around a screen.

It was a news program. "By now you've probably heard about the murder of Tina Eckans early this morning. The young woman was found dead in her bed from respiratory failure caused by, of all things, a snakebite. Though the Police have not yet issued a public statement concerning the case, Corporate Sector Security has already voiced its suspicion of the famed private detective, Sherlock."

"Consulting detective," Sherlock muttered. Carson and I rolled our eyes.

"Sherlock was present at the scene of the crime," the young anchor continued, "and the details of the murder closely resemble that of another murder, the one detailed in the mystery story, "The Adventure of the Speckled Band." The story was written by Arthur Conan Doyle in the nineteenth century—"

"*Sir* Doyle." Carson and I shushed Sherlock, who half-grinned.

"— and is one of many stories featuring the character Sherlock Holmes, who our own modern-day Sherlock is said to have based his career on. Some even speculate he has based his whole life on the character, possibly even believing himself to be the character made real. We managed to get a brief interview with the victim's brother, Kris Eckans, just a few hours ago."

The scene shifted to the living room of the Eckans apartment. "Why was Sherlock here?" the interviewer asked.

"Tina asked him to come. She… my sister was, ah, paranoid. She had these delusions, and she thought she was in danger. That someone might be trying to kill her."

"Kill her?"

"Yeah," Kris shifted uncomfortably, "I tried to tell her to get help, but she never listened. So, she went out and asked that detective to come and figure out who would want to hurt her. And he came over, saying that if she was in any danger he would know it after spending the night here. Well, this seemed good enough for Tina, and I was so relieved to have a chance to put her paranoia to rest, so I agreed. I thought he'd seen she was… disturbed, and was playing along to try and help."

"But she was dead in the morning."

"Yeah. Snakebite. The police found the snake in the guest room safe, where Sherlock and his friend, a doctor of some sort, had stayed the night."

"What happened when you found out she was dead?"

"I called Corporate Security, while Sherlock called his friends in the City Police."

"But surely he wouldn't call the police if he were guilty?"

Kris gave a very convincing hesitant shrug, "I don't know. I don't want to accuse anyone without proof, but… I mean, he's got connections. And this whole thing, a snake getting in and biting her? Who the hell would do that to kill a person? It's right out of a story."

Muttering started among the officers watching. Sherlock radiated fury.

The program returned to the anchor's desk, "Could he have done it? City Police have generally been supportive of the detective, who became famous after his exposure of Miriam Sangrave, former employee of the R.X. Corporation, and her illegal activities in the drug trade. He was reported to have died last year; a body that his friend — a Dr. James Watts — identified as Sherlock's was found at the bottom of a tall building along with that of Miriam Sangrave. Clearly, he survived, faking his death, and going underground for over a year. No one knows what he was doing in that time, or what sort of change may have come over the detective since."

The scene shifted to a laboratory room full of snake cages. "We talked to a herpetologist, a specialist in snakes, at the City Zoo to find out if murder by snakebite was possible."

"Well," the herpetologist said, "there are many snakes whose bites would be deadly to humans if left untreated."

"If someone were bit while asleep, for example?"

"Many bites are very painful. The victim would wake up, unless they were a very deep sleeper."

"Is there a species of snake that a person could sleep through getting bit?"

"I wouldn't know for sure… though, there have been stories of people who have slept through krait bites. Supposedly, they aren't always as painful as others."

"Do you know what the snake in the Tina Eckans murder was?"

The herpetologist hesitated, but nodded. "A krait."

The program returned to the news desk. "Sherlock has been in the custody of the police all day, 'held for questioning,' though no arrest has been made. We will watch and keep our viewers informed of developments. Tune in next hour when we'll discuss the possibility of believing yourself to be a fictional character with Dr. Govad Zdrav, psychiatrist and bestselling author of—"

Carson turned it off. The officers started to disperse, all of them stealing a glance at Sherlock. No one was quite sure what to make of him.

"Detective Jackson," Sherlock asked in a quiet, remarkably calm voice, "why has there been no official statement made from the police?"

We turned to see Jackson standing behind us. I'd been too absorbed in the news to notice his arrival. He shrugged, "Isn't much to say, is there?"

"Aside from all the facts against my guilt."

"Hey, *our* snake guy already cleared you. Said the whole idea of a snake getting in there, biting the girl and then getting back out again was ridiculous. If it actually happened, it was sheer dumb luck."

"But the press has no interest in what the police have to say."

Jackson shrugged again. "More interesting story if you're guilty."

"Apparently. Watts," my friend turned to me, "should our source give us a positive report back, would you be willing to contact your... ah, college friend, and borrow some supplies?"

I stared at him. "Try saying that again, only this time try to be a little clearer."

Sherlock half-grinned. "We're going to find out exactly how easy it is to smuggle a snake into the Eckans residence."

I knocked. A voice came over an intercom, "What do you want?"

"We need to talk."

Kris opened the door. "I don't see what about."

"You know exactly what this is about."

"As if I would let you in."

"Don't put on that act with me. I'm not even armed. You already opened your door. We're already talking right now."

He smirked and went back inside. I followed. "I don't know what you think you can accomplish," he said as he sat in a chair in the living room, "You know you look like hell?"

I sighed. The area around my left eye had turned a vibrant mix of purple and blue, with a bruise along the right side of my jaw. "Yeah, thanks."

He shrugged. "Anyway, it's completely out of my hands. The press make their own conclusions—"

"Conclusions that you supported with your ridiculous false evidence."

"False evidence?"

"You implied we put a snake in a safe."

He grinned, "Well, how else would it get there?"

I glared. "When you put it in there as we examined her body."

"A neat theory, but you can't prove it."

My hand started shaking. "Maybe but… but…" I cursed under my breath and started to open my cyberleg, "Sorry. Have to get something."

Kris scoffed. "Drugs or meds? Or since you're a doctor, maybe both?"

I rolled my eyes. "Hardly." Taking a deep breath, I opened my leg, reached in and tossed the snake at him as fast as I could. It landed squarely on his lap. Kris leaped up with a panicked yelp, throwing it to the floor at his feet. The snake, rightfully upset by its treatment, struck at his leg.

Kris went pale. "You're crazy," his voice shook as he slowly backed away from the snake. After a couple feet he turned and ran to the kitchen.

I closed my leg and was fast on his heels. I stopped him just as he was taking a small bottle out of the fridge. "What are you doing?"

"Back off!" he swung at me but missed. I twisted the bottle out of his hand, holding it out of his reach and pinning him to the kitchen counter with my knee. "You think killing me will do anything? Sherlock will still be thrown in jail, this will just convince everyone of his guilt!"

"Killing you?" I asked, "Oh, this bottle is antivenom. That's why you want it so badly." Kris said nothing. "Tell me, why exactly do you have antivenom?"

He blinked a few times, thinking furiously. "My sister was killed by a—"

"No," I shook my head, smiling as I did my best impression of Sherlock, "that won't do. You purchased this antivenom before she died," I reached into my coat pocket and dangled a print-out in front of him. "We have a record of the transaction from the pharmaceutical supply company you ordered it from."

He gaped, his snakebite forgotten. "How did you get that?"

"Tsk, really. What sort of detective would Sherlock be if he couldn't find so simple a thing as a transaction record? Oh, incidentally, the snake that just bit you isn't venomous. It's a wolf snake, a krait look-alike, but harmless."

Kris sputtered, astonished and outraged. "You - you - it doesn't matter! You still can't prove I killed Tina!"

"Why else would you buy antivenom unless you knew you'd be in contact with a venomous snake?"

"No one will believe you!"

I chuckled. "We'll see about that. Our whole conversation has been live streaming since I arrived. It should be all over the internet and a few news channels shortly, if it's not already."

He glared at my cyberoptic as I let him go and tossed the antivenom into the trash. "Pleasure talking with you," I said.

Looking back on it now, I realize that I may have been a little too cocky.

Some instinct told me to turn back around. I saw him coming at me just in time to deflect the knife aimed at my back, earning a slice across my ribs instead. With a firm kick of my cyberleg, his knee collapsed, sending the rest of him down with it. I promptly administered a sedative, putting him into a deep sleep for a while as I applied pressure to the slice in my chest.

I sat down for a moment to catch my breath. I needed to

get myself stitched up, but I could afford a moment to relax before calling the cops and going home. I almost didn't believe the snake had worked. It slithered across the floor, disappearing into another room. I decided I was not a fan of snakes, venomous or not. As I picked up my phone, Sherlock tore open the front door.

He took one look at the unconscious man in the room, pointed him out to the police officer behind him, and knelt by my side. "Is it serious?"

"Caught me across the ribs."

He cocked an eyebrow. "That doesn't answer my question."

I smiled. "I'm fine. Just a little short of breath," my smile faded, "which probably isn't serious, but—"

"But considering you have just suffered a chest injury, we should get you to a hospital to be certain. Can you walk?"

I sighed, "I hate hospitals. How'd you get here so fast?"

"Are you kidding?" Detective Carson asked. I hadn't even noticed him come in. "You never turned your camera off. The instant Sherlock saw you get attacked, he ordered us to get our asses over here on the double."

"My language was somewhat more restrained," my friend drawled, grinning. "Watts, as you have not confirmed you can walk, I am forced to assume you cannot and I shall have to carry you out."

"I'm fine," I slowly got to my feet, and remembered to turn off the video feed. "Let's go."

"Hang on," Carson stopped us, "what happened to the snake?"

"It went in there," I gestured to the room it had slithered into. "Sherlock, I've decided I hate snakes."

"I don't blame you," he nodded, "though it's hardly the snake's fault for this mess."

"Doesn't matter."

He smiled as we asked an officer for a ride to the hospital, "My dear Watts, don't tell me you're ophidiophobic?"

"No. Just don't particularly ever want to touch one again."

He chuckled. "I apologize for putting you through such a traumatic experience."

"That would be more effective if I didn't know you were being sarcastic."

"Mm, honestly though, I am sorry you were nearly stabbed in the back."

"And I had to carry a snake in my leg," I shuddered.

"That bothers you more than the stabbing?"

"Of course it bothers me more, I'm used to nearly getting killed!"

Sherlock laughed.

Kris Eckans was arrested for the murder of Tina Eckans the next day. The day after that, the news channels were filled with the thrilling story of how Sherlock and I had solved the case despite being under suspicion… all without acknowledging the fact that most of that suspicion had come from the news channels themselves. Fan sites for Sherlock (and myself, I was surprised to learn) erupted all over the Net. Ghost assured us that most of them already existed, traffic had simply surged. The video feed online added fuel for the flame.

"Some of the comments on this thing are amazing," I said, jacked in on the sofa.

"I can only imagine," Sherlock muttered, lighting his pipe.

"It's kind of bizarre watching what I saw in a video. Nice to see my eye's picture quality's still decent."

He sat next to me, warily curious. "My entrance is much more dramatic from this perspective."

I smiled. "You do love to make an entrance."

We sat silently together until the video ended. I turned off the computer and took it back to my room. When I came back, Sherlock was in the kitchen, rifling through the cabinets. "Looking for something?"

"Tea," he said from around the pipe stem still in his mouth. "We appear to be out."

"Might be. Didn't keep much in stock when you died."

He paused a moment, just a moment, but it was enough. That weird wall was suddenly up between us again. Hadn't we joked about him coming back from the dead just a few days ago? Everyone had been talking about it. Why the hell did me not buying tea make the air just a little tenser?

"Sherlock?"

He closed the cabinets. "Yes?"

"Was falling out of the window part of the plan?"

He met my eyes for a long moment. He put the pipe down, "Not originally."

"You really did tackle her to save me?"

His brow furrowed, "Why would you ask that?"

"You left."

He flinched. "I never intended for you to see it. News would circulate, my letter would be delivered, and—"

"And hopefully I'd get the idea that this was suspiciously similar to a scene in a book," I sighed.

He nodded once. "I didn't expect her to kidnap you that very day, neither did I expect to live. Adrenaline and mad desperation are the only reasons I survived. I managed to stop my descent with the blade in my arm and a fortuitously placed window ledge, though I nearly ripped my arm off in the maneuver." Morbid humor pulled at the corner of his mouth. "I added quite a few scars to the collection."

"Thank you." It wasn't adequate, it didn't begin to be adequate, but it was all I had.

He smiled, softly. "How could I do otherwise?"

I cleared my throat, "This doesn't excuse you being dead for a year and a half."

He glanced away, and we were back to the same tension as before. "I don't expect it to."

I sighed, frustrated. "What the hell were you doing all that time?"

"You met him. I needed a position amongst criminals that would gain information while maintaining my independence, and take advantage of my rather unique skill set. 'Eccentric information dealer and occasional bounty hunter' seemed to fit."

"I can't even imagine what that must have been like."

"I don't want you to," he said, quietly. "I may as well have been dead. I was another person. I couldn't risk anyone seeing the slightest similarity between Sebastian and myself." After a moment, his eyes met mine. "I knew you would be hurt, but I never imagined how much. Of all the horrible things I've done in my life, nothing is as reprehensible as hurting you." A small, sad smile touched his face. "I plan to spend the rest of my life trying to redeem myself."

I believed him. Maybe I shouldn't have, but right then, seeing so much guilt on his face, that same vulnerability I saw the night he came back… I knew he meant every word. He'd spend his entire life trying to gain my forgiveness if that's what it took. "I don't think it's going to take that long." He studied me, searching my face for some hint of sarcasm or humor. I shrugged, and utterly failed to conceal a smile.

Warm relief filled his eyes, all his tension melting, and it was so good to see. "Thank you," he said. "Is this what you didn't want to discuss at the police station?" I nodded. "I can see why you wouldn't care for the setting."

I laughed a little. "Yeah." We stood in silence a moment. "Do you want to go out tonight?"

He blinked, uncomprehending. "Out?"

"Out, as in outside the house. What normal people do."

He smirked at my sarcasm, "What did you have in mind?"

"Dinner and a show?" He raised a skeptical eyebrow. I shrugged, "We don't do stuff like that often, thought it might be a nice change of pace."

He couldn't tell if I was serious for a moment, but then he smiled, in that miniscule way of his. "Did you want to go now, or were you hoping to catch the late-night street crowds?"

"You'd enjoy that. Strut down the street, the gossip from your latest case still circulating."

"I do not 'strut,'" he scoffed, grabbing his hat and stick.

"Sometimes you do."

He shook his head, a tender expression on his face. "Dinner and a show is a fine plan for the evening, James. Let us take advantage of it before some tantalizing mystery or terrible tragedy drops on our doorstep."

Corporation vs Colony

Sherlock's fame was already on the rise after the Almandine Drive, but after the Eckans business it simply skyrocketed. References to him started showing up in mainstream media, interview requests came in from every news and entertainment outlet, and on the other end of the spectrum were a whole host of conspiracy theorists and reactionary trolls who did everything they could to prove he was a meddler at best, a psychopath at worst.

Sherlock ignored all of it, at first. When Ghost pointed out that it was easier to interview ahead of rumor, instead of after, he reluctantly agreed, but still found the idea of being a source of entertainment repulsive. Then the host of a long-running but small audience talk show wrote him an honest to god letter, on paper, politely asking if he would consent to be interviewed, with the understanding that he could leave the interview at any time.

We watched a few clips of the show online. It was very basic, just the host and guest sitting at a table, talking to each other for twenty minutes. Sherlock agreed. The show's ratings exploded. Sherlock's fame was even more firmly established... and every single news and entertainment outlet was remarkably jealous. Coverage was suddenly a lot less constant, and much more neutral in tone. It probably hadn't helped that he'd specifically mentioned the role of mainstream media in his frame-up for murder during his interview. Sherlock was thrilled with the result.

I suppose it was about time for someone to take a shot at him.

I leaped up from the sofa when I heard the gunshot, rushing to him… and stopping with a lurch as I saw him unharmed, glaring at the crack in the window directly in line with his head where he sat in his chair.

He slowly exhaled a cloud of smoke, speaking around the stem of his pipe, "We'll have to get that fixed."

"The window's bulletproof?!"

"Of course. You didn't think I'd spend every day sitting in a place I could be easily shot, did you?"

I shrugged, deflated, "Honestly, I never thought about it."

He half grinned, putting the pipe down to consider the window again. "Media representative, or criminal?"

"Teenager hoping for fame."

He stared at me. "That is a horrifying idea."

"But a valid one."

"I have enough people trying to kill me without trigger-happy youths taking shots at me."

I sat back down, "I gotta say, there've been surprisingly few attempts on your life recently."

"You've been busy with patients. There've been more than you think." He smiled at my frown. "I shouldn't have said anything. Don't worry Watts, nothing serious. An attempted assault on the street, the shot through the window you just witnessed, little things."

"Yeah," I said, flatly, "they only want to mostly kill you,

not completely kill you."

"That might not be far from the truth." He resumed smoking, "With my name in lights, most of the recent attacks have been from those who wouldn't care about me whatsoever if I were unknown. It's not my death that they're after so much as the effect my death would have, at least for five minutes of news coverage."

"Come on, you'd get at least fifteen."

He laughed. "Thank you, I think."

There was an urgent pounding on the door. I checked the security cam, and showed Red in. "Evening, Red."

"I just heard a gunshot…" she froze as she saw the window. She looked at Sherlock, her brow raised, arms crossed. "You planning on closing those curtains?"

"Why? The damage is done, they know they can't shoot me."

Red rolled her eyes, and closed them anyway. "Don't taunt the people trying to kill you, Sherlock."

"Do you think it's dangerous?" he drawled.

"It's tacky."

Sherlock chuckled, standing up. "And to what do we owe the pleasure of this visit?"

"Just got off duty, figured I'd drop by, make sure you hadn't gone crazy," she said. "Apparently, I should drop by more often, just to be sure you aren't dead."

He grinned. "Your faith in my sanity is remarkably reassuring. You're always welcome here, of course. Something to drink?"

"Please," she took a seat on the sofa as he poured her a

bit of scotch. "You sure know how to spoil a girl."

"I'm merely attempting to bribe my official liaison in the only way she might accept such a thing," he smiled.

"You're weird," she said, sipping appreciatively.

"So you've implied on multiple occasions," he sat back down. "While I realize it is customary for a host to inquire after a guest's personal life and attempt introductory small talk, I must admit my greatest curiosity lies in what precisely brought you here, apart from my questionable sanity."

"Like I said, I'm just here to make sure you're ok, and drink your authentic alcohol. I know fame doesn't mean interesting cases." He sighed. "Though, now that you mention it, I might have something up your alley."

Sherlock clapped his hands once and leaned forward eagerly. "Yes?"

I shook my head, smiling to myself as I had a seat next to Red. Sometimes the man's like a kid in a game shop.

"Heard from an old friend of mine yesterday," Red said. "We were at the Academy together. He lives out east in a city called Ashland, seems like he's doing fairly well for himself. Anyway, we were chatting last night, and he mentioned they've been having trouble with the local Colony."

Sherlock cocked his head, "What sort of trouble?"

"Seems the local branch of Dynamo wants to expand their energy farms. Unfortunately, the location they want borders on the Colony, and the Colonists currently use the land for livestock. It's a pretty large Colony, too, so they've got the manpower to do a little preventative sabotage. They're outside the city, so the police don't technically have any jurisdiction, but that's not really a factor when Corporate suits are breathing down necks. My friend's in a tight spot and can't get any sort of compromise going. He's been assigned to try and resolve the whole mess, since no lawyer is going to get involved on behalf of the Colony." Red took a sip of her scotch before stating a little too casually, "I told him I knew an expert on Colonists who could help him out."

Sherlock was skeptical and unimpressed. "I am hardly a diplomat."

"Maybe not," Red shrugged, "but you *can* understand both sides. Plus, you can figure out who's doing the sabotaging."

"You implied it was the Colonists."

"I said the Colonists could easily pull it off. They deny any involvement. Dynamo, however, is getting irritated. They want the saboteurs taken care of, and they aren't afraid to take on a whole Colony to do it."

That gave Sherlock pause. "You're not seriously suggesting they would attack the Colony?"

"They're pushing as hard as they can in that direction. Like I said, my friend's in a tight spot. Besides," Red grinned, "might be good for you to be someplace else for a bit. The City will survive a couple days without you, I promise."

Sherlock half grinned. "I can't deny that the idea holds a certain appeal. However, I do not guarantee that I will be able to help your friend. I know nothing about his city, or the Colony in question."

"An attempt is all I ask."

"An attempt you shall have. Watts, can your practice do without you for a few days?"

"It'll take a little arranging, but I should be able to make it work."

"Excellent. Now Red, tell me more about this friend of yours and his city."

Sherlock started packing while I bought plane tickets. "Have you ever flown before?" he asked.

"Once, when I was little. The whole family went with Dad on one of his business trips in the summer. Haven't done it since."

"Is it as terrible as I'm imagining?"

"Probably," I laughed. "Getting through security is tedious and the seats are cramped, but we'll be there in a couple hours."

He leaned in the doorway to my room. "Security?"

"They verify your I.D, scan you for concealed weapons—"

He chuckled, "Perhaps you had best cancel those tickets, Doctor."

I smirked, "Your blade isn't an issue, worst case scenario is that they'll make you use an activation monitor."

"And the identification?"

"It's a retinal scan. Mostly to make sure you aren't banned from flying." He was pensive. I stared at him. "Sherlock, what possible reason would you have for being on a no-fly list?"

"I'm not, to the best of my knowledge."

"So why are you worried?"

"I am concerned that any attempt at verifying my identity will fall short of bureaucratic necessities."

"You have a bank account, you have to be in the system."

"The process by which a Colonist rejoins civilization is incomplete at best. I had documentation of my birth in the Colony, which was sufficient verification of who I am to open the most basic of accounts, sending and receiving funds, which in turn was sufficient for leasing a home from a private agency." He thought a moment, "There is a police file with my name on it, perhaps that will suffice." At my sigh, he smiled. "There was a misunderstanding early on, I'd only been in the City a few months at that point."

"Right. Well, after the Eckans business, you're sure to have some sort of official record anyway."

"Don't put too much faith in my fame. All we need is one overzealous officer to throw the rule book at me."

"I'm sure it will be fine."

I wasn't nearly as confident as I think I sounded, but it was enough to get him to stop worrying. The airport was a confusing mass of businessmen and rich families going on vacation. I was glad we didn't have to worry about luggage, our bags small enough to come onto the plane with us. Flight numbers and departure times were regularly updated on the screens overhead, boarding announcements echoing semi-regularly for those infrequent travelers who didn't have the app installed.

Security moved slowly, but as efficiently as possible given the amount of people being processed by a small staff of workers. When it came time to verify Sherlock's identity, the retinal scan displayed a 'no data' message. The officer rolled his eyes, took a look at the line, and looked at Sherlock's name.

"Either the machine is malfunctioning, you've just had illegal new-grown eye transplants, or you're exactly who you say you are."

"One of those options involves considerably less paperwork, I imagine," Sherlock said.

"They're all a pain in the ass," the officer grumbled. He called over another officer, "No data on the retinal, send him through if fingerprints work."

Fortunately, there wasn't any further problem, and we were soon on board. I've heard Corporate flights are practically flying hotels, all the comforts a person might need thirty thousand feet in the air, but for those of us who can't afford to travel multiple times a year, or even decade, airplanes are just flying cans packed tight with passengers. They're fast, but that's about it.

We were too distracted to complain much. Sherlock's white knuckled grip vanished once take off was over, marveling at the sight out the window, though every spot of turbulence made his hold on my hand a little tighter. He kept up a running commentary on anything that came to mind to keep my attention off the weird physical unease I was experiencing. It wasn't awful, all things considered, but we both prefer traveling with our feet on the ground.

A dusky middle-aged black-haired man dressed all in denim approached us as we exited the gate. "Excuse me, but was one of you sent over by Maureen Murphy?"

"Red requested I come," Sherlock nodded. "I'm Sherlock. This is my friend and associate Dr. Watts." He gestured to the badge hanging around the stranger's scarf. "You are Detective Warrin, I presume?"

"I am," the detective shook our hands, "Have to say, when Red said she was sending an expert, she neglected to mention your, ah, primary occupation."

Sherlock chuckled, "I assure you, sir, I am here to give advice first and foremost. Should you wish to take advantage of my services, I will gladly render them to you, but I have no intention of stepping on toes."

Warrin smiled, "Ok then. I took the liberty of reserving a hotel room for you. Then we've got an appointment with Mr. Ritch, Dynamo representative."

"How did you find out about my line of work?" Sherlock asked as we got to the car.

"Internet, of course. You've got a global following."

"… Global?" Sherlock paled slightly.

"Rumors spread fast online. Almost all the fansites are based and accessed from your city, but there's some decent traffic from around the country and a few sites even have international followers. Japan, England—"

"I see. And what was the impression you received from these sites?"

Warrin smiled. "You think you're Sherlock Holmes, but you're brilliant at it." Sherlock chuckled. "Doesn't matter to me," Warrin shrugged, "what I want to know is what makes you an expert on Colonies?"

"I grew up in one."

"Really? Oh, so that's why you're so old-fashioned."

"It's one reason," I said.

Sherlock didn't comment. "Colonies vary, so I will need

as much detailed information as possible on the local people and their history."

"Not a problem," Warrin said as we reached the hotel, "you can take the tour."

"The tour?"

"I'll explain later."

Edward Ritch, of the Ashland branch of the Dynamo Corporation, was waiting for us in his office. Warrin gave the introductions, "Mr. Edward Ritch, this gentleman is Sherlock, and this is his associate Dr. Watts."

"Hello," Mr. Ritch gestured we should sit, "Detective Warrin tells me you're some sort of expert in Colonists?"

"I grew up in a Colony, which gives me some unique insight," Sherlock said.

Mr. Ritch's eyebrows shot up. "You're a Colonist?"

"Not anymore."

"Why did you leave?"

"It was necessary. I was given to understand you are having problems with Colonists who refuse to leave?"

"We don't want them to leave, just to keep their sheep somewhere else! Their farmland or ranch or whatever the hell it's called borders our energy fields. We need to expand, and have even offered to pay the Colony for the land, even though we are not legally required to."

At Sherlock's look of puzzlement, Warrin explained, "It's federal land, technically, but Dynamo has the rights to develop on it."

"So I assumed," Sherlock replied. "What I do not

understand is what a Colony would do with credits?"

Warrin chuckled at Mr. Ritch's shock. "You don't know?" Ritch exclaimed, "This isn't some backwater commune, it's a goddamn tourist attraction!"

Sherlock quirked a mildly offended brow, but said, "Yes, Detective Warrin mentioned taking a tour. Now I understand what he meant."

Warrin clarified, "The Colony has a bank account that they use to purchase medicines and the occasional luxury item. It's funded by their tourism business."

"Interesting. Mr. Ritch, I imagine your goal is to discover who has been committing these acts of sabotage against your expansion efforts and convince the Colonists to cooperate?"

"At this point, I doubt it'll happen. We've already threatened to shut off power to their rail, with no effect."

The look Sherlock gave him was something you'd give to a silly child. "I suggest finding a new tactic. Threats are rarely effective against idealists." We stood to leave, "Now, Detective Warrin, show us this tour."

Warrin took us to a small subway station on the edge of one of Ashland's Corporate Sectors. Unlike our City, Ashland's sectors are interspersed with each other, fitting together like puzzle pieces, the borders not always obvious. It was disconcerting to say the least. I was glad for the guide. The sign overhead read Colony Station.

"Not very imaginative, but it gets the point across," Warrin said, "There was an attempt at putting in a rail transit system ages ago, failed horribly due to lack of funding. When the Mayor of the Colony at the time approached the city with a proposal for a tourism project years ago, this tunnel was restored and put into working order. Reaches all the way to the Colony."

We boarded the single, empty car. "Not exactly busy," I said.

Warrin shrugged, "Popularity has fallen a bit, though there's still a decent crowd on weekends, especially around holidays and in the summer. You just missed the nostalgic Christmas rush a couple months ago."

Sherlock and I glanced around as we shot down the tunnel. We'd never been underground before. It was strange, and a little claustrophobic. "Why a subway?" I asked.

"Saved the need for any new construction, apart from restoration costs. Safer than a shuttle through the rough parts of town, and it makes for an impressive effect at the end."

We soon found out what he meant. As we climbed up the steps at the end of the line, we found ourselves in a small old brick rail station out of a pulp western film. A ruddy older man in a white shirt and black suspenders was reading a book behind a small window with a sign that said Tour Tickets and Colony Cash.

"A striking transition," Sherlock mumbled.

"Good morning, Detective Warrin," the man in suspenders said, "You sure are persistent."

Warrin chuckled. "Yeah, well, your Mayor sure is stubborn. This way, gentlemen, unless you want an official tour?"

Sherlock shook his head, "Just a chance to walk around."

"What's 'Colony Cash?'" I asked as we stepped out of

the station.

"Tourists can use credits to purchase 'cash', which can be used in any shop with a Cash sign in the window. The shops keep a record of every cash purchase, and get a receipt from the station for that amount of credits. They can then use that much credit out of the Colony account for purchases in the city."

"Medicine and luxury items?"

"Primarily."

"Then people who do not own shops do not benefit from the tourist industry?" Sherlock asked.

"No, they do, just not as directly. A percentage of all transactions is set aside for 'general use', and if any shop-owner were to significantly benefit more than his fellow townsfolk, well. The Mayor would take actions to, uh, redistribute the wealth."

"And if the shop-owner defied the Mayor?"

Warrin grinned. "When you meet her, you'll see why that's not likely to happen."

We strolled down the main road, giving Sherlock a chance to duck into the occasional shop and chat with people on the street. This Colony was larger than Sherlock's, and tended more towards a small town feel than an old-west outpost, apart from the train station. The people, used to tourists, were much more pleasant to outsiders… though it felt like the same sort of generic pleasantness you get when you call customer service. Everyone we talked to was obviously humoring Detective Warrin, and obviously thought he was wasting his time with these visits. They eyed Sherlock with curiosity, and me with mild dismissal. I was just another tourist type, but they could tell

Sherlock was different.

As we neared the Town Hall, Sherlock suddenly asked if we could see the site of the sabotage. A little surprised, Warrin took us to the edge of town where construction vehicles sat waiting to be used. The land had been cleared, but work had stopped before the new construction could begin.

"Every time Dynamo gets their equipment back in working order, it breaks down again. Calling in new equipment or repairing the old both cost money they would rather not pay, hence the halt in the work," Warrin explained.

"What was this land used for?" Sherlock asked.

"The whole area around the edge of town is used for livestock to graze. The families who used this section distributed their animals to neighbors."

"I see. Shall we meet the Mayor?"

The Mayor sat at her desk in the Town Hall office, bent over an array of documents, her pen tapping frustratedly. She wore a blue suit, chocolate curls obscuring her dark features. She glanced up as we walked in, and frowned. The pen stopped tapping. "Oh. You. Detective, I know you're just doing your job, but it doesn't matter how many times you come back here, my answer is not going to change and frankly I'm getting tired of talking to you."

"Would you be willing to speak to me instead?" Sherlock asked.

Warrin smiled. "Gentlemen, this is Elea Caine, Mayor. Mayor Caine, this is Sherlock and his associate Dr. Watts. They're here as consultants from—"

"Consultants? For what? Are they supposed to tell you

the best way to get us to cooperate?" she glared at Sherlock, "Do you make a living of off taking Colonist land?"

"No, and I have no intention of starting now. We are not here at the request of a Corporation, we do not work for a Corporation, and we are not paid by anyone to be here. We are here as a favor to a friend, to ensure this conflict can be resolved before Dynamo does something rash."

Mayor Caine frowned. "Rash." Sherlock nodded. She studied him for a moment before gesturing that he should sit. "What the hell sort of a name is Sherlock, anyway?"

"Literary."

"Let's try this again. Who are you, and why are you here?"

"My name is Sherlock. I am a detective. Detective Warrin is friends with one of the police detectives of my city. She asked me to come and act as... diplomat, I suppose."

Mayor Caine leaned back, flabbergasted. "What?"

"He's a Colonist," Warrin put in.

"Former," Sherlock corrected, "I was born and raised in the local Colony, but have lived in the City for several years."

"And you think that you being from a Colony means what? That we'll be willing to listen to you?"

"Not at all. I fully expect you to treat me with the same stubborn dismissal with which you treat Detective Warrin. And I fully expect that nothing anyone from outside your town does or says will have any effect on your opinion until it is too late. Dynamo is going to take that land, no matter what you do. It's just a matter of time."

Mayor Caine stood, "Then there is no reason for you to

be here, and I will ask you to leave."

"No."

The silence stretched. "I beg your pardon," the Mayor demanded softly.

"Madam," Sherlock stood to look her eye to eye, "you are in a bad situation. Your stubbornness is going to get your people hurt, maybe even killed. The land that Dynamo wants is not essential. The animals have already been moved, the land has been cleared, it is of no use to you anymore," he held up a hand to forestall her protest, "I know that giving in to their demands sets a dangerous precedence, but you are not seeing the larger picture. You are not just a Colony, you are, as I was told earlier today, 'a goddamn tourist attraction.' You are not taking full advantage of your status."

Now she was listening. "What do you mean?"

"Why have you not reached out to your public? Alert the tourists to your plight, cast Dynamo in the role of the terrifying, overbearing villains. Contact Dynamo's competitors, ask for their support. They would love a chance to smother Dynamo with bad press, no matter what sort."

"Put ourselves in debt to just another Corporation."

"You don't have a choice. You are too close to the City. Developers will want to push you out, if not Dynamo then somebody else. Someone will always try to control you. The only thing you can do is delay the inevitable."

The Mayor sighed. She suddenly looked exhausted. "I know it."

"Why don't you buy the land?" Everyone looked at Detective Warrin. He shrugged, and repeated, "Well, why not?

You'd have to save up, but you've already got a significant amount in your account. Make the government an offer and secure your Colony's land."

"Even if that works, what's to stop Corporations from ignoring it?" the Mayor scoffed.

"That is something to worry about later," Sherlock cut in, "resolve the matter with Dynamo, and then you can consider Detective Warrin's idea."

Mayor Caine nodded. "I'll call a town meeting early tomorrow morning. Now then, gentlemen, if you'll excuse me, I have a lot to think about and a lot to do."

There was nothing else we could do for the Colony's problems, so we left. Sherlock thought the saboteurs were likely Colonists, but he had no inclination to find the guilty party for Dynamo. We went back to the hotel and explored the area for the rest of the day while Detective Warrin reported back to the increasingly impatient Mr. Ritch.

Ashland was a little smaller than our city, but the interspersed districts took some getting used to. Twice, we walked down a street only to turn right back around again, neither of us in any mood to wander through a rough part of a strange town. Still, it was neat to explore and play the tourist for a day, especially since it was the first time Sherlock had ever been in a new city, and the last time I traveled was when I was little. By the time we got back to the hotel, it was getting late.

"I just realized no one in that Colony said anything about our cybernetics," I commented as we removed our coats.

"As a tourist destination, they're surely used to seeing metal on other people, though they don't use the technology themselves."

"Makes sense," I yawned. "Alright, I'm headed to bed."

"Goodnight," he said as he looked out the window.

"You coming?"

He raised an amused brow. "I think you would find me to be a poor bedmate."

I rolled my eyes and started getting ready, "You know what I mean. Are you going to sleep at all tonight?"

"Possibly."

"We spent the whole day walking around town, you have to be at least a little tired. Don't give me the 'I walk all the time' line," I cut him off, "and I know you don't sleep when you're on a tough case, but this thing is hardly complicated... what?"

He was watching me, a small smile on his face. "Very well, Doctor," he went to his bed, tossing his suit jacket over a chair, "I'll turn in. It's clear you won't sleep until I do."

"Good," I smiled. "Sleep won't kill you, you know."

I woke with a jolt, a bloodcurdling sound ringing in my ears. I leaped out of bed in the dark, confused, before I realized what was going on. Sherlock was screaming.

"Sherlock!" I shouted, shaking his shoulders, "Wake up!"

I dodged a swing as he sat up, eyes open but unseeing. I heard his blade extend and leaped back. "Sherlock?" I called across the room, my voice catching in my throat. I carefully approached his left, flesh and blood, side. "Sherlock, wake up!"

He jumped as I touched his shoulder, finally waking. "Watts?" He started to lift his right hand and froze, the blade catching the streetlight through the window. He retracted it, confusion turning to terror. "Why… oh. Oh, god, I almost—"

"You didn't," I sat next to him, an arm around his shoulders. He was shaking. "I'm fine, you didn't hurt me."

"I'm sorry," his voice was taught, "I'm so sorry, they… they were tearing me apart, one limb after another, and I thought you were—"

"It's ok," I held him tight as he fell against me, "We're alright."

"I could have killed you."

"Don't think about that. Just try to relax." He managed to take a deep, shuddering breath, tension slowly fading. "Hell of a nightmare."

He scoffed with a smile. "You are a master of understatement, my friend."

"Think you can go back to sleep?"

"I'll try." He gripped my hand tight, "I would never forgive myself if I hurt you."

"I know."

Soon, his breathing was slow and regular, his body relaxed. I closed my eyes, relieved.

It was past dawn, but probably still morning. I hadn't looked at the clock yet, just saw the sun shining through the window. Sherlock looked peaceful, one of the few times I've ever been able to use that word to describe him.

His eyes opened. "Watts."

"Good morning."

"Good morning." A tiny grin pulled at his mouth, "You

survived the night."

I smiled, "How are you?"

"Embarrassed, but rested."

"Does that happen every night?"

"Frequently, though last night was a particularly bad example. My nightmares don't normally involve me trying to kill my best friend."

"You weren't trying to kill me, you were defending yourself."

He smirked, "Watts, please don't be saccharine first thing in the morning."

"I'm being comforting!"

"Is that what that was?"

I shoved him, "You can be such an ass sometimes."

His grin faded as he took my hand. "I'm sorry for frightening you."

"Scared the hell out of me is what you did. I've never heard you scream bloody murder before."

"Now you know why I was reluctant to sleep."

"Ha, yeah. We'll have to see Rip when we get home, get a sleep override installed in your arm."

"A what?"

"Some sort of manual trigger to unlock the blade so it can't happen on accident."

He blinked. "Do you plan on being in my bedroom more often?"

I rolled my eyes, getting out of bed. "If I hear you scream like that again, I'm going to come running no matter how bad an idea it is."

He smiled a little, and nodded, "Very well. I am sorry."

"I told you, it's fine. It's not like you meant to do it."

The phone rang. Warrin was on the other end. "How good is your detective?"

"One of the best," I said.

"Come out to the Colony, now. There's been an explosion."

We caught the train straight away.

The man in the ticket window greeted us, "Detective Warrin said to keep an eye out for you two. He's out by the construction site."

We found him with half a dozen Ashland cops and a crowd of townsfolk. "Mayor Caine, I appreciate you calling me so quickly," he was saying, "and I realize it was purely diplomatic, but no one else sets foot on that site until my consultant gets here."

"Consultant? You've already got cops here," the Mayor protested as we pushed our way through the crowd.

"They're here for extra hands if I need them." Warrin pointed to us, "*They're* here to solve this thing."

Everyone muttered in surprise. Something clicked in the Mayor's memory. "Sherlock Holmes."

Sherlock bowed. "Just Sherlock."

"You've got to be kidding."

"Not in the least."

"This being both a Colony and City matter," Warrin said, "I thought it best to bring in an independent party."

"Your superiors will not be pleased," Sherlock said.

Warrin shrugged. "My superiors won't care as long as

they don't have to deal with this mess."

Sherlock grinned and set to work. This was something new, and he had an audience. He loved it. "Kindly describe the events surrounding the explosion."

"One of the trucks had a bomb planted on it," the Mayor drawled.

"As I assumed from the burned remains," Sherlock bit back, "I was hoping for more detailed and informed information. Surely someone in this town is slightly observant?"

Someone said, "We were in a town meeting when we heard it."

"And everyone flocked to the scene. You put out the fire, but it was too late to save the person inside. A worker, I presume?" Sherlock turned to Warrin for confirmation.

Warrin nodded. "Looks like a basic car bomb set up. Turned on the truck, triggered the explosion."

"Why was he the only one working?"

"According to the company records, he and a few others were scheduled to come out today to start hauling supplies back. Guess he came out early, or there was a mix up in the schedule."

"Did anyone in town know about this?"

"How would we know?" the Mayor demanded, "Dynamo didn't tell us when they decided to take the land, why would they tell us their work schedule?"

"If the trigger was the truck starting, then whoever planted the bomb did so with the intention of killing. If it was a Colonist, then that means it was done under the assumption that workers would be returning to finish the job. Not an unreasonable assumption, given the circumstances."

"You said 'if' it was a Colonist," one of the cops said, "who else could it be?"

Sherlock grinned. "Indeed. Mayor Caine, I need a list of everyone who has come to town in the past few days, everyone who was at the town meeting this morning, and a list of the town's transaction history for the past few weeks."

"We're also gonna need a lot of coffee and room to work," I added with a sigh.

No large tourist groups had visited and no visitors had wandered off through town, except us, of course. That meant whoever planted the bomb either wasn't recorded coming into town, or was a townsperson. The transaction records didn't suggest anyone with an interest in bomb-making, but Sherlock did find a strange purchase for machinery textbooks and magazines.

To my surprise, instead of talking to the family, Sherlock went back to the Mayor. "Why does the Roberts family have an interest in machinery?"

She looked up at him from her desk blankly. "What are you talking about?"

"Someone in the Roberts family has been purchasing mechanical texts."

The Mayor blinked. "Oh. That would be Sophie most likely. She's got an e-reader, downloads all sorts of things from the Ashland library and bookstores. And before you ask, she lives across the town from the construction site."

"But she could easily go there."

"Not without anyone seeing her."

"Would anyone who saw her say so?"

Mayor Caine sighed, "Look. I'm not trying to be difficult. I know you're doing your job, but I have to do mine, too. And that job is to look after my people."

"I have no interest in turning a resourceful young lady in to Ashland authorities. I am interested in catching a murderer."

"You can't think Sophie has anything to do with that."

"As I have never even met the girl, I certainly can. However, she is not high on my suspect list. I would like to take her off it."

"So why are you talking to me instead of her?"

"Because I think you've known the whole time who the saboteur was, and if that's true then you likely know who planted that bomb. Sophie wasn't at the town meeting, nor were several other young people who may be just as enterprising."

Mayor Caine stood up, "None of them had anything to do with it. Even if someone in this town knew how to blow up a truck, they never would."

"Are you certain?"

"I have been keeping Ashland off our backs for a decade. Everyone in town knows that a stunt like this would only bring more trouble, which is exactly what we don't want."

Sherlock smiled. "Excellent. Well, given this information, I shall have to call home for assistance."

I dialed Ghost's number and handed him the phone.

Later that day, we met with Mr. Ritch. "Don't know why we couldn't have met in my office," Mr. Ritch grumbled as he entered the small conference room. "I was just about to go home, couldn't this have waited?"

"We have good news for you," Sherlock said.

"Oh? You've found the saboteur, then?"

"Better. We've found the man who planted the bomb, killing one of your workers."

Mr. Ritch blinked. "Ah. And?"

"And I hope for your sake you have an extremely compelling reason for it. One that will make me feel the tiniest bit of remorse when I see you put away for life. It would be refreshing."

Ritch chuckled. "Oh, please."

"You were late getting into the office today. Why?"

"Car trouble."

"You don't usually drive to work, you live close enough to walk. You don't even have a parking pass."

The Dynamo man blinked. "How... why does it matter why I was late? I slept in -"

"Your record is outstanding. You don't sleep in. Shall I tell you where I think you were? I think you were at the Colony. You took the train, knowing the Mayor had called a town meeting because Detective Warrin told you so yesterday. The train is automated; the Colonists can control it of course, but so can Dynamo. Without anyone at the ticket window there was no one to see you arrive. You went to the construction site, planted a bomb on the truck you knew would be moved offsite today. Then you left. What you hadn't counted on was a worker arriving early, before the town meeting was over, which narrowed the suspects considerably. The Mayor, realizing the sort of trouble this could cause, alerted Detective Warrin to the crime. He in turn alerted us."

"You can't prove any of this," Ritch grumbled.

"True, there is no hard evidence connecting you to the crime, but it is the solution which makes the most sense. You grew tired of waiting and decided to take matters into your own hands. A murder on the scene would force the police to take sides, perhaps even gain the limited attention of the federal government. You could then easily have the Colonists pushed out. So, you took your chance, and a man died."

Ritch scoffed. Then he started to laugh. "I did a little research on you. That whole R.X. business. Gave you a little reputation as a Corporation killer. I think you've let it get to your head. You catch one company being sloppy, and you think every businessman has something to hide."

"As a Corporate man once told me, everyone has secrets," Sherlock had dropped the false nicety of earlier. "Yours is that I terrify you."

"Please. You flatter yourself," Ritch sneered. "I was concerned. I knew there was no way you were going to be impartial. That silly detective wanted your advice so bad, he'd take it no matter who you said was to blame. If there was any chance the police could be moved to act in favor of the Colony, or even just take a flat neutral stance, there was no way our expansion could go smoothly. It would be a P.R. nightmare. Even if this all did work out, what then? We'd just have to do it again in a year or two. Better to just kill their image and then get rid of them."

"Thus, you tried to frame a whole Colony."

"You said so yourself, there's no evidence connecting me. I'd say that's a successful frame-up."

Sherlock grinned. "And I'd say that's a clear confession of guilt."

"To an out-of-town crazy ex-Colonist? No one will believe you."

"They don't have to."

"We'll take it from here, thanks," Detective Warrin said from the conference room speakerphone.

Mr. Ritch gaped at it.

Sherlock chuckled. "Ah, Watts. Let's leave them to it, shall we?"

Sebastian

We returned home to a list of messages Ghost had saved from potential clients. Anything that seemed urgent had been directed to Red in our absence, and of what remained, not much was challenging. The City was business as usual, with the small exception of Corporate Security in a bit of an uproar. Apparently, they'd unsuccessfully petitioned the Mayor to give them greater control of the Corporate Sector, essentially shutting out police authority. The Mayor gave them a little, but not everything they asked for, and that was all anyone in Non-C really cared about it, but it saturated the Corporate-run news for a couple days nonetheless.

The personal paranoias of the elite were the last thing we cared about. A far more pressing concern for us were rumors of increased Crusader activity. They hadn't bothered us yet, but we weren't sure where we stood with them after the battle with Sangrave's cyborgs and Sherlock's return from the dead.

"Do you think they're actually more active, or are their hunts just becoming more noticeable?" I asked over coffee.

"Likely a bit of both," Sherlock muttered as he lit his pipe. "Their numbers continue to grow because they fill a gap. Most members aren't interested in purging humanity, they merely want a meal, some fellowship, and perhaps they truly are drawn to the idea of a tech-less existence. Yet, for every few that join, one seems to take to Joshua Hall's more violent rhetoric."

"Why don't the sane Crusaders go somewhere else?"

"Where would they go? Until some organization or very rich individual sets up a similar practice, without the fundamentalist message, there aren't many options."

"A Corporation would have to set up a charity."

"Or perhaps a church," he scoffed, "not that there are any of those left large enough to compete."

I smiled. "Or a church with a fairly rich patron."

He looked at me dubiously. "Perhaps. What are you thinking?"

"Just seems like something worth suggesting."

He sighed a cloud of smoke. "Watts. Who on earth are you hoping to convince to create a new home for the nonviolent Crusaders?"

We'd met Henry Williams when his friend, Father Lewis, asked us to look into his 'ghost' problem. It turned out the haunting was really a butler with access to hallucinogens, and a family of raccoons. Since then, Henry had been dabbling as a socialite, placing his inherited fortune into safe investments, and donating to a variety of charities without much fanfare. He was mildly eccentric, but not enough to garner press, and he was, it soon became clear, terribly bored.

"Sherlock! Dr. Watts! This is quite a surprise. Please, come in!"

"Thank you," Sherlock said as we stepped inside, "but we can't stay long. We have a favor to ask of you."

"How can I be of service?"

"Are you familiar with the Crusaders?" I asked.

"Yes, the people with the red armbands. Anti-tech and

whatnot. Don't they do some sort of homeless work?"

"Their appeal covers the social spectrum, but the focus is on the lower classes, yes," Sherlock said. "There's a fundamentalist faction that is gaining traction. The best way to discourage it is to give people someplace else to go. Such an endeavor would require a rather wealthy patron."

"You want me to start a shelter?"

"Essentially."

Henry thought for a bit. "Hell, I think it's a great idea, but I haven't the slightest idea where to start."

"Do you know anyone who might have experience in this sort of charitable outreach?" I asked.

Henry shrugged, "There's Fr. Lewis, of course, though it's been awhile since his church did this sort of thing. Heck, maybe we can convince him to use the church to host it. We could go talk to him now, if you like."

"An excellent idea," Sherlock smiled.

Father Lewis was reluctant, not about the idea of setting up a shelter so much as just how quickly it had to happen. "An operation like this takes time, and manpower, to set up successfully. The church has the space for it, but the parish doesn't have the funds it once did. It'll take time to raise enough donations to pay for the supplies we need."

"Donations?" Henry protested. "What am I here for?"

Fr. Lewis smiled. "Money is necessary, but so are people."

"Get the thing started, talk to your dwindling supply of parishioners, and we'll work it out as we go."

Fr. Lewis laughed. "I won't argue. We have a lot of

planning to do."

"Excellent," Sherlock grinned. "Thank you, both. We'll leave you to it."

"This should have been done ages ago," I said as we left.

Sherlock nodded, "Hopefully, with an alternative in place, the Crusaders will see their numbers drop. This is hardly a permanent solution, however."

"It's a start."

We made our way home in silence. As I parked the car, Sherlock said, "I'm glad the Crusaders have at least left you alone."

I shrugged, "I've had a couple of them as patients. And we did nearly die saving the Crusader church. Figure that should give us something of a pass on the whole hunting thing."

"Until we do or say something to remind them why they hate us," Sherlock muttered, glancing around the street before we went inside. He was checking for lookouts and spies.

I hung up our coats once we were in, and locked the door. "Did you have any run-ins with them while you were dead?"

"Not much. I avoided the hunting parties when I could, though I didn't see them that often." He grinned, a touch wickedly, as he went to his room. "There are places in the City where even a holy warrior won't tread."

I sighed, skeptical. "You're going to be dropping vague hints like that for the next year, aren't you?"

I heard a short laugh, but he didn't answer me. I rolled my eyes, and someone knocked.

The man at our door was all in black, nondescript casual clothes under a roughed-up coat. His hat was pulled low, and the smell of cheap cinnamon aftershave hit me like a brick wall. "I'm here to see Sherlock. I've got a business proposition."

That didn't sound encouraging, but I showed him in and asked him to have a seat. He refused, instead standing near the door, looking around the room with idle curiosity. I leaned on the arm of the sofa, and kept a casual eye on him. Something didn't sit right.

When Sherlock came in, he froze in surprise. It was brief enough that I don't think the stranger noticed. Sherlock went straight to his pipe on the mantel, filling it without even looking at the man.

"Here I was, expecting you to show off," the man said.

Sherlock chuckled, his pipe lit, "Mr. Kirby, I do not show off."

Kirby gave a start, then laughed. "Well, fine. Since you know who I am, we can get straight to business."

Sherlock stood perfectly straight, exhaling a cloud of smoke, "I am in the habit of catching criminals, not helping them."

"You'll look the other way now and then, for a greater good or whatever. Done a little law-bending yourself, I understand. Touch of vigilante work?"

"Mr. Kirby, the only reason you are not behind bars at this moment is because I have not yet seen fit to ruin you. I suggest you come to the point."

"I'm going to die if you don't help me."

This neither surprised nor concerned Sherlock. "I'm afraid you will have to be more specific than that."

"Kishore is going to kill me for going behind his back."

"And you are going to offer information to ensure his arrest?"

Kirby grinned. "You wish. I'd just be signing my own death certificate from someone else. Back-stabbing is expected. Rats are exterminated."

"Then the solution to your problem lies in blackmail or murder, neither of which I am willing to supply."

"Not asking you to. What I want you to do is find the man who can supply what I need."

Sherlock blinked. "I don't follow."

"There's a guy I know who could take care of Kishore, get me the protection I need, without involving the police or any private detectives. But he disappeared, shortly after you came back. I figure that means you know what happened to him."

"Simply because of the coincidence? Mr. Kirby, even if I knew to whom you referred, why would I find him? If you were truly frightened for your life, you would leave town. Or turn Kishore in and then leave. Why come to me, to send me on a wild goose chase?"

"Wild what?"

"It's a bird. He means this is hopeless, never going to catch anything," I muttered.

"Oh. Well, fair question. You're going to help me, Sherlock, because I know where your kids live."

"His what?" I exclaimed.

"The kids working for you," Kirby clarified.

Sherlock glared, deathly quiet. "Am I to understand that you are threatening the lives of those children?"

"You are. Anything happens to me, something happens

to them."

Sherlock was stone. "Who do you want me to find?"

"A guy named Sebastian."

My jaw dropped. Kirby didn't notice, focused on Sherlock. Sherlock betrayed no hint of recognition. "Describe him."

"Information dealer. Never took credits, payment by goods only. Dressed in bright colors, bit of a dandy. Partial to Blue, but if you could get him genuine cigarettes, he'd do any job you wanted. Or treat him to a good meal, fancied himself to be something of a gourmand. And that's all anyone knows about him, apart from knowing anything about everyone in the shadows, and if he didn't know it, he could find out fast."

"Why was he permitted?"

"Why didn't someone take him out, you mean? Well, simple, isn't it? He was useful, to everyone. Take him out, and you'd be removing a valuable source of information. Like having a free spy at your beck and call, provided you didn't mind wining and dining him. Never turned on a client either. Smart business move."

"And then he disappeared."

"You came back, and he hasn't been heard from. Either you caught him, or he's gone into hiding til he can figure you out."

"Mr. Kirby, you have the advantage here. Why are you sending me out to find this Sebastian, instead of simply ordering me to get what you want?"

"I know better than to trust you. I don't want any cops involved in this, or detectives who work for cops. You find

Sebastian, tell him I have a job for him, and I'm willing to pay. Then you leave me alone, permanently."

"Very well. You leave me no choice."

"Fast, Sherlock. I don't have a lot of time. And neither do the kids." Kirby paused halfway out the door, "If you try to relocate them, I'll know."

He was gone. I stared at Sherlock. "Blue?"

"The Irregulars' lives are in danger, and that's what you ask me?" he snapped.

I frowned, "I'm just as worried about them as you are. One exposure to Sunshine nearly ruined you, so yeah, I'm a little concerned about hearing you use Blue."

He shook his head, calmer. "There's no need for you to worry. It was a convenient and acceptable currency."

I sighed. "What are we going to do about the Irregulars?"

"*We* will do nothing. I will resurrect Sebastian, and eliminate the threat."

That gave me pause. "Eliminate?"

"I will not kill him, no matter how difficult it is for me to resist the temptation."

I put a hand on his shoulder. "I'm sorry."

He covered my hand with his, "You have nothing to be sorry for. Now, I must prepare."

"Can't I come with you?"

"No. It would raise suspicion. Sebastian works alone. Kirby is a low-level middleman in the drug trade, with delusions of grandeur. This will not take long. I will give you a full account when it is all over."

***

First came the "search." Sherlock went in disguise for a couple days, prowling about the underworld, creating just enough hint of a rumor of his investigation to make it look like he was seriously engaged in tracking down "Sebastian." Then Sebastian came out of hiding.

His first stop was to his favorite bar.

"Where the hell have you been?" the bartender asked.

"Heard there was someone looking for me," Sebastian grinned.

The people around him scoffed and chuckled. "Rumor has it Sherlock's out to find you."

Sebastian shrugged. "I was wondering when he'd get around to it."

"You're not worried?"

"Oh, really, now. What do you think I've been doing all this time?"

"You've got something on him?"

Sebastian didn't answer. He just smiled and tossed back his drink. "Be seein' you gents." Talk would spread. People would know he was back, and that he had something worth knowing on Sherlock. That would keep everyone speculating, and likely line up some assignments, none of which he intended to take seriously, but it would keep the attention off his ultimate goal - Kishore and Kirby.

Kishore controlled the Blue trade for a quarter of the city. Most of it was delegated to other dealers, but everything came back to him... and his wife.

"Sebastian," she cooed, "how nice to see you. It's been so long."

"It has," he kissed her hand, "I must say, madam, you grow more radiant each time I see you."

"Tch, flattery," she grinned. "Shameless at that. You must be desperate for something."

He shrugged. "No use denying it, but it's true nonetheless."

"What is it you're looking for this time, Sebastian? Information on my husband, no doubt."

"Nothing you aren't willing to give," he humbly bowed, looking up at her with a mischievous grin.

She laughed. "It'll cost you."

"I expected so," he nodded.

"Last time you got off easy," she gripped the silk scarf around his neck, pulling him close to her. "I was feeling generous, and so lonely. But then you didn't come to call again."

"Business, my dear. A man must make a living. Is the life of a kept woman still so horribly dissatisfying?"

She sighed. "Yes. All this money and no one to have fun with. Tell you what," he repressed a shudder as her fingers slowly trailed down his chest, "you come with me and we can discuss my husband, and you can tell me a little bit about what you've been doing after disappearing."

He smiled. "Sounds like a marvelous plan."

She took him to the bedroom. They were alone in the house, Kishore was out overseeing his "empire" as he thought of it, likely from the comfort of a gentlemen's club.

"What did you do with the info I gave you last time?"

"Sold it to a competitor of yours, of course."

"And now you're on assignment again."

"You are the most reliable source concerning Kishore's business. You are the power behind the throne, as it were, and you don't particularly mind the fact that you're selling out your husband. Besides, Kishore doesn't like me."

"True. You're too flamboyant for his taste. And much more attractive than him." She leaned back on the bed. "So. What exactly did you want to know about this time?"

Sebastian chuckled at her display, shaking his head. He lit a cigarette, offering her the pack.

"One of these days I'm going to see you with your clothes off," she pouted, taking a cigarette.

He lit it for her, "Business before pleasure."

She sighed. "Fine. But only because you're cute. Fire away."

"Why does he have a worm like Kirby working for him?"

She scoffed, "I ask myself that question a lot. Bad enough Kirby was skimming off the shipments, but then he went and told Taran how to intercept the next one. Pain in the ass for us, death wish for Kirby. I'm sure Taran paid well, but he's not going to have long to enjoy the reward."

"When is Kishore taking care of him?"

"Soon as we find the bastard," she grinned, "you wouldn't want to tell me where he's been hiding?"

"Oh, a fellow like Kirby's not hard to find. Your own men should do just fine. In fact, why haven't they?"

"Kirby says he's got something on Sherlock. Kishore wants to know what it is. Only thing keeping him alive right now. But my darling husband is getting impatient. He's going to kill Kirby, whether he tells him what he knows or not."

Sebastian blinked and forced a grin. "Is that right?"

"Mmhm," she chuckled, "but, as I understand it, you've got something on the Detective, too."

"Ha, I might at that. Took me awhile, but I've got a lovely bit of gossip on the man."

"Ooh. Do tell."

"I'm not sure I will."

"I answered your questions, you answer mine. Quid pro quo."

"Kirby for Sherlock? Hardly. Sweeten the deal, and we'll talk."

She took a long draw from her cigarette. "What about... for a few doses of Sunshine?" Her hand languidly reached toward the side table, opening a hidden drawer. She wavered, eyelids suddenly heavy. "You... you bastard..."

"I apologize. Drugged the cigarettes, except for mine. You'll be fine in a little while." He saw the vials of Liquid Sunshine in the drawer, his gaze lingering. They seemed to glow gold under the fluorescent lighting. A memory of euphoria swelled up, and he wondered what it tasted like...

He ran out of the building, ducking through every alley, weaving a fast path through the City until he came to a bolt-hole. Making sure he hadn't been followed, he dashed inside, tearing away his beard and collapsing on the cot. His whole body shook.

"What the bloody hell was that," he muttered, "I haven't had a craving like that in a year." His stomach turned. He washed his face and hands in the small sink, the cold water shocking some rationality back to his senses. After a proper cigarette, he reapplied his beard, adjusted his clothes, and grinned a touch maniacally at the mirror. "Alright, Sebastian. Time to eliminate the threat."

Kirby came home that night to find a visitor sitting in his living room. He swore, "You startled me. Couldn't keep the lights on?"

"No."

"… are you drinking my wine?"

"It's genuine, rather than synthahol."

"Which makes it ridiculously expensive."

Sebastian grinned. "Indeed. Take it out of my pay."

"Ha. Fair enough." Kirby had never dealt with Sebastian before, but from everything he'd heard, it was easiest to appear a generous host and do nothing to upset the man. He was the best information in the City, but he was also a little crazy. "I need blackmail on Kishore. Or just take him out completely."

Sebastian shrugged. "So I heard. I also heard there's going to be a hit on you soon. Given the urgency of the case, what I can offer you up front is blackmail on Kishore's wife, which I already have in my possession."

"He won't budge for his wife."

"He will when cops raid his home and find Liquid Sunshine in the bedroom."

"He'll pay them off."

"Not if it's the right cops."

Kirby frowned. This was not what he had in mind. Too many ifs. "What else you got?"

Sebastian grinned again. It was not a friendly expression. "More information on Sherlock than you could dream of."

"That's not helping me right now."

"Kishore is going to kill you no matter what, because you were stupid and reckless. There is not a single piece of information in the world that will stop this. However, what I am offering you is a chance to become a valuable informant, if not to Kishore then to someone else."

"I'm interested."

"You pay me for information on the Detective fellow. I relay it to you, exclusively. You then sell yourself as an informant to Kishore, and pray he thinks you're more valuable to him alive than dead. Or you sell the info to someone capable of protecting you from Kishore, either way."

"And what's this information going to cost me?"

"Do you really want to put a price tag on your life?"

Kirby chuckled. "Ok. Don't see that I have much choice."

Sebastian sipped his wine. "You show me the pay, I'll give you info accordingly."

"Extortion."

"If you like. I prefer to think of it as 'saving your ungrateful tail,'" he smiled.

Kirby sighed and brought out a case from a hidden safe. "Here. Blue, Blood, Flash, and a little Sunshine."

Sebastian peeked inside and closed it. "Lovely. One quick question, how'd you get that private detective with delusions of Victorianism to track me down?"

"I told him I knew where his brats were."

"The kids who work for him?"

"Yep." Kirby was clearly pleased with himself.

Sebastian smirked. "And you were dangling this in front of Kishore to keep him off your back long enough for a solution to fall into your lap."

Kirby shrugged. "Gamble, but it worked."

"Were you bluffing?"

"Nope. Had my best man keeping watch. Anything happened to me, his orders were to take the kids out."

"Mm. Well, it's a good thing I took him out."

Kirby blinked. "What?"

"Crippled him. Delivered him to the police, telling them Kishore's missus uses Sunshine, and his agent Kirby deals with Taran and has been skimming off shipments."

"What!" Kirby's outrage was cut off as he was thrown against the wall, an impossibly strong grip holding him in place.

"You threatened my children," Sebastian growled.

"Your…?" Terror creeped into Kirby's face as he realized who had him by the throat.

"What did you think I'd been doing that year I was dead?" His response was choked off again as Sherlock threw him to the floor. He tried to get up. Sherlock sent him back down. "You would have killed those children in cold-blooded murder."

"Hey, now," Kirby coughed, hand reaching inside his coat, "nothing personal. Just business."

He pulled his gun as the blade shot from Sherlock's forearm.

***

I hate waiting. I tried to keep myself occupied, but images of Sherlock lying dead on the street kept going through my head. I knew he had to do this alone, but I hated it. I couldn't stand thinking about him dead, again, but I couldn't stop myself.

I leaped up from the sofa when he finally got home, but the expression on his face stopped me in my tracks. He looked hauntingly disconnected. He silently went straight to the shower, changed into a new suit and took up his violin.

"Did the move go as planned?" he asked as he settled the instrument on his shoulder.

"Everything was fine. The Irregulars are safe in a new building. How did it go with you?"

"I was successful."

"Good… right?"

His response was dissonant music. That worried me, but I let him play. It wasn't until a few hours later that I got an explanation. Red stopped by.

"Got a strange tip today," she said to Sherlock, clearly not happy about it. My friend stood by the window, setting down his violin. Red continued, "Followed up on it, of course. Found Pete Kirby, drug dealer, works for Jack Kishore… but you already know that. He was cut up pretty bad. Unconscious, but alive. He's recovering in the hospital now. The bullet in the wall says he put up a fight, bad luck for him that he missed. No evidence to suggest who did it, of course. I've got a warrant out for his boss and top competitor. We've found enough evidence to charge them for drug trafficking at least, though no guarantee we can make it stick."

Sherlock nodded again. "Of course."

Red sighed. "Look, if we can get Kishore in jail, I'll be as happy as anyone. Kirby's alive, I don't know what he did to justify the blood on the floor, but I'm honestly not going to worry about it much. What I am worried about is a friend of mine developing something of a vigilante streak."

Sherlock smirked. "Really, Red."

"Don't laugh. I thought Sebastian was retired."

"He is. It was required he come out of retirement for this single case. He never will again. He is dead."

Red nodded. "Ok. What about you?"

"What about me?"

Red turned to me. "He ok, doc?"

I shrugged. "Been better. It was a... personal matter. He's not crazy though, so that's good."

She was doubtful. "At least there's that. Well, sorry to have taken your time. I get worried. I like you two. Don't get into trouble I can't ignore."

"We always do our best," I said as she closed the door behind her. "Are you ok?" I asked as I stood beside him at the window.

His voice was quiet. "I nearly killed him, Watts. It would have been so easy."

"But you didn't."

"I wanted to. Even had he not been armed, I might have..." He shivered as I held his hand, "It is rare that I've ever felt so enraged. It seems the more I let affection into my soul, the more of a monster I become."

I frowned. "How would you have dealt with this situation

a few years ago?"

"What do you mean?"

"You once told me that before we met, you were becoming more machine than human. You hadn't laughed in years. The case was more important than the people. Would you even have cared if your Irregulars had been threatened back then?"

His brow knitted, mildly offended. "Of course I would."

"And how would you have kept them safe?"

Sherlock was speechless.

"Well?" I asked, a touch pleased with myself.

"I would have killed him," he softly said, "I would have killed him and thought nothing of it." He shook his head, "That doesn't excuse—"

"That's not my point." I squeezed his hand, "My point is that you've got a great heart to go with that great mind of yours, and maybe you shouldn't blame it for all your moral shortcomings. It's kind of what's keeping you human."

He was silent a moment, lost in his thoughts. "It isn't the only thing." His eyes met mine, "I would be nothing without you, James. I owe you my life, and my sanity." His grip on my hand tightened when I shrugged, "I am perfectly serious."

I was perfectly awkward. "Yeah, well. You're my friend. Seems the least I can do is keep you alive, when you let me." He sighed. "Manage to stop beating yourself up?"

He smiled, just a little. "For the moment."

"Good enough. Come on, we could both use a drink, and you haven't eaten anything since you got home."

"Why are you constantly concerned with how much I

eat?"

"You'd forget to do it if I didn't remind you. Man cannot live on bread and water alone."

"That rather depends on the man, and the bread."

"I've seen the nutritional content of our bread. It's not enough."

He chuckled, and let me drag him to the kitchen.

Kitty's Back

Sherlock went to see the Irregulars in their new Hideout twice over the next week to be sure everything was secure. Whether he was satisfied or whether Wendy told him to stop worrying, I'm not certain, but I suspect it was a bit of both. The Sebastian business had really shaken him, not just because of the threat to the Irregulars, but because he'd gone back into a character that he'd been for so long and thought he'd purged. He wasn't quite comfortable in his own skin afterward. So, I did the only thing I could think of, and took him to the Symphony.

There weren't any Crusaders hawking pamphlets this time, and the selection was more modern, but it was still classical-style music and for an hour Sherlock was in a state of utter relaxation, a gentle smile on his face. He put a hand on my shoulder as we left, "Thank you. I needed this."

I smiled, "I'm glad it helped."

As we made our way out of the Corporate Sector, a voice called out, "James Watts! Is that you?"

I spun around. There she was, as gorgeous as I remembered her. Long black waves shone in the sun as her amber cat eyes seemed to sparkle. I remembered when she bought those eyes. Her model buxom figure fit perfectly in her green dress, her matching two-inch heels lifting her an inch above my height. Smiling her perfect smile, her sculpted legs were carrying her straight toward me.

Oh, hell.

I was frozen between fight and flight. What was she doing here? Her arms flung around my neck in a far-too-fond embrace. Her perfume shocked my body into mild arousal. I looked around for Sherlock, embarrassed. He was waiting for me down the street, smoking a cigarette with an amused look on his face.

I gently pulled her off of me. "Kitty," I said, still stunned, "hi."

"It's great to see you," she smiled.

Somehow, I doubted that. "I haven't heard from you in years."

"Been seeing the world, came back to meet some friends, never dreamed I'd see you on the street!"

"I bet."

"What are you doing tonight, we should get together," she gasped as if struck by genius, "Dinner at the Greco-Italian restaurant, what's it called, the one across the street from the mall and between the margarita bar and the fusion steakhouse, and then after-dinner drinks at my place!"

My head was screaming 'Bad idea!' "Uh, sure," my mouth said. Traitor.

"Great! Meet me there at seven?" She kissed me quick and took off before I could answer.

"Damn it," I muttered, face in my hand as I joined Sherlock, whose amusement now held some concern.

"Problem?"

"I just made a date with my ex-wife."

He stopped, shocked. "Your wife?!"

"Ex-wife!" I walked faster.

"I had no idea you were married!" He easily caught up to me.

"We split up a year before I met you."

He was understandably very confused. "And now you're seeing her tonight?"

"Yeah. I'm an idiot."

"If you didn't want to, then why—"

"Because she's as perfect as I remember, and I'm impulsive enough to blindly agree." I stopped, furious at myself, head in my hands as I leaned against a wall.

I felt Sherlock's arm around my shoulders. "Come," he said, "when we get home, you can explain everything."

"Her name's Kitty Cortez. We met at a party for a mutual friend. She looked exactly as she does now. She took me home with her, we started regularly sleeping with each other. She was funny, gorgeous, and spectacular in bed. I was a fairly well off medical man who was open to anything."

I sighed. "The only reason we got married is because she thought it would be fun and I didn't think twice. Didn't last long. She got bored, left to see the world, we divorced, and now I see her out of the blue and I freeze up, just as smitten as the first time I saw her."

I looked over at my friend. He was filling his pipe, listening closely. "Watts, if you hate this woman, then simply don't go."

"I don't hate her, I'm angry at myself for being such a sap. I'm over her, but I'm…" I stopped talking, trying to figure out how to explain. He did it for me.

"If you feel you have to see her, then go. Give yourself the closure you never had the chance to before, show her how superior a human being you are, whatever the impulse may be," he smiled, "and then come home. I'll even wait up for you, if you like."

I laughed a little, "Thanks. I don't imagine it'll be a long date."

Knowing he was waiting for me actually helped. Kitty was in top form, using every seduction trick she knew and a few I hadn't seen before. Once I realized what the game was, I was able to actually enjoy myself, the thought of Sherlock in the back of my mind.

At some point during the meal, she realized something was different. We'd made small talk about her travels and how great she looked, and after she asked about people I hadn't heard from in years, and I'd made a slight glance at my phone, she asked me what I was doing these days.

"Ever become a real doctor?"

I grinned, "Not exactly. I went rogue."

Her eyes went wide. "How exciting!" I couldn't tell if she was being serious or not. "What's that like?"

I shrugged, "Different. I have some regular patients, and my name has got around enough to keep me busy."

"I guess that means you aren't living in this sector, then."

"No, I share a place across the border."

She smiled. "Life on the dangerous side. You'll have to show it to me sometime."

I coughed. "I don't think so."

She was surprised, but remained playful. "Too

dangerous?"

"No… well, not during the day. And not at night if you stayed close to the border."

"Why not then?" I started to answer, but she cut me off, "I know it's been a long time, but we used to be friends. I'd like to get reacquainted."

I was amused. "Still always thinking of the next man in your bed."

She laughed, "That's rich, coming from you."

She had a point. "I'm not who you remember," I said.

"James—"

"Watts," I snapped a little, surprising myself. "Sorry. Everyone calls me Watts."

She blinked, stunned. "Alright," she leaned back, amazed. "So. Are you exclusive?"

"I'm not that different," I smirked. "I'm just choosing not to get involved with an ex."

"Then why come out?"

I shrugged. "I was curious. You completely dropped out of my life when you left, I wanted to know if you were how I remembered you."

"Did you expect me to keep in touch?"

"No. You said you came back to see some friends?"

"Mm. Not really. I came back here to try starting over from square one again. Seeing you on the street, well. It was like old times. Old habits." She smiled, "We did have fun, didn't we?"

I smiled, in spite of myself. "Yeah. Yeah, we did."

"Unlike some of your former lovers."

"Oh, god," I rolled my eyes.

"Let's see, there was the pompous ass from med school…"

"Kitty."

"Multiple of those, come to think of it."

"Kitty?"

"Then the woman who took you to the 'gala' that ended up—"

"Please stop," I groaned.

"I only just started!"

"That's why I want you to stop!" I laughed.

She relented with a smile. "Oh, fine. Spoilsport."

"You're the only person who ever accused me of ruining their fun."

"That can't be true."

"It's close."

"Hm. So. Watts. Can I ask how you lost your first name?"

"I was always Watts in school. Carried over to the medteam, and just sort of stuck. I liked it."

"Bit distant, only using your last name."

"Just means the people who call me James are close to me."

"So, no one calls you James."

"… pretty much."

She leaned in, chin in her hand. "*Does* someone call you James?"

My fingers drummed the table. "You are going to make way too big a deal about this."

Girlish delight filled her face.

"No," I immediately tried to control the situation, "it is not whatever you're imagining."

She pouted skeptically, which is a facial expression I don't think I'd ever seen before, and was right back into a more subdued gossip mode. "Man, woman, other?"

I sighed, resigned to my fate. "Man."

"Is he cute?"

I laughed. "No, 'cute' is not an adjective I would ever use to describe him."

"Then how would you describe him?"

"He's very… refined. Old fashioned."

"Old fashioned can be cute."

"Not the way he does it. He has a very dry sense of humor, zero interest in popular culture, and is one of the most difficult people to have as a housemate, possibly in the world."

"Then why do you stay?"

It took me a moment to put the words together. "He's a good man. Not just the sentimental thing people say, I mean I think he's honestly a good person, who tries to do what's right. It doesn't always work, but he tries. He's brilliant, and human, and… we've been through a lot. He's my best friend."

Kitty was watching me closely, not an ounce of skepticism or gossip on her face. In fact, it might have been the first time I'd ever seen her sincerely smile. "He must be a hell of a man."

I wasn't sure what to make of her mood shift. "He's one of a kind, that's for sure."

She laughed a little. "Tell him I said I'm sorry for

keeping you away." At my confusion, she leaned across the table to give me a peck on the cheek. "Go home, Watts. It was good to see you."

I heard his violin from the steps. It was an actual piece of music instead of his usual emotional outpouring, though I didn't recognize it. He stopped playing the instant the door opened.

"How did it go?" he asked.

"Better than expected."

"Good," he put away the violin, "do you have any other former wives I should know about?"

I chuckled, "No."

"Husbands?"

"No!"

"It's a reasonable question."

"Sherlock, Kitty is the only person I have ever married. If I meet any more of my former lovers, I will not have anywhere near so dramatic a reaction."

He grinned. "Good."

I went to my room to change into a t-shirt. "She told me to tell you she apologized for keeping me away," I called out to him.

"She what?"

"I don't know what spurred it. I was too puzzled and anxious to come home to ask." I joined him on the sofa, "Now that I think about it, she probably thinks we're dating."

Sherlock's expression was an amusing mix of surprised humor and discomfort. "What on earth did you say to give her that impression?"

I smirked. "I snapped at her when she called me James."

He was bemused. "That is your name."

"Yeah, but you're the only one who uses it."

"I wasn't aware I'm the only one in the world permitted to."

I shrugged, "Feels weird if anyone else does."

He softly smiled. "I'm flattered."

Someone knocked on the door. Sherlock sighed before checking the security cam. "This will be interesting," he muttered before answering. "Can I help you?"

"I'm looking for someone called Sherlock?"

I knew that voice.

"Please come in," Sherlock said as I stood, "I'm Sherlock and you already know—"

"Watts!" Kitty exclaimed, shocked.

I stared. "What are you doing here?"

"The police told me..." she glanced at Sherlock as he closed the door, "*He's* the one you were talking about?!"

I sighed, "Yes."

"That's not quite the reaction I anticipated," Sherlock said.

I wasn't sure if he was talking about me or her, but either way I cleared my throat, "Um, Kitty, meet Sherlock. Sherlock, Kitty Cortez."

"Good evening," he said, not bothering to hide his amusement. "I take it my name never came up in your conversation."

Kitty shook her head, "No, he didn't mention it. I didn't

think I'd ever meet the mysterious boyfriend, so I didn't ask."

Sherlock looked at me, astonished. "Boyfriend?"

"At no point did I ever say I had a boyfriend!" I protested.

Kitty waved away my protest, "Who cares what you call it, it's true."

"I have rather a strong opinion on the subject," Sherlock drawled sardonically. "'Boyfriend' makes me sound like a lovesick schoolboy."

Kitty and I blinked. "I can't tell if you're joking or not," I said.

"I'm not, I genuinely don't like the word, and it does not accurately describe our relationship, besides." Sherlock gestured Kitty should take a seat on the sofa as he went to the mantle for his pipe, "Now then, Ms. Cortez, perhaps you could explain what brought you to our door in the first place."

She sat down with a nervous glance at me as I leaned on the arm of Sherlock's chair. "I had a message at my hotel today from Drake, my second husband. It said… sorry, let me start over. I remarried after Watts and I got divorced. We had a daughter, Adanna. We were very happy, but it all fell apart after she died. She was 5 months old. That was four years ago. We split up soon after. I travelled a lot, eventually made my way back here. This evening, just after I met Watts, there was a message on my phone. It was from Drake. It said, 'I know about Adanna.'"

Sherlock's brow knitted. "Know what?"

"I don't know," she said, exasperated.

"And yet you went to the police."

She sighed. "You don't know Drake. He was tons of fun at first, he loved being a dad, but," she hesitated, "he had a darker side. When he got angry, when he took something personally, he was terribly unforgiving. He could be terrifying. If he thinks I was somehow responsible for Adanna's death…"

Sherlock was perfectly emotionless behind the veil of smoke, "Were you?"

She looked like she'd been smacked. "No!"

"Yet you assume that's what he means."

"What else could it be?"

"What happened when you went to the police?"

"I tried to explain it, but it didn't work. They couldn't do anything with just one vague message. Someone made a joke that they should send me to you. I was desperate enough to try anyone."

Sherlock scoffed, in a rare display of vanity. "I am hardly 'anyone.'"

"You've been out of touch," I explained, strangely proud, "His cases regularly make the news. Did you hear about the R.X. trial a couple years ago? I thought that got some international press."

"I remember hearing about it, there was some mention of a private detective that exposed them, but I don't remember anything else. That was you?" she asked him.

"It was, but we're getting off track," Sherlock went back to being coldly professional. "How did the child die?"

Kitty blinked at the topic shift, "Sudden infant death. We woke up one morning and found her in her crib… gone."

"Hardly something that can be blamed on you."

"He did anyway. Not directly, he never accused me of anything, but it was there. The way he treated me afterward, as if I'd somehow done something wrong. When we divorced, I thought that was the end of it, but now it's four years later and he's tracking me down. I'm worried. I want to know what's going on, so I thought I might as well take the cop's suggestion and talk to a…" she paused.

Sherlock half grinned, "I imagine the adjectives used were less than complimentary."

She smiled a little. "Well, they did say you were crazy."

He scoffed. "Only crazy? That's refreshing. Why haven't you asked Drake what he meant?"

"I tried, multiple times, but he hasn't responded."

"Hm. This will require some research. All you can do at this point is return to your hotel and try to relax. If you feel you may be in danger at any time, call. I will try to discover what I can, and hopefully we can sort this out."

With a nod, Kitty stood. "Need company back?" I offered.

"I think I'll be alright," she said. "The car's still out front."

"One moment," Sherlock stopped her just before she left, "You never mentioned Drake's last name."

"Cayne."

"Thank you. Goodnight."

"Goodnight," Kitty said, and closed the door behind her.

"An interesting woman, your ex-wife," Sherlock said as he sat down in his armchair.

I sat down on the sofa. "Do you think she's really in any

danger?"

"Difficult to say. 'I know about Adanna'… certainly a unique challenge, to say the least. I'll start the investigation with Mr. Cayne, try to learn what sort of man would track down an ex-wife to harass her about a child gone four years."

"Not a good one."

"No. I'll of course have to look into Adanna's death."

"You don't think Kitty had anything to do with it?"

"Not in the least, but I have to cover every possibility if I'm going to discover what this mysterious message might mean."

Sherlock left first thing in the morning. I had patients to see, which kept my mind off Kitty. It was a little weird, thinking of her as a mom. It wasn't something I'd ever imagined her as while we were dating, or married. I was also trying not to think of her second ex-husband. I wasn't surprised she'd remarried. I was surprisingly pissed off at the fact Drake was bothering her.

My mood wasn't improved by her calling me late that afternoon. Again, it wasn't the calling that put me out of sorts, as much as the reason.

"There was a note in my hotel room," she said, "It's in Drake's handwriting, and says, 'We will talk.'"

"Not as bad as I expec—"

"It was in my room! He knows where I'm staying, he got into my hotel room when I wasn't here, and he still won't tell me what the hell is going on!"

I sighed, and swore. "Sorry. Come to the house, I'll be home soon, you can stay there for a while if it helps."

"I don't want to be in the way—"

"You're not. 122 Break Street is one of the safest places you can be right now."

"Thanks, Watts," she was clearly relieved, "When can I come over?"

"I'll be there in an hour."

I half expected Kitty to be waiting for me outside the door, but fortunately she wasn't. I went inside and found Ghost at the kitchen table. "What are you doing?"

"Eating," she said around a mouthful of cereal, "like you're always telling me to do."

I went to my room to put away my gear. "My ex-wife will be here in a few minutes."

Ghost swallowed. "Why?"

I smiled as I came back to the table, "She's one of Sherlock's clients."

"Your ex is one of your boyfriend's clients."

"He's not my boyfriend."

"Yes, he is."

"No, he doesn't like the word."

Ghost blinked, and grinned. "You know, waiting on the reserved asexual from the Victorian Era to make the first move might not be the most brilliant idea."

I sighed, "We're not dating."

"Of course you're not dating. You're practically married."

"Given my record, I hope not."

Ghost laughed. "I'm not making fun of you, Doc, I promise. Well, maybe a little, but just because you're good for each other." Someone knocked on the door. Ghost stood up, taking her bowl of cereal with her.

"Sure you don't want to meet her?"

"Sure don't. Have fun."

I waited till the attic door closed, and let Kitty in. "You ok?"

She shook her head, "Right now I feel silly, but I was so freaked out earlier."

"It's fine, really. Sit down, relax a bit."

"Thanks," she sat on the sofa. "Were you talking to someone just now?"

"Just the ghost in the attic."

She chuckled, "I do that sometimes." I took a seat next to her, "You look good, Watts."

"Um, thanks."

She grinned, "I don't mean physically. Well, that too, but it's more than that. You look… I don't know. Happy."

"And this is new?" I asked, a bit surprised.

"Kind of, yeah. You were always in a good mood while we were together, but never really in a good place, do you know what I mean?"

"Not really, no."

She laughed a little, "Never mind. He's obviously good for you, is what I'm trying to get at."

I smiled. "Maybe we've been good for each other. Can I get you anything?"

"I'm fine right now, thanks. Has he read all these books?" she gestured to the shelves.

"Most, at least."

"How did he get them?"

"I have no idea."

"They must have cost a small fortune."

"I think most of them were payment for services. He probably brought a few from the Colony, too."

She stared at me. "He's a Colonist?"

"Former. And speak of the devil."

Sherlock paused as he came inside and saw Kitty. "Has something happened?"

"There was a note in my hotel room. I freaked, and asked Watts if I could hide out here for a while," she smiled apologetically. "Sorry."

"Don't be ridiculous, there's no reason to apologize," he sat in his chair. He was in modern casual clothes, black denim jeans and a grey shirt under a black jacket. He took off his gloves as he sat, tossing them to the floor.

"This is the first time I've ever seen you wear jeans," I said.

He sighed heavily as he pulled out his cigarette case, "While a full disguise wasn't necessary, I needed something that wouldn't be instantly recognizable as the 'crazy detective.'"

"It's a good look."

He rolled his eyes with a grin as he lit his cigarette, and turned all his attention on Kitty. "You said there was a note?"

She nodded, "It said 'We will talk.'"

"I don't suppose you brought it with you?"

"I did, actually," she pulled it out of her purse and gave it to him. "It's his handwriting. It was in my hotel room, on the bed where I wouldn't miss it. None of the staff admitted to letting anyone in, and no messages were left."

"Apart from this," he muttered as he held it up to the light. He took it to his desk and minutely examined it with his magnifying glass. "Does Drake own a pen?"

"Yes," she said, surprised. "It's a fountain pen. He's ridiculously enamored with it, uses it every chance he gets. Why?"

"This note was not written with a ballpoint, which is what all the hotels in the City use. It is, however, standard synthetic stock, the sort of thing one would find on a hotel manager's desk for making quick notes while on the phone. In which hotel are you staying?"

"The Palladium."

He put down his lens and leaned back in the desk chair. After a long draw on his cigarette, he said, "You managed to marry a very dangerous man, Ms. Cortez."

Kitty's eyes widened. "Drake? He runs an investment company."

"He's under suspicion by a variety of international legal entities for fraud."

"What?"

"In connection to his dealings with the Mafia."

"What!?"

"You upgraded from 'aspiring doctor' to 'mob boss?'" I said.

She hit my arm, "Shut up."

"He's not a boss, Watts, he's an associate," Sherlock corrected.

I shrugged, "Whatever. Bottom line, we should take his

notes as threats, right?"

"Given that he has been unresponsive to Kitty's attempts at contacting him, yes. He has a reputation for brutality outside his legitimate business ventures. I'm still no closer to finding out exactly what it is he wants from you, Kitty, but I hope to shed some light on the matter this evening."

"How?" she asked.

"I'm going to look at Adanna's medical records."

Kitty blinked. "How? She was born, and died, overseas."

He half grinned. "If I told you, I'd be putting a very valuable resource at risk."

"You're going to hack the hospital?"

"It's faster than waiting for them to approve a request from you, and it provides comprehensive access, rather than a specific piece of information. Do you have an alternate place to stay for the night?"

"I'll just have to get another hotel room."

"He's proven he can track you to one, why not another? You don't have any friends you could stay with?"

She shook her head, "Most of them haven't kept in touch, or I haven't kept in touch with them. The ones I did manage to contact haven't been encouraging. I cut a lot of ties when I left the country."

"Then you'll stay here," I said, surprising myself as much as it did her.

To our further surprise, Sherlock agreed. "Of course."

"I've already been enough trouble."

"It's not trouble," I said, "it's not safe for you to be where he can find you, and if he tracks you down here, he's in for a hell of a surprise."

"Thank you," she sighed, giving me a quick hug, "I really appreciate it," she said to Sherlock, who modestly inclined his head.

"I'll leave you and Watts to see to the arrangements," he said, standing and going into his room.

"I like the suit better," she commented.

"Me too, but he never wears modern clothes, not without being in disguise. Come on, let's head back to the hotel and get your stuff."

Fortunately, Kitty travels light. "You can take my bed, I'll stay on the sofa," I said as I pulled her suitcase out of the back of the car.

"I don't want to inconvenience you."

"You're not, honest." I paused in front of the door, "How do you feel about the violin?"

"Violin?"

"Sherlock plays sometimes."

She rolled her eyes. "Everything's going to be fine, Watts, stop worrying. It's just one night, hopefully."

I showed Kitty to my room and left her to get settled while I went up to the attic. "Progress?" I asked.

Sherlock, back in his usual clothing, shook his head. "I have a theory that Miss Ghost is looking into. Thus far, her research hasn't yielded results."

"Patience," Ghost muttered.

Sherlock came back downstairs with me. "Kitty's getting set up in my room," I said, "I thought she'd want some privacy.

So, what's your theory?"

"I'd like to keep it to myself for the moment." He half grinned at my expression. "I'm not being dramatic, this time. I really do think it for the best."

"That's a little worrying."

He sighed, "Please, Watts."

"Ok," I warily agreed, "I'll wait."

"After I have Miss Ghost's results, I'll have to confront Mr. Cayne."

"You mean 'we.'"

"And leave fair maiden unguarded?"

"Are you teasing me?"

"A bit."

"Where else was she going to go?"

"Nowhere," he said with a placating smile. "It's simply an amusing situation," his gaze shifted to my door behind me, "Good evening, Kitty."

"Hello," she said, "Thanks again for taking me in for the night."

"You are welcome. Has Drake attempted to contact you at all?"

"No," she huffed, "I wish he'd stop being so creepy about it and just tell me what's going on. But then, he never was one for reason when he was pissed off."

"You hadn't been married long before Adanna was born?"

"A little under nine months. He really wanted kids, and Adanna was early."

"I see." He gestured that she have a seat on the sofa,

"Would you mind if I ask a few questions about Mr. Cayne?"

She shrugged and sat. "Go for it."

Sherlock selected a pipe, leaning against the mantelpiece as he filled it, "We've established that he had a temper and could be ruthless, but would you describe him as easily jealous?"

"Yes."

"May I ask why you married him in the first place?" She blinked, and started to answer him, "The real reason, if you please, Ms. Cortez. It is important."

She stared at him as he lit his pipe, offended. It didn't last long. "I met him on a trip to Europe with friends while Watts and I were married. He was suave and different. I was bored."

"Ouch," I said, sarcastically.

"Oh, hush, we didn't marry until after you and I divorced, and it's not like you didn't have your own flings."

"Like what?"

"That thing you had going with the exotic, or—"

"That was with your permission!"

"Focus on the issue at hand!" Sherlock commanded. "Kitty, you started seeing Drake while married to Watts. Did Drake know you were married?"

"No."

"Did you continue using contraceptives the whole time?"

"Sherlock!" His hand cut off my protest, his eyes never leaving Kitty.

Kitty paled. "Oh my god," she whispered.

"Sherlock. What's going on?" I demanded, a sinking feeling in my stomach.

He turned to me, "While Kitty thinks the messages

reference the child's death, I think they reference the child's origin."

"You think Adanna was mine?"

"I knew Drake wanted kids," Kitty said, "so I went off my birth control, but then the night before I left town…"

"Yeah," I sighed. "Adanna wasn't early, you just started counting from the wrong date."

"And somehow, he found out," Kitty was starting to look truly scared.

"We don't know this is true," I pointed out.

"Not yet," Sherlock conceded, "but as Kitty said when she came to us, what else could it be? Adanna died with no indication of foul play, and every possible test was done."

I poured two drinks and handed one to Kitty.

"I didn't know," she said.

"I know you didn't." My computer dinged.

"The results," Sherlock said quietly.

I printed them out. "You were right," I shrugged, "so now we just have to explain the situation to a jealous mobster."

"Oh that'll go real well," Kitty scoffed.

"I'll consider our options," Sherlock said. "For now, I recommend supper and sleep," he gave Kitty a small, genuine smile, "as you look about ready to collapse, if I may be so bold."

Kitty laughed a little, tossing back her drink, "That sounds about right."

I fixed a quick meal and Kitty disappeared into my room as soon as she'd eaten. Sherlock wordlessly helped me clean up, and then followed me to the sofa. "Are you alright?" he asked as he sat next to me.

"I'm fine. It's a little weird, but even if Adanna had lived, she'd have been better off with them than me."

"A jealous, possessive mobster, and a woman who impulsively tries everything she can just for the thrill of a new experience?"

"Versus a wannabe-hero hedonist with commitment issues? At least they actually wanted to have kids, which I never did."

"Regardless, based solely on his behavior toward Ms. Cortez, you would have been infinitely better."

I smiled a little, not believing him but pleased. "Moot point now, I guess."

We sat in silence for a while.

"I thought you didn't find exotics attractive," Sherlock commented.

I coughed. "I'm not a fan of fur or feathers." He closed his eyes, face in his hand. "You asked."

"I've learned my lesson," he groaned. He looked up, confused as I leaned against him. "What are you doing?"

I shrugged, and suddenly my voice wouldn't work.

He relaxed with a small sigh. "You aren't actually alright with all this, are you? Kitty and Adanna?"

"No. I don't think I am."

He carefully put his arm around me. "Does this help?" I nodded. "Then I will stay as long as you need."

I woke to the smell of coffee.

"Good morning," Sherlock said as he brought me a cup.

"Hey," I yawned. "Anyone else up?"

"Ghost came down earlier and went right back up again. She took an apple with her, and I quote, 'just so Doc won't scold me.' She even made a production of taking a bite out of it."

I smiled, "Good. Kitty up?"

"She just finished with the shower."

"Probably used all the hot water," I grumbled into my coffee.

"It'll be good for you."

"Are you implying I take unreasonably long hot showers?" I joked.

"I would never imply such a thing," he said, perfectly deadpan before finishing, "I'm telling you that you take unreasonably long hot showers."

"You never said anything before!"

"It never came up, and you always look infinitely better both physically and psychologically, so there's no sense in stopping you."

I didn't know what to say to that, so I had two more sips of coffee before changing the subject. "Plan for the day?"

"If you're free this afternoon, I'd like to call on Mr. Cayne and put this business to rest."

"You know where he's staying?"

"Of course."

"Just us?"

"I'd rather keep Kitty out of potential harm's way."

"Good. Ok then," I stretched, standing up from the sofa, "breakfast, more coffee, mobster. Sounds like a fun day."

"A fairly typical day, at least."

Of course, our days often don't go according to plan.

Kitty and I were finishing breakfast while Sherlock lit his morning pipe.

"Mr. S!"

Kitty jumped, "The hell?"

Sherlock spoke into his hand's communicator, "Miss Wendy?"

"Car down the road. Man that got out matches the description. Incoming."

"Thank you. It would make me very happy if the four of you would be absolutely unseen."

"Don't have to tell us twice."

"Which four?" I asked as he exhaled a cloud of smoke before putting down his pipe.

"Wendy, John, Captain and Twist."

"What just happened?" Kitty asked.

"My lookouts," Sherlock explained. "Mr. Cayne is—" someone pounded on the door, "— here." Kitty stood and stepped back. "You will come to no harm while under this roof, Kitty." The calm conviction behind those words reassured her enough to sit back down. We watched him go to the door, radiating lethal confidence, despite his dressing gown.

He opened the door, blocking the entryway. "Drake Cayne, I presume."

I couldn't see him, but his voice was clear. "Good, you know who I am, you can tell me where Kitty is."

"It is unseasonably warm for May."

"What?"

"Hopefully June will not suffer for it."

"I know she's here," Cayne growled. "I will see her, and

you will not stop me."

"I most assuredly will," Sherlock stated quietly. "I will not permit a ruffian across this threshold. You will behave as a gentleman, *sir*, or you will find yourself back out on the street a great deal worse for wear than when you came inside."

"How dare you—"

"You have driven a woman half mad with fright thanks to your scare tactics. Taunting her from a distance," the disdain dripped from Sherlock's voice, "and ignoring her repeated attempts at contacting you to set things right? You have given no indication that you are any better than the common thugs your Italian associates would employ to shake down a rat."

The following silence stretched, unbearably tense.

At last it broke. "May I talk to her?" Cayne said, managing to hide most of his distaste under a layer of dignity.

Sherlock stepped to the side, and gestured that he enter.

Drake Cayne was as tall as Sherlock, with greying black hair, but while my friend is deceptively lean, Cayne was clearly muscular. The blue business suit was perfectly tailored, and ice blue eyes practically shone from his tanned face. He fixed his gaze on Kitty immediately. Kitty sat up straight, determined not to be intimidated. "Hello, Drake."

"Kitty."

"You want to tell me what the hell's going on?"

"I'm not in the mood for games."

"It isn't a game."

"I admit I let my temper get away with me, but don't expect me to listen to you mock me."

Kitty slowly stood, leaning forward on the table. "I don't

know what you're talking about. What could you possibly have to say to me about Adanna, years later?"

"She wasn't mine!" he finally shouted, "You lied, you were seeing another man—"

"You were the other man!" she shouted back. He stared at her. "I was married, Drake. I was married when we started dating. I got my divorce just a few weeks before we married. I didn't know I was already pregnant. I thought she was yours, and I never bothered to confirm it. I didn't know."

Cayne was just barely keeping his rage contained. If Sherlock and I hadn't been there, I'm certain he would have attacked her. "You've made a fool of me."

"How?" she demanded. "What possible significance could this have on your life? So she wasn't yours, so what? You still loved her! You still blamed me when she died, you still berated me constantly for every fault, and you still chased me across the world to what, get even? You opened old wounds, just because I hurt your pride? Go home, Drake."

He glared at her before quickly walking to the door. Sherlock held it open. Cayne paused in the doorway, just a moment, seething. He turned, and everything happened very fast.

"Down!" Sherlock shouted as the gun came from Cayne's sleeve. I tackled Kitty to the floor as he swung his arm up to aim, Sherlock intercepting and thrusting it up, the gun going off, the shatter of a lightbulb and a gasp of pain.

Drake Cayne fell to the floor. Sherlock looked down at the knife sticking out of the mobster's back and quickly scanned the street. He spoke into his communicator, "Was he alone?"

"Apart from the driver, yeah," Twist's voice confirmed.

"Where is the driver now?"

"Still in the car… wait. He just got out. Boss, he's got a gun."

I grabbed mine.

Wendy's voice came on over the comm, "He's scanning the street. I think he saw where the knife came from." Her voice shook, "He's looking for Jon."

I pressed up against the doorframe. I'd have to time it just right, and not miss.

Someone started whistling outside.

"Captain," Sherlock swore, but I didn't hesitate. The rash teen had distracted the driver. I took my shot. I didn't miss.

I carefully approached the body, and called back to the house, "Head shot. He's down."

Sherlock flew out of the door and across the street, headed straight for Captain. "What in the name of the devil were you thinking!"

Captain was startled, but defensive, "I saw Doc in the doorway, I knew he couldn't get a shot off without getting shot at, so I distracted the guy!"

"You put yourself directly in harm's way, what I specifically ordered you not to do!"

"You said be unseen, and we were, until we couldn't be anymore. Next time, I'll just let your boyfriend die."

"He's not— That's not the point!" Sherlock fumed, trying to regain his usual detachment and failing. The other three came out of hiding. "And you!" he gestured at Jon, "What do you have to say for yourself?"

Jon tried to look amused, but it was ruined by a shiver.

Sherlock deflated and put a reassuring hand on Jon's shoulder. "You acted swiftly, and likely saved if not my life, then that of Watts or Ms. Cortez. Thank you." He looked around at the rest of them, "Oh for heaven's sake, come inside, all of you. You've nearly given me a heart attack, but I'm proud of you, and immensely grateful." Sherlock even gave Captain a mock salute, which the teen returned with a grin. "And do not *ever* do anything so foolishly courageous again!" He nodded, satisfied, at their slightly penitent expressions.

"Have to get the dead body out of the doorway," Wendy pointed out.

"I'm half tempted to have Will sell it for parts," Sherlock grumbled as he stepped over it, "but I suppose I should inform Red."

Kitty slowly stood up from where I'd left her in the kitchen.

"You ok?" I hugged her.

"I'm fine, just shaken. I didn't think he'd try to kill me."

"He couldn't abide being humiliated," Sherlock said. "A misogynist serpent, all honey and false promises until you make him mad."

Kitty sighed, "He wasn't always like that... though I guess I didn't know him very well," she trailed off, noticing the Irregulars for the first time. "Sherlock. Don't tell me you use kids for lookouts."

"Very well, I won't," he said as he went to his room.

Kitty stared accusingly at me.

I held my hands up, "Hey, they were already on his

payroll before I moved in, and my reaction was the same as yours."

"They are invaluable," Sherlock said as he came past again, "as they proved today. I provide them with shelter, food, and money, and they act as scouts, spies, and lookouts."

"They're kids… what are you doing?"

Sherlock was kneeling by the body, handkerchief in his hand. "Removing Jon's fingerprints," he said as he wiped down the handle sticking out of the corpse's back. "It was an admirable throw," he commented, "perfectly aimed."

Jon sighed.

"That sounded disappointed," I said.

"He'll lose the knife if Mr. S calls Detective Red," Wendy explained.

"*Him?*" Kitty looked at me, aghast, "The teenager threw a knife and killed a man."

Jon shrugged.

"These four have been doing whatever they have to to survive for most of their lives," I said, "though this is the first time I've seen one kill someone."

Jon held up two fingers.

"This is the second one?" I asked.

He nodded. "First was to save my life," Wendy translated, "second to save Mr. S," Jon gestured to me and Kitty, "and you guys, too."

"I don't know how to feel about this," Kitty muttered.

"Welcome to Non-C," Twist smirked.

Sherlock did call Red, despite Captain's rather

imaginative ideas for how we could dispose of the bodies. He promised to replace Jon's knife, a small comfort to the silent Irregular. I made sure everyone's physical needs were met, told Jon he could talk if he needed (you know what I mean), and sent them back to the Hideout.

Red arrived with a clean-up crew. She listened to Sherlock's story wordlessly, perfectly neutral. "Make sure I've got this right," she said at the end, "Ms. Cortez here was being stalked by Mr. Cayne. Cayne tracked her here, when his driver stabbed him in the back, literally and figuratively. You spotted the man as he was headed back to the car. He pulled a gun to eliminate the witness, Watts shot him in the head."

Sherlock nodded once.

"Ok. Why'd the driver kill him?"

"Mr. Cayne had numerous connections to the Mafia. It was a hit."

"Proof?"

"None, but it is the likeliest scenario."

"Wouldn't get paid until after the job was done, so no need to worry about a paper trail," Red nodded. "No prints on the knife, so just your word for it. I'm not happy about it, but it'll do." She looked at Kitty. "How'd he track you here in the first place?"

"I don't know," Kitty said. "No one knew I was coming. I don't think I was followed."

We all looked at Sherlock.

Sherlock cleared his throat. "I've given the matter some thought."

"You don't know?" I was stunned.

He rolled his eyes. "I'm not omniscient."

"Despite appearances," Red scoffed.

"There is of course the obvious possibility," Sherlock continued, "and that is a tracking device of some sort."

"I haven't seen him in years, how could he hide a tracker on me?" Kitty asked.

"That is the primary problem with the theory, yes," Sherlock was irritated. "You're the cybernetics expert, Dr. Watts, surely you must have some sort of suggestion?"

"I'm not an expert in cybernetics," I crossed my arms, "I just know enough to... oh. Oh! Kitty, when did you last go to a doctor?"

She looked at me like I was crazy. "Years ago."

"Before you divorced Drake?"

"Probably," she shrugged.

Sherlock clapped his hands together, "Ha! Of course! Watts, I am impressed."

"You think a tracking chip was installed?" Red asked, skeptical.

"Makes sense, doesn't it?" I said. "This guy was jealous to a paranoid level, why not bribe the doctor or nurse to chip her? Wouldn't hurt more than getting a shot, and anytime he wanted to know where she was, he could track her. He'd still have to be within a certain range, but he could hire a runner to find her general geographic location."

Kitty grabbed my arm. "Fix it," she demanded.

I shrugged, "Sure, step into my office. All my supplies are in the bedroom."

"That ties it all up nicely," Red said. "Well, nice enough

for paperwork, anyway. And one day, Mr. Detective, you can tell me what really happened."

Sherlock just smiled.

Red and the clean-up crew left, leaving nothing but a slight stain on the carpet behind them. I removed Kitty's tracking chip and disposed of it immediately. With a sigh of relief, she started packing her things.

"Thanks for your help," she said.

"Anytime. Any idea what you're going to do now?"

"No, but I'll find something. I always do."

"If you need anything, you can call."

She smiled, "I appreciate that. Good luck with everything. I don't understand this life of yours, this world you live in, but you found a place that fits you."

"I guess I did." I followed her out.

"Leaving so soon?" Sherlock stood up from his chair.

She laughed a little, "I've intruded enough, and I'm anxious to get back to my side of the border. I'm very grateful to you, for everything." She shook his hand. "It was nice meeting you, Sherlock. Take care of Watts."

"My dear lady, he is typically the one taking care of me."

"Then you're in good hands."

"The best," he smiled. "If there is any way we can be of assistance in the future—"

"I'll let you know," she grinned. "Goodbye."

I walked her to the door and watched as she put her bag in the car. Once she drove away, I closed the door and turned to Sherlock. "Red took your story well."

"She wasn't particularly happy with the details, but it

was short notice," he slightly shrugged, sitting back down in his chair.

I sat on the sofa, "Thanks for this."

"For what?"

"Helping Kitty."

"I did the same I would for any client."

"I don't think you'd invite a regular client to stay the night."

"I didn't invite her, you did."

"But you approved… right?"

He smiled. "Yes. I rather like her."

I laughed. "You aren't anything alike!"

"You and I aren't particularly similar either."

"We're more alike than people think."

He half grinned. "We complement each other well, at the very least. Had you any plans for the day?"

"A few appointments later. Why?"

"I wondered if you might care to go out." I blinked, and laughed. My reaction puzzled him, "What is it?"

"Maybe I should just give up on telling people we aren't dating."

He thought about that for a moment. "Is a date an outing between two people with the purpose of getting to know each other and enjoy each other's company?"

"… essentially."

"Then I'd say we've been dating for years."

"Dating is usually romantic."

"Surely not initially?" He continued as if presenting the facts of a case, "First dates are hardly ever romantic, are they?

Romance doesn't come until after a solid foundation of friendship and mutual respect has been established. If rather than romance you are trying to argue that dating features sex, I counter that neither sex nor the pursuit of a relationship are necessary for the other."

"I… don't have an argument against that."

He smiled. "Excellent. I'll get dressed."

The Mayor's Letters

A slow stretch followed in Kitty's wake, which meant I was trying my best to keep Sherlock from becoming bored. Even though he was short on clients, I still had patients to tend to, which meant I came home every day hoping he managed to keep himself occupied without damaging the house, or himself.

Now that spring was securely here, the sicknesses of the winter were giving way to the more violent injuries common to the warmer months. It's a trend I've learned to live with. Still, no amount of expectation could have prepared me for seeing a man fried by his own cybernetics.

The victim's friend, who'd called me to the scene, described it as "he just burst into flames." By the time I got there he was long gone, and I doubt I, or anyone for that matter, could have helped if they'd been there sooner. When I asked why no one called an ambulance, the friend shrugged and said he couldn't afford it. An all too common answer in Non-C sector, and the reason rogue medics like myself can make a living, unfortunately.

Even an ambulance wouldn't have been much help, though. Without anything to smother the flame, the friend had just watched helplessly as the victim ignited and fell to the ground convulsing until he stopped. He'd called me immediately since I was the only 'doc' his family had ever worked with that didn't try to screw them over.

"I knew it would be too late by the time you got here.

Too late the moment he caught, I bet."

I nodded. He was taking this with the same nonchalance towards sudden and random death many people on this side of the Corporate border develop. "What do you want to do with the remains?"

"Practically cremated already. I'll let his dad know what happened, if you can tell me. I don't think 'burst into flame' is going to go over well. The man's not sentimental, I don't guess he'd much care about the body. Couldn't even sell it for parts like that."

I sighed, and knelt down. The clothing had burned off, leaving a clear view of the whitish brown third-degree burns across his skin. "Did you see anything before he burst into flame?"

"We were just walking, then I saw a flash out of the corner of my eye and heard a sound like a fire starting, turned my head, and there he was on the ground, spasming. Called you immediately."

"A flash?"

"He was covered in fire, man."

"But people don't just spontaneously combust." The victim had a cyberarm, with some swelling around the contact site. His legs were both flesh and blood, and the lower portions had only sustained second-degree burns. I pulled out my scalpel.

"What are you doing?"

"I need to see how deep the damage extends. If these burns were caused by the fire, then there shouldn't be any damage to the tissue underneath… but there is. The subdermal tissue is severely damaged, more than the surface burns warrant."

"Say what?"

"I'd put credits on this being an electrical burn. The flash you saw was an arc, which caused a flash burn which ignited his clothes."

"Well damn. But where'd the electricity come from?"

"That I don't know. Must have been a malfunction with his tech."

"Can that happen?"

"Maybe? I've never seen anything like this before, it's the best I can come up with."

"Yeah. Well, thanks, Doc, at least I've got something to tell his old man. What's the fee?"

I waved it aside, "No charge. Take care."

I headed back to Break Street. My path took me by the Crusader church, an area I hurried through as quickly as possible. I hadn't seen the place since before Sherlock faked his death. Apparently, they'd put up a new steeple in the year and a half since the last one was destroyed by one of Sangrave's cyborg monstrosities. They'd have loved the idea of a cybernetic frying its owner.

I put them out of my mind, and focused on getting home in one piece. The strains of a wailing violin greeted me as I approached my front door. Sherlock was bored.

"What about that tech leak?" I suggested as I put away my things. A new neuroprocessing chip had appeared on the street market, top notch quality, and very probably stolen from Desai Amalgamated Technologies' latest shipment to the City.

The violin paused long enough for Sherlock to scoff, "It is not my job to track down company leaks, even if they wanted to hire me, which they don't. A multinational corporation will make slightly less profit from our corner of the globe. Oh, the injustice."

"Ok then," I sat on the sofa, "how about spontaneous combustion?"

He made a face, "At this point I would even look into alligators in the sewer system if…" He stared at me, "Dear god, you're not joking." I told him about the man who'd burst into flames. Sherlock's brow knitted. "Do you really think it was a malfunction of his tech?"

"Can't think of what else it could be, can you?"

"No, though I may have to reevaluate my opinion on the possibility of sewer-dwelling reptiles…" his attention drifted to the window. "Speaking of reptiles."

A small black car had just pulled up. A man in black with a hat pulled low over his face hurried to our door, rushing inside as soon as I opened it. He was careful not to stand in front of the window and waited for me to close the door before removing the hat, revealing the face of a late-middle aged man, his blue eyes and fashionably greying dark hair instantly recognizable from campaign ads. On a more personal note, we had called on him once late at night, shortly after discovering his involvement with Miriam Sangrave.

"Mayor Artasin," I muttered a choice swear or two under my breath.

Sherlock returned his violin to its case and sat down in his chair. "What tragedy could possibly make you desperate enough to seek my aid?"

The Mayor acknowledged our disdain with downcast eyes, then went straight to business, meeting Sherlock's cold gaze. "Someone's trying to kill me."

"Mr. Mayor, I imagine a great many people have tried to kill you. It is an election year, after all."

The Mayor shook his head. "The battles are always between the parties backing the candidates. They can't directly attack a candidate, not physically, because then it's all too easy for the other side to call foul play and corruption—"

"An altogether hypocritical accusation."

The Mayor ignored him, "—and while death threats are common forms of intimidation, the ones I have recently received feel too genuine. And then there is the evidence of too many 'accidents' happening of late."

"What sort of threats?"

The Mayor pulled a slip of paper from his coat pocket. "Step down, or we will scatter your innards through the streets as carrion for the scavengers to prey upon."

"Certainly more poetic than the usual 'your time is up' rigmarole," Sherlock suppressed a yawn, "but hardly cause to come to me."

"This is not the only letter I've received. They all say the exact same thing, and they're numbered."

That caught Sherlock's attention. "Numbered?"

"The first one started at seven. The one I have just read is number four. They're counting down."

"An effective intimidation strategy."

"But what if it isn't simply intimidation? I've received

one of these a day. What if, after three more days, my time is up?"

Sherlock held out his hand for the slip of paper. "It is not remarkable in any way. No distinguishing mark, the letters are printed with a ballpoint pen, no fingerprints, not even a smudge… How was it delivered?"

"Taped to my window."

"Surely you have security measures?"

"The cameras show a dark figure by the window. No attempt at entry was made, so no further measures were triggered."

"I see. Each has been delivered the same way?"

"No. One was on my car, another at the office, they pop up randomly."

"But always where there is minimal security and when a passerby might go unnoticed."

"Yes."

"You mentioned accidents."

"I've had a close call each day I've received one of these. Objects falling, close calls in traffic, lots of little things that might be nothing. Even so, it's enough to make me jumpy."

"Mm. The next time you receive one of these, call me immediately. Do not move from the spot, do not move the note, do not let anyone trample all over the place." He jotted down our number on the back of the note and handed it to him.

The Mayor nodded. "See you tomorrow."

"At least it's something to do," I said after the Mayor was gone.

Sherlock chuckled. "Exactly. I believe the Mayor tends

towards paranoia, but at least finding the writer of those notes will be an entertaining challenge."

Who doesn't want to kill the Mayor, especially in an election year? The cops hate him for his corporate brown nosing, and Corporate Security hates him because he refused to expand their influence over the official police. His leading rival candidate and the crime family backing him would love to see him disappear. The man has managed to alienate a lot of people. The only reason he hasn't been taken out already is that he's got Mafia blood, and sometimes it's easier to live with an annoyance than taking out an entire hornet's nest.

That being said, everyone who wants him dead wouldn't bother with intimidation. We were looking for someone who didn't just want him dead, but wanted him to be scared, all the way to the end. Assuming whoever was responsible was sane in the first place.

We heard from the Mayor the next day. His latest threatening note had come from above, attached to the brick that fell from a building as he was driving past. It landed on his car and put a nasty dent in the hood. No one was seen, and the note was exactly the same as the others.

"They're able to intercept your movements because you have a predictable pattern," Sherlock said as he studied the note in the Mayor's office, "which is how these notes keep being delivered in such convenient fashions."

"Convenient?"

"For the delivery person, at least. And again, the note is without any distinguishing feature. I shall have to try another tactic. Have a pleasant day, Mayor, at least you can rest assured that there will be no further interruptions for you today."

We left him flustered, and went back to Break Street to summon the Irregulars. While Sherlock waited for them, I took instructions up to Ghost.

"You anyplace you shouldn't be?" I asked as I entered the attic room. She was lying on the loveseat with her feet over the end as usual, jacked into her cyberdeck. Her eyes flicked back and forth, reading invisible text.

"Just checking out the news," she sighed, "though I was planning on hitting a financial corp's mainframe later today, something with really amped up security."

I folded my arms, unimpressed. She smiled, still not looking at me. "Joking, Doc. It's a lazy day for me. I like to hang out and surf too, y'know."

"Well if it's not inconvenient," I grinned, "Sherlock would like you to do a check on the Mayor, see if there's been someone in particular he may have pissed off recently."

"Will do."

"Anything interesting in the news?"

"Not much local. Just DesAm moaning about their stolen tech."

"That's not surprising," I said and went downstairs. Aidan and Nadia were already there, waiting for the rest of the Irregulars. The white-haired pixie twins had been on watch duty today, so they'd been close at hand. The rest of the dozen trickled in from around the City shortly after. Sherlock assumed his usual position before the fireplace, the commander in front of the troops. The young, mismatched, smart-ass troops, two of whom were struggling to stay awake.

"Long night, Captain?" Sherlock asked the teen in the long naval officer's coat.

He shrugged. "Worked the club circuit. Took a while for a payoff."

Sherlock's gaze shifted to Muse, practically hiding under her tattered magenta coat. She also shrugged. "Long night."

He studied her for a moment and moved on. "The Mayor has been receiving threatening messages and wants me to find out where they came from."

"He wants you to help him?" Wendy, the leader, was skeptical.

Sherlock half-grinned. "That was rather my reaction as well, but—"

"It's a slow week," she finished for him, smiling.

He didn't comment. "As these notes have no feature to suggest any point of origin, I want you to shadow his movements and see if you can learn who is leaving these messages. Track them as far as you are able without unnecessary risk."

He assigned positions to everyone and dismissed them, quietly asking Muse to wait. Once everyone was gone, he walked up to where she waited by the door. "Are you alright?"

"Why?"

"You can barely keep awake. Captain maintains his night work picking pockets of club patrons, but you are not a night owl."

"Just a long night," she shifted, annoyed and uncomfortable. "Can I go?"

He frowned. "Muse, I only wanted to make sure—"

"I'm fine."

"You've lost weight, you haven't slept, your whole body is tense and you're breathing faster than usual, no, you are certainly not 'fine.' You do not have to do this job if you need time to settle matters at home." She looked away, tense and nonresponsive. Sherlock sighed, and spoke gently. "Your lives are your own, but I do worry about all of you. Please let me know if there is anything I can do to help."

Muse nodded and hurriedly wiped away a tear. Sherlock was stunned.

"What's happened?" I asked, "I've never seen any of you kids cry."

"My brother," she whimpered, and the floodgates opened. I got her back to the sofa where Sherlock joined us. Her brother had been on and off drugs of all sorts, but had managed to finally get clean and seemed to be making an effort to help Muse and her mom. The minimal job he managed to get wasn't doing much good, so he turned to dealing black market tech, and sampling some of what he was dealing. Muse and her mom didn't know what was going on until a piece of new tech malfunctioned, killing him. "We don't even know what it was that malfunctioned, we just saw the flash and—"

"You don't have to say more," Sherlock stopped her, sensing her hysteria, "Breathe, Muse."

She took a breath, and fell against him. He was surprised, but put a reassuring arm around her as he looked at me. I smiled and gestured that he was doing fine. His relationship with the Irregulars is more complicated than 'employer-employee,' but he'd never been a shoulder for one to literally cry on before.

Muse calmed down, and realized who was holding her. "Oh!" she sat up, wiping her tears and sniffling, "Sorry, Mr. S."

"Don't apologize," he gave her a handkerchief, "you have nothing to be sorry for. How is your mother taking all this?"

She shrugged. "Working. She cries a lot when she gets home."

"If either of you need anything, tell us," I said. She nodded, and I put a hand on her shoulder, "I mean it, Muse."

She nodded again, this time with a small grin. "I know, Doc. Thanks. I feel stupid sitting here crying."

"Sitting and crying is probably what you needed," I smiled.

"Yeah. I guess so," she stood, "Thanks again."

"Of course," Sherlock saw her to the door and was better prepared this time for the hug just before she left.

"Do you think it could be related?" I asked him.

"What?"

"Her brother's death. Do you think it could be related to that spontaneous combustion case I had yesterday?"

He cocked his head, "Do you?"

"I don't know. Just seems odd that I should hear about two tech malfunctions involving a flash and ending in death so close together."

"Coincidences have been known to happen," he said, but I'd got him thinking. "Watts," he said, slowly, "I think I may look into that technology shipment that went missing after all."

"Really? What about the Mayor?"

"His countdown won't end for another few days, and there's no further step we can take without more data anyway."

"DesAm won't let you in."

"They don't have to." He went upstairs. I heard him ask Ghost to find everything she could on the DesAm tech theft, and then he came down and grabbed his stick and hat. I grabbed my jacket and guns.

"Where are we going?"

He grinned. "We're going to see Will."

I sighed. Walking into Jackal territory was not my idea of a pleasant time, and I couldn't fathom how the scavenger gang could have been involved with the DesAm shipment.

"Have a little faith, Watts," Sherlock shot me a wry grin as he read my thoughts, "Who better to see when corpses are involved?"

Of course, we didn't just walk into Jackal territory. That would be silly. Sherlock *sauntered* in. He deliberately walked slowly, his stick clicking loudly with each pace on the asphalt. We didn't know exactly where, or how, to find Will, so the brilliant detective decided to just attract the attention of everyone.

I was less than thrilled. "Sherlock, you're going to get us killed."

"Why?"

"What if the Jackal who finds us isn't keen on taking us to Will?"

"I find that unlikely."

"What if it's a new recruit?"

That gave him a moment's pause. "Even so. I believe I could talk us out of any unpleasant confrontation. The last I talked to Michael, his brother was still the leader of the Jackals, and if Will is leader, then we should be left relatively unmolested."

"Should be. Relatively." He nodded once. I sighed. At least it was daylight. "Why didn't you ask Michael where Will is?"

"He doesn't know. Will keeps him as distant from the gang as he can."

We hadn't walked far when a man and a woman with jackal faces on their biceps approached us. The woman's left cyberarm was covered in translucent plastic and the man's right was dull chrome. She had a glowing green cyberoptic; he had a chrome left leg from the knee down.

"Good evening," Sherlock said, "I'm looking for Will."

"Who the hell are you?" said the man, but the woman rolled her eyes.

"That's Sherlock, moron. Will's brother works for him."

Sherlock placed a finger to the brim of his hat and bowed slightly to her. "You have the advantage of me, madam."

She shook her head, but at least it was with a grin. "You really are as crazy as they say. What do you want with Will?"

"His professional opinion."

She waited a moment for him to elaborate. When he didn't, she shrugged, "Follow us."

They took us to an old apartment building that looked like it had been evicted years ago. The inside had a lobby on the ground floor, filled with tables and stacks of collected tech. Standing by one of the tables, talking to another Jackal, was Will. Michael's older brother had the same cyberarm as before, covered in translucent orange plastic, but he'd acquired a new pair of eyes since we'd seen him last, irises glowing a mellow blue. To my relief, he gave us a wry grin as we walked inside.

"Well, now. What brings Mr. Detective down here?"

"Hello, Will," Sherlock answered as we approached, "I need some information."

"What sort, and how badly do you need it?"

"I've heard of a few cases of tech malfunctioning, with deadly results."

"More specifically?"

I cut in, "Have any of your people found bodies that look like they've suffered severe electrical burns, or possibly just any bodies that have been severely burned?"

"And if so, did they have the new DesAm chip installed?" Sherlock finished.

"You think the deaths are related to the chip?" Will asked.

"I think the deaths are caused by the chip," Sherlock said.

Will was surprised. So was I. "How?" he asked.

"How many bodies, Will?"

Will frowned, hesitating slightly. "About a dozen each day for three days."

"Where?"

"Scattered."

"Any pattern to their placement?"

"I don't know."

Sherlock produced something from his pocket and a pen. "Show me."

"What's that?"

"It's called a map."

"On paper?"

Sherlock opened it with a roll of his eyes and handed Will the pen. Will studied the map and made a few marks. "I can't remember all the locations. We don't usually worry about that sort of thing."

The woman who guided us before came over. "I found a couple here and here."

"There was one over here, too," said her companion.

"Do you remember when you found them?" Sherlock asked.

Their estimates were over the past few days. Sherlock frowned. "I need more data points. I need to know how many your people have found, and where and when."

"Is the chip dangerous?" Will asked.

"Yes. Have any of your people incorporated one?"

"As far as I know they've all been burnt out, nothing but scrap, but I'm not a hundred percent positive."

"Ask. Have everyone who has found one mark the time and place on this map. Bring it to me at Break Street when you've finished."

Will nodded. We were escorted out of Jackal territory and made our way back to Break Street.

"He didn't even try to bargain," I said.

Sherlock grinned. "His concern for his people came first."

"How'd you figure out the chips were causing the deaths?"

"I didn't."

"... pardon?"

"I needed a reason for him to help. I thought there was likely a connection between the sudden disappearance of a high-demand technology, its illegal sale on the street, and the multiple occurrences of unexplained technical malfunctions, but it was more of a hunch than anything else."

"You guessed."

He sighed, and muttered under his breath, "If you want to define it that way, yes."

I smiled. "So is it just bad tech?"

"We'll know for certain when Will returns my map."

Will sent one of his Jackals to us later that night. Sherlock immediately spread out the map on the kitchen table. It was covered in marks with dates and rough times noted by each one.

"The locations are completely random," Sherlock said, "which decreases the chance of these events being triggered remotely... I hope?"

I nodded, "Unless each chip can be individually triggered, or an army of saboteurs is walking around randomly zapping people. So, if the locations are random, then what? The chips go bad after a certain amount of time?"

"Yes." Sherlock nodded once, slowly. "I need to know more about that stolen shipment." I followed him upstairs. "Miss Ghost!"

"The mayor hasn't pissed off anyone in particular, not more than usual," she said without looking at us, "Doing a pretty good tightrope act. Election year and all. The DesAm theft was an inside job. The suspects all have alibis just convincing enough to keep anything from being pinned on them. Someone at the warehouse let someone else in and a crate was replaced. It's already turning up in used-tech shops."

"Damn, it's far too available now. You have to spread the word that the chips are not to be dealt with."

"What?"

"Every chip from that stolen shipment is malfunctioning, with fatal results. Not instantly, but after a period of a few days they become deadly."

"Hell. Ok, then, I'll spread some rumors. Solid proof to point to would help."

"Rumors will have to suffice for now. Hopefully…" Sherlock froze. "Miss Ghost, the suspects with just convincing enough alibis. Is there any indication they might belong to some sort of criminal organization? The theft is not a one-man job, and neither is the alteration of so many chips, and their distribution around the City."

"I'll see what I can find."

"It could still just be bad tech," I pointed out. "Something went wrong in manufacturing, and the thieves had bad luck. Besides, why would the Mafia or Yakuza or whoever else want to spread a fatal chip?" I asked.

"To spread panic and fear, as a demonstration of power. Or it could be an anarchy group bent on simple destruction. Even if the product itself is the result of a manufacturing flaw, the fact remains that the theft and distribution is too big for a handful of warehouse workers."

"So what's the plan?"

"We wait until we have information we can work with."

Reports of strange deaths made it into the news the next day. Hospitals were getting a sudden surge of mysterious electrocution victims, and no one knew what was causing it. There weren't quite enough cases to warrant a panic, yet, but there were enough to attract attention and make people worry.

Ghost's rumor of the chip being the cause started to gain traction, a rumor which DesAm firmly denied. Their denial was countered with a whole new branch of rumors, everything from DesAm hiding something, to the shipment being stolen and used by terrorists. We still didn't have a clue to who took the damn things in the first place.

Sherlock hates waiting. He decided to spend the day smoking and torturing his violin's strings, and by noon I was sick of it. "I'm going for a walk, want to come?"

The bow fell to the side as he scoffed from his armchair. "I'm not in the mood to be so easily distracted."

"Mr. S!"

Sherlock jumped at the sudden shout before he rolled his eyes and swore as he put down the violin. "Miss Jeneva," he scolded through the communicator in the back of his brass hand, "surely there is a subtler way of—"

"We found him!"

Sherlock blinked. "Him?"

"The ones after the Mayor! Twist and Yuki are tailing him right now."

Sherlock had obviously completely forgotten about the Mayor. "Ah. You said 'him?'"

"Looks like a man, at least," Jeni said. "Just saw him take

a shot at the Mayor while he was on lunch, then ran. Up on a roof, so not much chance of anyone catching him."

"As long as you can follow him, and safely. Do not put yourselves in any danger, do you understand? The Mayor is not worth it."

"No arguments from us. Let you know what we find?"

"Yes."

There was a bit of dead static and a click. Sherlock let his hand fall to his lap, a slight frown on his face. "That is far more direct than any of the attempts have been previously."

"Kind of hard to leave a note via bullet," I said.

"Doubtless one was left while the Mayor was distracted trying to protect himself. I'm sure we'll hear from him shortly."

The phone rang. I put it on speaker. The Mayor was... irritated.

"What the hell is the point of hiring you if I'm just going to be shot at! Are you even trying to find the people responsible?!"

"Honestly, Mayor. If you were in danger, you'd be dead," Sherlock was condescending, and bored. "I presume a note was left?"

"Yes, but—"

"Then they intentionally missed. You still have time."

"And how close are you to finding out who it was?" the Mayor demanded.

"I've had other matters to occupy me, but I believe I should have an answer for you soon."

"Other matters!"

"I'm not going to put my entire practice on hold simply

because you're being threatened. As it is, I'll find them before you're dead, don't worry. Of course, if you don't believe me, you could always resign." The Mayor growled a string of colorful and physically impossible expressions. "Do let me know if I can be of any assistance in the future, if you have one."

"Wait!" The Mayor shouted. "I'm sorry. Damn it, man, you try being shot at…" he realized who he was talking to, "I mean… oh, hell, you know what I mean."

"I do," Sherlock conceded. "I realize the stress you're under, but do be patient. You have time, and I have not completely forgotten about you." I smirked. "You'll hear from me." He hung up. "What I wouldn't give for a fresh bit of evidence," he muttered.

"At least we should hear from Twist and Yuki soon."

He half-grinned. "Still. It is mildly vexing to be unable to glean any sort of clue from a bit of… paper." His eyes went wide, "Good lord, have I been so blind?" He bolted up the attic stairs.

"What is it?" I followed.

"Paper, Watts! Real paper! The note from the Mayor wasn't synthetic, it was genuine!"

"And…?"

"And as you regularly remind me, paper isn't cheap. Who would bother obtaining the real thing, only to use it for a note to the Mayor? Such a dramatic detail would be wasted on him, he wouldn't notice the difference."

"So, the people responsible buy a lot of paper?"

"And who in the City would do such a thing?"

"Besides you?"

He rolled his eyes. "Ghost! Another assignment. I do apologize for the haphazard way I've been requesting your assistance."

She scoffed. "What else is new?"

"I need to see pictures of all the warehouse workers at the Desai Amalgamated warehouse the shipment was stolen from. Then I need you to get me the transaction reports of Waters & Mark."

"Who?"

"The sole company in the City that sells authentic paper."

"Oh. How long ago you want them?"

"The last month should suffice."

"… all transactions in the last month."

"Yes."

"Ok then. You gonna jack in to view this, or you want me to send it to the printer?"

He sighed. "I suppose it would be more efficient if I joined you."

"Extra cables are on the shelf by the cot."

He emerged from cyberspace grinning. "Any word from the Irregulars yet?" he asked as he came down the stairs.

"Jeni called. Apparently, you turned your comm off. She was kind of mopey about it."

He gestured I get to the point, "And what did she have to say?"

"Twist and Yuki tracked the guy to an apartment building, but that's not the important part. Twist said he was wearing a—"

"Red armband."

I frowned. "The Crusaders buy a lot of paper, don't they?"

"Indeed they do."

"The Crusaders are after the Mayor."

"Understandable, given his indirect involvement with the cyborg army that nearly destroyed them."

I shrugged, "So what are you going to do about it?"

His grin faded to contemplation, "What indeed. These are deep waters, Watts, this has to be handled carefully."

"The Mayor could just resign."

He made a dismissive gesture, scoffing, "I couldn't care less about him. The chips, Watts, the chips!"

I blinked. "I missed something."

"One of the warehouse workers is a new hire by the name of Joe Clark. He bears a striking resemblance to another man of our acquaintance, by the name of Gabriel."

I gaped at him. "No. No, Crusaders wouldn't mess with chips."

"Wouldn't they? I think Mr. Joshua Hall would find great poetic justice in a bit of technology destroying those who used it."

"But could they do it? Do they even have the numbers for this?"

"I doubt most of them even realize what they're doing. The Crusaders appeal to people across the social spectrum. All they need are a few recently unemployed members, ply them with food, a place to stay, fellowship, and promises of more to come."

"Hall's insane. If he really did all this just to kill tech users… wait, why is he shooting at the Mayor, too?"

Sherlock lit his pipe. "As I said, he has good cause to hate the man. And it is possible he was trying to distract me."

I stared at him. He was perfectly serious. "Even if this Joe Clark guy really is Gabriel, you're still saying the Crusaders managed to get one of their guys hired at DesAm just in time for a recalled shipment to come in. That seems a stretch."

"They had to have advance knowledge of the shipment. Someone told them it was coming, and likely pulled a few strings to see Gabriel hired."

"Who in their right mind would do that?"

"That is the essential question, and one which I have Miss Ghost investigating. For now, however, we must deal with the immediate threat of the damage these chips cause. Rumors haven't been enough to deter people from using them."

"Of course not, but if Ghost shared what you just found out—"

"Then the Crusaders would be branded as terrorists."

"Why is that a bad thing?"

"It wouldn't be, necessarily, but the backlash against them might."

I sighed. "The people who just want a meal and a place to stay."

"Exactly. The vast majority of the Crusaders are innocent in all this. It is the fundamentalist faction that must be eliminated. Unfortunately, the public at large have a very difficult time distinguishing shades of grey." He sighed, "At least the chips are destroyed in the malfunction. Once the batch is finished—"

"We can't just sit back and wait for hundreds of people to die! DesAm won't take responsibility, so the malfunctions will keep being unlucky coincidences until enough people have died to prove a pattern, or until someone famous tells people why they should stop."

Sherlock froze. "Ah."

"Oh god what did I say?"

"Hm?"

"You have that look on your face you get when you have a ridiculous idea."

"There's nothing ridiculous about it. I'm simply going to collect on a debt."

"From who?"

"Whom."

"You're so annoying."

"Yet you stay by my side," he smiled.

"Yeah, well, I might be crazy."

He laughed. "I'm going out. There's someone I have to see, and then I'm going to spend the night spying on the Crusaders."

"What? Why would you risk going there?"

"Hopefully I'll hear something, anything, regarding the Mayor or how they knew about the stolen chips. I'll do my best not to be killed."

The next day, I stopped home for lunch between appointments and found Sherlock in the kitchen smoking a cigarette in his dressing gown as he made tea. "Did you just wake up?"

"I had an unproductive night. Unfortunately, the fundamentalist faction keeps their activities closed off from the rest. However, it is worth noting that many more Crusaders are now uncomfortable with the knowledge that hunts still go on. A hunting party was apparently caught on camera and broadcast before they removed the camera from the owner's skull."

I went straight to my computer and checked the news. None of the mainstream sites had the video itself, but they all had a short blurb of a story. The independent blogs, on the other hand, had recorded the feed and had it up with a warning of "disturbing content." They weren't kidding.

"If that doesn't spark a panic about Crusaders, I don't know what will," I said.

"Indeed. I managed to spread the word about Fr. Lewis and Mr. Williams's new shelter, so hopefully Crusader numbers will drop dramatically."

"We just talked to them about starting the thing a few weeks ago, how fast could they possibly..." a headline on a media site caught my eye. "Sherlock! Get in here!"

He came in, curious. "Yes?"

"Is this your doing?" I started the news clip.

Aria Variel stood with a reporter in front of her corporate offices. Her ruby hair shone in the morning sun, her business suit perfectly form fitting. I was glad to see that the blackmail business a couple years ago hadn't come back to haunt her.

"Miss Variel, why this unprecedented and sudden support for such a new and small operation as the St. Jude City

Outreach?"

"Fr. Lewis and Mr. Williams are trying to make a difference in the City, providing a place where people who need help can get the help they need. A safe bed, a warm meal, and someone who treats you like a person, can make such a difference in a life. It was far past time a project like this was started."

"Then your support is keeping with Marova Unlimited's general mission statement, your claims to be a conscientious corporation?"

Aria laughed. "That, and it's just the right thing to do." She looked directly at the camera, a knowing smile on her face. "A Corporation is not by necessity evil. In fact, I hope to show the opposite is true."

Sherlock half grinned.

Aria continued, "Supporting this new charity is just one of many ways we can support our neighbors in Non-C, who, no one likes to admit, support us. How many people in suits do you think would be willing to work in warehouses, collect trash, fix the machines we rely on for manufacturing? The fact that so many companies rely on smoke and mirrors, doing anything they can to avoid blame instead of taking responsibility for their mistakes, is appalling and ultimately harmful to everyone."

"You sound like you have someone specific in mind."

"I think it takes a certain amount of willful ignorance not to connect the sudden surge in deaths due to a tech malfunction with the sudden availability of a new chip from Desai Amalgamated, a chip that wasn't supposed to be on the market yet. This was clearly a bad batch that should have been recalled and either wasn't, or some fell through the cracks due to sloppy oversight. DesAm refuses to admit this because they don't want to lose profits on the chips that are perfectly fine."

"That's a bold claim."

"You don't have to be Sherlock to figure this out, just use your head!"

Sherlock covered his laugh. "I didn't expect her to be quite so... vehement. What is the public's reaction so far?"

"Well liked, comments along the lines of DesAm rumors being true, what are they hiding, etc. Also, people saying she's a hypocrite, pretending to be nice for money. Most importantly, a couple other Corporations have taken her lead and called out the "harmful tech leak" as "concerning" and want more details from DesAm."

"Excellent. If popular opinion follows, DesAm will have to make a statement. I don't expect that statement to be true at all, but hopefully all of this will discourage more people from using the chips."

"Hopefully. Any word from the Mayor yet this morning?"

"Not yet, but I'm sure we'll have an irate phone call any minute now."

It was an hour later when the call came.

"Tomorrow!" the Mayor shouted, "Someone's going to try to kill me tomorrow, and you have no idea who or why!"

"On the contrary, Mayor. It will probably be a Crusader, and the reason why is that you encouraged a madwoman to wipe out their entire population."

Mayor Artasin was quiet for a few moments. "Ah. Well,

about time you had some information for me. I've asked Corporate Security to provide a few guards tomorrow, in addition to my usual bodyguards. I'll let Mr. Cole know his men should be on the lookout for Crusaders."

Sherlock was concerned. "Cole?"

"Thomas Cole, he's the current Chief of Security. He worked his way up fast, became Chief just a few months ago. I'll let him know what you found out. Hopefully, I survive tomorrow."

He hung up.

Sherlock bolted up the stairs to the attic. "Ghost!"

"Hey!" I chased after him, "What's going on?"

"That name! Joshua Hall buys the largest amount of paper in the City by far, but there was another name for a small purchase, just a few days before the threats to the Mayor started."

Thomas Cole, new Chief of Corporate Sector Security, had purchased some paper. Before he became Chief, he had been in charge of the Almandine Drive's security. We first met him on the stairs in the building where Jonas Wakeman had been shot by one of Sangrave's lackeys to keep him from talking to us about her cyborg army.

"How the devil did he get promoted to Chief?" Sherlock wondered aloud.

"Good at shifting blame," I muttered.

"His brother works at DesAm," Ghost said. "Runs the warehouse. He'd have known about the shipment."

"And told the Crusaders?" I asked.

"I thought the Mayor was the distraction, when all this

time the chips were meant to keep me from saving the Mayor," Sherlock said. "And now he's surrounded himself with Corporate Security, and I sincerely doubt he will be willing to dismiss them, especially as I just told him the threat was from the Crusaders."

"There has to be some way we can keep him safe," I said. "Don't you know anyone who'd be willing to help?"

He thought for a moment. "No, but we might be able to pay someone to help."

"You want to hire a mercenary to protect the Mayor," I stared at him.

"Want to? Of course not. Unfortunately, I can't think of any other option. We're out of time. Come on, Watts, we're paying a visit to Ms. Jann. If anyone can get us the person we need as fast as we need them, she can."

Ms. Jann was in the same place she'd been when we'd gone to her for information on Sangrave. Her corner table in the bar was just as shrouded in shadow, her amethyst hair creating an eerie effect around her unnaturally pitch-black skin and clothes. Sherlock had told me once that she was the ambassador between all the crime families that did business in the City. She was also a source of information if you could pay, and if you were one of the few people she liked dealing with. Apparently, Sherlock was one of those people. I have no idea why.

"How was being dead?" she asked as we sat down.

"Exhausting," Sherlock said.

"I bet. You started cutting into a little bit of my business."

"Are you certain it was me?"

"Who else would make Theo Foretti pay for information, that his partner was planning to trap him behind a wall, with a vintage bottle of authentic amontillado?"

Sherlock half grinned, "I'm here for a recommendation."

"On sherry?"

"On mercenaries. The Mayor is going to be attacked tomorrow, by Corporate Security. We need to stop it."

"Interesting. I imagine you want someone who can protect the Mayor, without anyone knowing they're there. Do you know how it'll be done?"

"No."

"High versatility, then. Freelancer that can handle any threat, on short notice. You'll want someone with zero pre-existing loyalties, too, and you're not the richest client." She leaned back and thought silently for a moment. A soft chuckle came from the shadow. "I thought of someone, but you won't like it. She's a cyborg."

Sherlock frowned. "Can she do the job?"

"She's more than capable." There was an odd humor in Jann's next words, "Only ever failed to finish an assignment once, and that was just because she got cocky. She's got a few chips loose, but she'll do the job to the best of her ability, which is considerable."

Sherlock nodded. "Fine. We don't have the luxury of time to be selective."

"I'll have her contact you immediately."

"Thank you."

I whispered to him as we left, "Why didn't I like the way

that conversation ended?"

He sighed. "I don't know what she has planned, but I'm certain it will be unpleasant."

"You think we've been set up?"

"No, that's what puzzles me. Ms. Jann delights in being mysterious, but she's never put me in direct danger without warning me before. Whoever she has in mind, they are everything she said... and yet..." He shook his head, "There's little point in worrying about it now. Let's head home."

The rest of the day was without incident. It wasn't until later that night that we finally heard from Ms. Jann's freelance mercenary. We'd been expecting a phone call. Instead, she arrived at our door.

Sherlock went to the security camera, and leaped back with a shout.

"What's wrong?" I jumped up from the sofa, alarmed. I'd never seen him react like that before.

Sherlock swallowed once, taking a deep breath. "I believe... Ms. Jann's cyborg connection has arrived."

"Ok..." I trailed off, waiting for an explanation for the panic.

Sherlock composed himself, setting his shoulders straight, his right hand clenched tight. He opened the door, revealing a slender cyborg just a touch shorter than him, completely chrome apart from three quarters of her feminine, and terribly familiar, face.

My hand went for a gun that wasn't there. "Jessie."

"Hey, little brother," she smiled, as if embarrassed to be seen. That didn't help.

"You're dead!"

"Your boyfriend's not the only one who can do that trick. Bullet destroyed the eye, second one triggered an emergency shutdown, but I rebooted after a while. Since I was dead, I was out of Sangrave's contract, so I just had to lay low. As soon as she died, I went back to freelancing. Single assignments these days, no more long-term contracts. Tired of taking orders." She noticed I hadn't relaxed. "I don't blame you for hating me, or trying to kill me for that matter. I was torturing your boyfriend after all," she turned to Sherlock, "but nothing personal. Strictly business."

"Stay away from him," I warned.

She smiled at me, slowly moving farther into the room, "You're adorable." Each step was nonchalantly cautious, as if the possibility of us suddenly attacking was an inconvenience she wanted to avoid. I suppose getting shot in the face hadn't been a pleasant experience. "Anyway, I'm here because apparently we've got a shared contact." She glanced around, the red of her right cyberoptic reflecting the lamplight. "That's a lot of books."

Sherlock closed the front door, harder than necessary. "If you would keep this visit 'strictly business' and as efficiently short as possible, we would both appreciate it."

"Sure. Jann says you need an extra guard for the Mayor, one no one can know about, and good enough to handle any threat. I'm your girl."

"And your cost?" Sherlock asked.

"You just cover any repairs I might need, plus a little maintenance, and we'll call it even. This is a one-day thing, after all. Consider it a family discount."

I bristled, my stomach knotting.

Sherlock didn't react. "All I know for certain is that the Mayor will be attacked sometime tomorrow, and that while the Crusaders will be blamed, the culprit will be Corporate Security. There are too many unknown variables for Watts and I to protect the Mayor ourselves, especially when he has surrounded himself with the very people who have been trying to kill him for a week."

"Alright. Not my usual style, but at least it's a challenge."

The chill of Sherlock's voice belied the smolder in his eyes. "I am well acquainted with your usual style."

Jessie smiled. "I'll be outside the Mayor's home at dawn. I'll keep in touch; the good doctor's phone number isn't exactly secret. I gotta say, I'm looking forward to seeing how you get anywhere near the Mayor with Security itching to toss you out." She left.

The tension in the room instantly lifted, both of us taking a breath. "You ok?" I asked.

Sherlock smirked, "She took my arm and would have tortured me to death in the street had you not shot her twice in the head, I am as 'ok' as can be expected. What about you?"

"I'm fine." I shrugged off his concerned frown, "I'm fine, just a little shaken up. She's not my sister anymore, and as soon as tomorrow is done I'll never have to deal with her again." I saw him wince as I went to the kitchen. "I'm not going to get drunk like when I thought I killed her. Just one to steady myself, and then bed."

He was quiet. "Good." I was about to close the bedroom door when he said, "Is there anything I can do?"

I managed what I hoped was a reassuring smile. "I'll be fine."

I closed the door and went to bed. I did not sleep well.

I opened my eyes with a shout, the dark of my room disorienting.

"It's alright," Sherlock's arms were around me, "you're safe."

I fell against him with a sigh of relief, tears on my face. "Damn it."

"Hell of a nightmare," he said softly.

I smiled, "At least I didn't try to kill my best friend."

"True, though you also don't have a weapon grafted to your body."

I laughed, a little. I was exhausted. "Did I say anything?"

"Incoherent shouts of despair, ending with a tortured 'no.'"

I shivered, pressing my face into his shoulder as if I could blot out the memory. "She was killing you again. This time I couldn't stop it."

His arms wrapped a little tighter. "Don't dwell on it. I'm here, and we're safe. Breathe, James."

I nodded and took a few deep breaths, my eyes already closing. I fell back into a dreamless sleep.

When I woke, it was against Sherlock's chest, his arm still around me.

"... Sherlock?"

"Good morning."

"Why are you in my bed?" I asked through a yawn.

"It helped when you stayed with me, so I thought I should return the favor."

I smiled "Thanks."

"You are amused."

"If we're going to be sharing each other's bed every time one of us has a nightmare, there's not going to be much point in separate rooms."

He chuckled, "I am well accustomed to my nightmares, company will rarely be necessary."

I stretched as I sat up, "I'll handle breakfast if you make coffee?"

"Agreed."

Breakfast was basic and the coffee was strong, which was just about perfect for the morning's mood. "I imagine we'll hear from the cyborg soon," Sherlock said as we sat down.

"You mean Jessie?"

"I refuse to be on a first name basis with the woman responsible for my arm, and I'd like to think as little on her relation to you as possible."

"Fair enough."

"Watts, if you ever want to talk about… anything, you can. I may not be much help, but I will listen."

I smiled a little, a bit uncomfortable, but pleased. "I know. I'm fine, really, but thanks."

An hour later, we were in a cafe across the street from City Hall. Sherlock had dressed us in business suits, streaked my hair with red and given himself a short beard. We slipped into the sector through a warehouse back entrance, gaining a number of bewildered looks from workers, but no one said anything.

"We're unexpected, but enough underhanded dealing goes on that no one will think too long on a pair of businessmen trying not to be seen," he explained as we calmly walked out into the street. He even tipped his hat to the guard.

"Your reliance on people not wanting trouble is going to land you straight into it," I muttered. He chuckled.

A bit of maneuvering around crowds kept us from encountering Corporate Security, and soon we were drinking coffee on Mayor Artasin's dime.

"Does the Mayor know you have his account information?" I asked.

"No, but it's the least he can do since I'm trying to save his life."

"You don't normally steal from clients."

"I also don't normally despise them."

"Good point."

Jessie had let us know the Mayor was planning on going to City Hall as usual today, rather than wait for an attack on his home. When I asked how she knew, her only answer was a sarcastic, "I'm really good at recon." So here we were, waiting for some sign of the Mayor, and the people who were going to kill him. My phone rang.

"Is that teen conveniently loitering on her phone on the corner one of yours?" Jessie asked.

I looked out the window. Wendy was leaning against a lamppost. "Yes."

"Your boyfriend would be upset if she got hurt."

"Very." I waited, but my phone was silent. Had she been checking to see if Wendy was a threat? "Why is Wendy here?" I asked.

Sherlock looked at me in alarm, and then out the window. He softly cursed. "Their refusal to follow instructions is becoming a liability."

"They want to help."

"As touching as that is, I'd rather not put them in even more danger than their association with me already... look."

The Mayor's car pulled up to City Hall. Mayor Artasin got out, his personal bodyguards flanking him, two Security guards coming down the steps to meet him.

There was a sudden crash and a startled scream, gunshots ringing out. Security chased after the shooter as the bodyguards got the Mayor back in the car.

Wendy was gone, the bodies of three men down on three different corners. Security had scrambled toward the one with an armband, clearly surprised to find him dead.

There was a small crater in the asphalt where Wendy had stood, as if something had fallen there. We rushed out of the cafe, hurrying down an alley and around the block.

"Wendy!" Sherlock shouted into his comm.

"I'm ok! I'm on a roof."

"A roof?!" He slid to a halt, and shifted direction. "Which one?"

"Uh... the third south from the corner I was on?"

"Are you safe?"

"Maybe? There's... she said her name's Jessie and she's

not going to hurt me but I'm kind of freaking out anyway."

We could hear Jessie laugh in the background.

"Stay calm, Wendy, we're on our way."

We reached the roof Wendy had described. Jessie and Wendy were sitting down, a distance from each other.

I smiled a little to see Sherlock restrain himself from rushing over, his relief clear. "Miss Wendy, what part of 'stay away from Corporate Sector' did you not understand?"

"You needed extra eyes, and you didn't tell us to stay away earlier!"

"Earlier was before the day there was to be a hit on the Mayor." He looked at Jessie as she stood up. "I take it you are the one responsible for her being on a roof."

"Couldn't risk her getting shot in the crossfire, and there were three shootists, so I covered her and took them all out. Here," she handed him three crushed slugs, "for the record, all three of them shot at me. No one was aiming for the Mayor."

"He was never in danger."

"But how lovely it would look for a kid to get killed in a terrorist attack."

A wave of conflicting emotions crossed Sherlock's face. "Thank you for saving her."

Jessie shrugged. "James said you'd be upset if she got hurt. Figured I could keep that from happening and still finish the job. Feel free to call next time you need a hand."

She gave a mock salute, and leaped across to the next building.

"She climbed up the building carrying me," Wendy shivered. "It was terrifying."

"I don't doubt it. Let's get you home."

"Mr. S? Was she the same one who ripped off your arm?"

"Yes."

"Why was she helping?"

"She's Dr. Watts's sister."

"... what?"

We got Wendy back to the Hideout, and turned on the news as soon as we got home. Mainstream media painted Corporate Security to be heroes, a single clip of chaotic gunfire edited to a view of a dead man with a red armband. The Mayor made a statement thanking Corporate Security for their efforts, and commenting that the Crusaders were becoming more of a threat to the City than ever before.

The very next news story was the DesAm theft. Desai Amalgamated was finally speaking up... and blaming the Crusaders.

The perky newscaster explained, "Desai Amalgamated has received a lot of criticism over the past few weeks for its silence on the matter of new chips that are suspected of malfunctioning, killing users. Now representatives of the company are speaking up, claiming that they recalled the batch immediately upon discovering its malfunction, with plenty of time for it to be returned before making it to its markets, but the batch was stolen and distributed independently. DesAm is further claiming that the Crusaders, known for their anti-tech message, infiltrated the company, stole the faulty chips, and distributed them as an act of terrorism."

"Turn it off," Sherlock said.

I took his hand. "You ok?"

"He played me." He sighed, "I can't do anything about it now, but it is a blow to my pride, nonetheless."

I smiled. "You aren't going to torture your violin or bury yourself in your chemistry set? Go out and discover everything you can about Chief Cole?"

He grinned a little, "No. I think I can restrain myself. However, we must keep an eye on Mr. Cole. His ambitions may be as simple as securing his Sector, making his job easier, or he could hope to one day run his side of the City under military rule, monopolizing resources and throwing the rest of the City to the buzzards."

"That's a cinematically specific theory."

Sherlock shrugged, "It's best to be prepared for the worst. For right now, all we can do is continue on as best we can."

"We always do."

Rescue from a Brothel

Immediately after the footage of Crusaders stealing the DesAm chips hit the Net, people went a little insane. The Corporate Sector became a hotbed of paranoia while Non-C residents were suddenly a lot less tolerant of the occasional red armband on the street. The Mayor, to his credit, made a speech about how important it was not to blame everyone in a group for the actions of a few people, and urged the public to stay calm. The police were on the lookout for Gabriel and the other Crusaders in the video, and even asked Sherlock if he could help. Sherlock told Red everything he knew about the Crusaders, but the church was empty, along with Joshua Hall's residence. Some Crusaders, appalled by the news (and possibly out of self-preservation) took over the church under new leadership, preaching a simpler anti-tech message that didn't include killing people. It didn't seem to help public opinion too much.

Even with the Crusaders split and DesAm taking heat for its botched shipment, Corporate Security pushed for stronger borders between sectors. The Mayor refused to instantly cave, but everyone knew it was just a matter of time. The strongest objections came from an unexpected source: Corporations. Plenty of them had dealings with Non-C, and saw restrictions on the border as an inconvenience that could cut profits, not to mention potential difficulties with black market dealings. However, even Corporations fell silent when they realized they were alienating customers.

Most Non-C residents didn't care one way or another; they had more important things to worry about than paranoid rich people. Some however, including Sherlock, saw this as an omen of further division, the money of the sector being entirely cut off from the rest of the city, ultimately leading to a failed economy in at least one, if not both, sectors. With Corporate Security randomly stopping people for 'proof of residency or employment,' we steered clear of the sector, focusing on our lives on the wrong side of the border.

One evening, I came home to find Sherlock practicing with his sword in front of the fireplace, his shirt tossed over the back of his armchair. I dropped off my stuff in my room and came out to lean on the back of the sofa, fascinated.

"Good evening, Watts."

"Hey. Do you mind me watching?"

"No." His movements became a little faster, a little more complex. "You've seen me fight before."

"In an actual battle. Hard to appreciate details when people are shooting at you." He half grinned at that. "Fencing?"

"Fencing, kenjitsu, various other forms of blade work."

I watched, entranced. His knowledge of historical and modern techniques created a bizarre dance in front of the fire. After a few minutes, he started to slow, bringing his routine to a close.

My attention drifted to the sea of lines decorating his wiry body. "How'd you get your scars?" I knew he didn't like to talk about it, but the question came anyway. I expected a vague answer, at best.

He surprised me. "Most of them came from my

instructor."

I stared at him. "Your instructor?"

"He used real blades, all the time."

"That's insane."

Sherlock shrugged slightly. "It wasn't as though I had many options."

"After the gash across your chest—"

"That one came from the skinning knife of a boy twice my size."

I blinked. "You were in a knife fight as a kid?"

"No, I was in a fist fight that ended when the other boy pulled a knife because I was beating him."

I grinned, "Somehow, that doesn't surprise me. What was the fight over?"

"He was bigger, and I was different. If there was any other reason, I don't remember it."

"Still, what the hell sort of teacher uses real blades with a novice?"

"He wasn't a teacher, he was a wanderer. I know nothing about him for certain, but I suspect he was at one time a professional killer. Blades were his specialty, though he also taught me how to use firearms." His voice was flat, but he flinched. I still don't know why he never uses a gun.

"You just took it and went home bleeding every day?"

"I bandaged myself up first, which is probably why so many of the cuts scarred."

My brow furrowed, "Wait, do your parents know you can fight?"

"In theory, though they haven't the slightest notion of

my skill."

"Why would you do that to yourself?"

"I was fascinated by the intricacies of the art, not to mention the man himself, though I never learned anything concrete about him. It became a form of catharsis."

Catharsis. "Why aren't there any scars on your face?"

"I didn't want to be burdened with having to constantly cover so distinguishing a mark as a facial scar. I begged my instructor that he not try to attack my face, at least not with his usual force. He found the reasons behind my request so humorous that he acquiesced."

"Bloody hell," I muttered. "What about the burns?"

That brought a tiny, self-deprecating grin to his face, "Not all of my early chemistry experiments went well, which taught me patience and the importance of the theory behind them, quickly."

I gestured to the wide splash across his left side, "That too?"

"No," his voice was quiet, eyes suddenly distant. He blinked and came back to himself. "That happened when my father, upset by my... obsession... and my plans to go to the City, interrupted an experiment. He had never taken my studies seriously, and was amazed when the beaker he splashed onto me in a fit of anger burned through my clothes, leaving a scar across my side and a part of my arm."

I had a sudden urge to leap over the sofa and hug him, just before I drove out to the Colony to break his father's jaw.

"An interesting array of expressions just crossed your face." He was watching me closely, curious.

I frowned. "I don't like the idea of you getting hurt."

"It happens often."

"It's your own fault now, not abuse from an immoral instructor or a negligent father."

He was surprised. Bemused, he sheathed his sword and returned it to its stand by the door. "It was several years ago."

I folded my arms, still upset. I may have been upset that he wasn't upset. "Just because it happened years ago doesn't make it ok."

There was a sort of tender confusion on his face for a moment. It vanished as Ghost came running down the stairs.

"You want to see this," she said, and ran back up. Sherlock grabbed his shirt and hurried after her, with me close behind. She thrust interface cables at us as we reached the attic and gestured to her gear on the table, "No monitor. Jack in, now."

We glanced at each other. This was unusual, even for Ghost. Her urgency was clear, and there had to be a good reason for it. With a heavy sigh from Sherlock, we jacked in and the world dissolved into grey static.

The static gave way to white. Ghost started to explain, "I found a message in one of Doc's emails, encoded in what I normally would have tossed as spam."

"You're going through my email?"

"Well, yeah. If you won't run a decent security program, someone needs to keep you from infecting your hard drive."

"You realize I'm not the computer illiterate one in this house?"

A figure blinked into existence, glitching between pixels

and picture until it solidified as a pretty young man of Asian descent. He was dressed in a simple blue skirt and tank top, dramatic eyeshadow and deep red lips.

"If you are watching this," he spoke, the image slightly out of sync with the sound, "then you have found a message for Sherlock. I cannot send a message directly, so I have hidden it within this email. If you are Sherlock, come to me tonight at 23:30. I will not look like this, and you should not look like yourself either."

He disappeared.

"That's where it ends," Ghost said.

"Where did the email come from?" Sherlock asked.

"Brothel. Part of a mass spam campaign to get new customers."

"He hid a message in a spam email, hoping it would get to us?" I asked.

"Must be pretty damn desperate."

"Why didn't he tell us where to meet him?"

"He didn't want to risk being identified," Sherlock said. "The image we saw likely is not his or her own, but a construction to protect their identity. As it was encoded in an email from a brothel, I think it safe to assume it's from one of the employees there."

"It's called Saboten," Ghost said, "Geisha-themed."

"I thought geisha were artisan entertainers, not prostitutes."

"Doesn't matter, just means the decor is vaguely Japanese and the avatars are any variation on Asian you want, from traditional geisha-types to modern anime girls. And guys."

"... avatar?"

Ghost sighed. "Yes, Sherlock. Your potential client works in a virtual brothel. Possibly one with ties to the Yakuza, though that's just rumor."

"Of course," Sherlock muttered.

"Would a flesh-and-blood brothel be better?"

"At least I could trust my senses. How can I be expected to read the tells of a person who is programmed to look like they're telling the truth?"

"Well, you can start with him." Ghost brought up the image of the young man again, this time with the sound muted. "We still don't know who he is or how to find him."

Sherlock was quiet. "Move closer, please." The image was magnified. "What are those small flowers on the skirt?"

"I'll look them up." Ghost ran an image search, "Either cherry blossoms or dogwood, it's hard to tell."

"Hm. Miss Ghost, I'm not going to understand what he's trying to tell us until I get inside Saboten."

"Ok. I'll design avatars for us."

"Us?" Sherlock asked as we jacked out.

"You aren't thinking of going in on your own," Ghost said.

"There is no reason for all three of us to go."

"No reason not to," I shrugged.

Sherlock half grinned. "I suppose you have a point. Very well, I leave the disguises up to you, Miss Ghost. Please, at least make them something with some dignity."

That night, we gathered in the attic. There were three

cyberdecks waiting for us.

"Everyone gets their own this time, but we'll be linked so we can interact with each other. I've pre-programmed the settings, should just be a plug in and go type of thing. We've got time for you to get used to it before the meeting."

Sherlock merely nodded and sat down in the chair as I joined Ghost on her loveseat. Once again, the jacks were plugged in and the world changed. This time, we found ourselves on the side of a street. Other people's avatars walked, ran, or flew by in a variety of forms, everyone unconscious of everyone else.

"We can see everyone going by because that's how the interface displays traffic, but we can't actually interact with anyone until we get on a site."

"Go in a building," Sherlock clarified.

Ghost smiled. "Exactly. So, what do you think?"

I laughed, "I think you've been watching too much old anime." She stuck her tongue out at me. I couldn't tell what I looked like, aside from the opera cloak, but she was in a grey one-piece outfit under a black trench coat and cropped purple hair.

Sherlock was examining his own appearance. "... Miss Ghost, am I wearing a tailcoat?"

"Maybe?"

"You dressed me as a Victorian era butler."

"Saboten's this way, boys," Ghost started moving. "Can't be late."

We followed Ghost to a nondescript building proclaiming "Saboten" in large calligraphy over the door. On the street it felt like watching a movie or playing a game. Inside, we were completely immersed in artificial reality. Sherlock stood stunned for a moment. Ghost led us to a quiet corner of the room. "You ok?" she asked.

He nodded. "This is much more realistic than I was expecting."

The room was done in stereotypical pseudo-Asian decor, complete with the smell of burning incense. The lighting was warm but kept a bit dim, encouraging intimacy even in the lobby in which we found ourselves. People stood and chatted, the employees clearly distinguished by a flower in their hair and a vibrant red collar around their neck. Off the lobby was a corridor that led to the private rooms.

"Private rooms can be reserved. If a client has an appointment, the employee will wait in the room for the client to enter, with the virtual reality scenario ready to go."

"How do you know so much about it?" Sherlock asked.

Ghost shrugged. "Research. This is the common room, where everyone chats and a record is kept to keep track of client interests for future reference and marketing."

"Madam, I have a distinct feeling I do not appreciate you as much as I should."

The realization all conversations were logged made me think very carefully about how I phrased my question. "Should we wait here for you while you keep your appointment?"

"If you like," Sherlock said, and disappeared into the corridor.

"Do you think that means yes?" Ghost asked.

I nodded. "Oh yeah. We'll hang out for a bit."

***

Sherlock stood in the corridor of doors, each one a different color. Many of them had softly glowing locks. It would be a locked door, that much was certain. The only distinguishing feature of the person in the message had been the blue outfit with the flowers, so he would look for a blue locked door.

Three doors were blue, each a slightly different shade. Two of them were locked. Fortunately, one was much darker than the other.

He wished he'd asked Ghost how to access the rooms. Hoping his hesitancy looked like that of a new client, he touched the lock, startled to feel a cool sensation of metal, and then clearly thought of dogwood blossoms.

The lock opened.

Sherlock stepped inside, into a log cabin with a blazing fireplace and every inch covered with some sort of animal's skin. Whoever had designed it had spent far too much time looking at the covers of twentieth century romance novels. The door vanished behind him. "Not a particularly helpful image, as far as gaining trust goes," he muttered.

"It can't be helped," a feminine voice said. "It creates the feeling of security. The knowledge that all actions within the room are completely secret."

"A pleasant lie, of course," Sherlock commented. "Do your clients even know the names of the dead animals they're lying on?"

"Probably not," an image of a young woman in a blue dress with the same dogwood pattern materialized before him.

This time she had pale skin and vibrant red hair, though her face wore the same makeup as before. "I know the striped one is zebra, but that's about it."

"Female this time?"

"It's not what I really look like. This meeting must look like an appointment. This is a commonly requested model. For a little while, there will be no record of our conversation."

"Then let's begin. Why did you contact me?"

"You came here with others."

"I wasn't about to attempt a foray into cyberspace to meet a mysterious stranger without backup, and you are wasting time."

"Sorry. I'm nervous. I need a distraction coordinated between the flesh and the Net and finally get free of this place."

Sherlock blinked. "I suggest you start again, a little further back."

"I started stripping to pay for college. That failed, debt piled up, and now I'm stuck in this virtual harem. I know a little bit about hacking, and I know just enough about how transactions work to have set up this fake appointment. There'll even be a fake payment to go with the fake client. I can show you how to get at the house's account to pay you—"

Sherlock held up a hand. "You went to all this great risk on the off chance that I might agree to help you get free?"

"You're the only one I could think of. The police can't help, and the other employees are useless."

"Are they in the same situation you're in?"

"Some of them. Most are too high to care much, when they aren't jacked in."

"Why aren't you scared?"

"I'm terrified. But I also can't do this anymore. I won't. You get me the diversion, I'll take care of cutting ties and disappearing."

Sherlock frowned. "I need as many details about your physical location as possible."

"2958 52nd Street. Office space and apartment complex. All the employees live onsite to guarantee we keep our appointments, and all the appointments are monitored by in-house security. There's a supervisor for each floor of the building and a couple of general security and a person who watches the monitors and tracks movements and whatnot. We're allowed out, but our movements are tracked."

"How do you plan to escape if you will be tracked?"

"I'll have to remove the chip when I get out."

"Never mind, I know someone who can take care of that. Can you send me a map of the building, with your quarters and security clearly indicated?"

She nodded rapidly. "I can do that."

Sherlock considered her a moment. It was terribly unsettling to view actual perfection, or some people's ideal of it, at least. As much as some of his richer clients strived to achieve it, simple physical interaction with the world invariably took its toll. There were always tells, a slight crease, a minute scar they probably didn't even realize existed, the way they held their eyes. The person before him — the projection of a person before him — may as well have been a blank slate.

"I am willing to help," Sherlock said, "but you must consider my point of view. I have made my career upon reading what people don't tell me upon their persons. I have no such ability with you here. To be blunt, how do I know your call for help is genuine, that you are not leading me into a trap?"

She blinked. "You think I'm trying to trick you?"

"No. I simply don't know." He permitted himself a small smile, "You may recall, I was framed for murder earlier this year. Forgive me if my suspicion is offensive, but I feel it to be justified."

She sighed, "Yeah, that makes sense." She thought for a moment, "I can't prove I am who I say I am, not now. But I can pay you. Not with money," she cut him off, "but information. Some of the major Corporate players are regular customers. I can send you transcripts of all their conversations while they're here. They like to use the private rooms for business meetings."

"Business meetings?"

"Whatever you just imagined, it's probably five times more extravagant."

Sherlock couldn't quite hide his disgust. "I see. That has potential, but it doesn't do much by way of gaining trust."

"I don't know what you want! I need to get out! Do whatever you have to, I'll give you all the information you ask for, just… get me out of here. Please."

"What's your real name?"

"Anthony Grant."

"You've lived in the City your whole life?"

"Yes."

Sherlock nodded once. "Very well. I believe that is everything I need for now. How will I contact you?"

"Make an appointment. Ask for Amanda."

The door reappeared.

"You could extend your time, but you'd have to pay of course."

Sherlock followed her lead. "Tempting. I'll call on you again."

"I look forward to it."

***

Sherlock reappeared with a flippant, "Details later," and left. We followed with typical protests, didn't see him on the street, and jacked out.

The instant we were out, Sherlock was up and lighting a cigarette. "Miss Ghost, I need to know everything about how Saboten is run. Where the employees stay, how transactions are handled, every last thing, but especially the identity of the worker Anthony Grant."

"Got it."

I hurried after Sherlock as he went back downstairs. "Can I ask something?"

"Of course."

"Why this case?" He stopped, waiting for me to explain. "I mean, a rescue is admirable and all, but what about all the other people in the same situation?"

"Does the fact that you cannot heal every sick person in the City keep you from treating the ones who seek you out?"

"No, but it's not usually your style. You help anyone you can, but there's also got to be an element of challenge. Besides the challenge of messing with Yakuza affiliates and escaping unharmed."

"History suggests 'unharmed' is far too generous an estimate," he half-grinned, "but I understand what you mean. There was no one else for him to turn to, so he came to me. I am the last resort, and as such, I will do the best I can. Besides, though there is little intrigue, the potential reward is enticing. I'll know more after Ghost makes her report." He pulled one of his scrapbooks from the shelf and sat at his desk.

I sighed and settled down for the wait, feeling a little like a third wheel. Fortunately, it didn't take too long for Ghost to track down Anthony's information.

"Anthony Grant, age 23, has been working for Saboten the past five years. Started as a part-time thing while he was enrolled in school, then suddenly enrollment stops and he's just barely paying off interest on student loans while working full time for Saboten."

"And now he wants out," Sherlock said from his chair. Ghost nodded as she perched on the arm of the sofa. "At least that much of his story is true. Any indication of previous affiliations with—"

"If you're asking if I saw any reason to think this guy has malicious intent, the answer is no."

Sherlock smirked. "Good. As for the other employee—"

"Whoa, boss, it's going to be hard enough getting one person out." Ghost ignored his frown, "Everyone who works at Saboten is an adult, and they're all under legally binding contracts. We're the ones committing a crime, technically. Something goes wrong, Saboten's owners could have our hides."

Sherlock huffed, frustrated, but nodded. "Very well. We

have a lot to plan for."

Three days later, a bored guard was watching the front door of the Saboten building. It was the dead of night; only three employees were awake, and they were all working the late shift, plugged into their stations upstairs. Down here on the ground floor, the guard was bored out of his mind... which might be why the sight of someone that looked a little like one of the employees walking straight toward him took him completely by surprise. "Tony? How the hell'd you get out past curfew?"

The dark-haired man in a blue skirt started in the opposite direction, not running, but as if he could just walk away. The guard sighed, and ran after him, grumbling the whole time. Just as they were outside the range of the security cameras, Anthony stopped and turned to face the guard.

The guard froze in surprise as he realized that the man in the blue skirt was not, in fact, Anthony. By then, it was too late. A couple swift strikes ensured the guard wouldn't be making any noise for a little while.

"You know," I commented as I came out of hiding, "that skirt doesn't do much for you, but I'm a fan of the eyeliner."

Sherlock rolled his eyes, "Now is not the time for sartorial commentary. Tell Ghost to disable the security system."

Once the cameras were paused, it was easy to sneak up to Anthony's floor. The map "Amanda" had provided told us which one was his. We headed straight for it, fully aware that our time was short. Anthony shared a room with two women and a man. Fortunately, everyone in the room was asleep.

I tried to wake him. "Anthony!" He stirred. "I work with Sherlock. It's time to go."

"Huh?" he looked at me, and then at Sherlock, confused.

Sherlock came over, "We haven't much time, Mr. Grant. You must rouse yourself and start moving if you want this rescue to be successful."

"Hey!" called a voice in the hall.

"Too late," Sherlock grabbed Anthony and hauled him to his feet. The other people sleeping stirred as we ran out the door and down the hall, a guard chasing close behind us. Sherlock suddenly halted, surprising the guard, and knocked him to the ground.

"He just roundhouse kicked a man while wearing a skirt," Anthony said, finally more alert.

"Yeah, he does that sometimes. Well, not in a skirt. First time I've seen that before."

"Turn right!" Sherlock ordered from behind. "Down the stairs!"

We turned right, right into a pair of guards coming up the stairs toward us.

"Hell," Sherlock and I said as they each drew a gun.

The lights went out. I shoved Anthony to the ground as a gunshot went off, the sounds of struggle on the stairs followed by the sound of something heavy falling down a series of steps and a cry of pain.

"Your sight, Watts?"

"Clear as day," I said, thermal imaging on, "Well, sort of. At least we won't run into any walls." I led everyone down the stairs, carefully avoiding the prone figures at the top and bottom. "Do you think Ghost hit the lights?"

"I set a timer on the power breaker," Anthony said.

"Mentioning that beforehand would have been helpful," Sherlock muttered.

"I wasn't sure what time it was. I was only going to pretend to sleep, but I drifted off. It takes me a while to wake up if I'm not jacked in."

We made it to the back door, and hurried down the street and around the block. We climbed through a window to a shop Ghost had disabled the security for. "I'm going to remove the tracking chip," I explained as we crouched down out of sight.

"They're going to find us here," Anthony whispered, harshly.

"No, they won't," Sherlock said, perfectly calm. "And if they do, they won't leave here again."

Anthony blinked, and looked at me. "He's kind of scary sometimes."

"Yep," I nodded as I got out my gear. "Wait, scary-scary, or scary-but-reassuring?"

"The second one? I think?"

Sherlock shushed us, and I focused on working quickly. I had nearly finished when they found us.

"In there!"

Sherlock silently moved to the door, his back to the wall. The first guard came in, leading with his gun. Sherlock disarmed him, and flipped him to the ground before kicking the other guard's gun from his hand. His blade extended. "I'd rather not kill either of you, but I will if you do not run."

At that moment their tracking monitor beeped. The signal from the chip had been lost.

"Well," one said, "looks like he ditched his chip."

"Easy for us to lose track, at night," the other nodded, and gestured toward his gun on the floor.

Sherlock gently kicked it to him. He slowly bent down to pick it up, and holstered it. This was repeated with the other guard, and together they left.

Anthony stared, disbelieving. "That's it?"

"One employee isn't worth losing their lives over if they can convincingly lie," Sherlock said. "Excellent timing, Watts."

I shrugged, "You know where to go from here, Anthony?"

Anthony nodded. "Thanks."

"Good luck."

We went our separate ways, Sherlock and I taking a public car a few blocks down the street. The ride home was quiet, both of us coming down off our respective adrenaline highs. As I pulled up to our front door, I said, "That went pretty well, but I'm kind of disappointed."

"Disappointed?"

"What are the chances I'm ever going to see you fight in a skirt again?"

He rolled his eyes, a small smile on his face, and got out. I followed him up the steps, "No, seriously. It was impressive."

"Thank you. I think." Once we were inside, he admitted, "I don't know if you're teasing me or being serious."

"Both?"

He sighed, and went to his room, "Sometimes you can be infuriating."

I smiled, and went to my room to get ready for bed. I glanced at my computer, and noticed an email. "Sherlock, look at this," I called.

"A moment!"

Once he was in his dressing gown, he came to look over my shoulder as I scrolled through the attached file. It was a transcript of online chats at Saboten over several months. Corporation representatives had been meeting with Yakuza reps in Saboten's "private" rooms for years. The file was attached to a short message; "Thank you. - Amanda."

Sherlock half grinned. "I told you the reward was enticing, did I not?"

Lights Out

Sherlock spent the next week going through all the new information in that file. It was difficult for him to tell who was who in the conversations because everyone used an alias, but the one fact that was clear was that Corporations weren't happy with the sudden enthusiasm of Corporate Sector Security. With Chief Cole pushing to become the literal law of the sector, Corporate heads were starting to envision doing business in a police state. I think Sherlock felt some satisfaction at seeing his own concerns about a Corporate Security takeover echoed, even if it was coming from Corporates.

It had been raining steadily all day. I sat on the sofa with the computer while he read over the notes he'd made from the file at his desk, reorganizing the information into his index. He would occasionally comment on a fact or two, using me as a sounding board as he tried to interpret the importance of each statement in every chat log. I was only half paying attention.

"One Corporate representative mentions a new contract from Corporate Security for genetically enhanced guard dogs, and trying to conduct business through the usual channels right under Security's nose… but I'm distracting you."

"No, it's fine," I tried not to smile.

"Mhm. What are you watching?"

"Chief Cole talking to a bunch of reporters."

"What?" He rushed over to join me on the sofa. "When was this recorded?"

"This afternoon."

Cole stood in the lobby of Corporate Sector Security Headquarters, a guard on either side of him. "Given the recent attempted assassination on the Mayor, it clearly is no longer efficient for Corporate Sector to be policed by two separate organizations. I will continue to petition the Mayor to grant full autonomy to Corporate Sector Security, and let the City Police be concerned with Non-C and the Outskirts. This will relieve some pressure on City Police, which I think we all agree is much needed among other things, while ensuring Corporate Sector's safety. The Corporate Sector needs a reliable force backed by the latest technologies, without worry of corruption or ineptitude, and without relying on independent private investigators with their own agendas to do the job."

Sherlock scoffed. I figured we'd heard enough and turned the computer off. "Well," I leaned against him with a sigh, "at least Chief Cole sticks to his tune, no matter what."

Sherlock laughed, "His bull-headed opinion based purely on heresy is not a trait I think one can consider positive, in any light."

I shrugged, "I tried."

"And you succeeded in eliciting a moment of humor from me instead of sheer annoyance at the man, for which I thank you," he smiled, just as the power went out.

"Weird. I didn't think the weather was that bad."

"It's not."

Ghost shouted from the top of the stairs. "Why the hell did my deck just switch to battery and what happened to the lights?"

"The power is out, Miss Ghost," Sherlock called back, "It's only temporary, I assure you."

Ghost swore, and from the sound of it tripped on her way back to her loveseat. She swore some more.

"A sailor could take lessons," Sherlock smirked.

The darkness lasted ten minutes, and then everything was back as suddenly as it had turned off. I switched on the news, figuring it would be the top story, and was not disappointed.

"The question on everyone's mind tonight is "who turned out the lights?" Dynamo Corporation has issued a statement concerning the massive blackout that left most of the City without power for ten minutes. Fortunately, emergency generators in hospitals functioned as they should, and there were only seven incidents due to blacked out traffic lights, resulting in only minor injuries.

The cause of the blackout was a failure of a central substation that was unable to compensate. Dynamo is citing mechanical malfunction as the likeliest cause. Some residents, however, are not convinced. Ninety-six percent of the Corporate Sector was affected by the blackout.

Chief Cole of Corporate Sector Security stated briefly, 'The possibility of sabotage should not be ignored. I hope they're right, that it was just mechanical, but to simply assume a coincidence seems foolish.'

To get some feedback from Dynamo, we have with us one of Dynamo's chief operating officers, Mr. Raul Kazo. Mr. Kazo, what do you think of Chief Cole's concerns?"

The camera turned to a man with golden eyes and silver

hair in a royal blue suit, emerald green tie vibrant against his shirt. I remembered him from a few years ago, when he came to Sherlock for help finding a missing statue of an elephant. He laughed a little, "I think it's admirable to see a security chief so worried about city infrastructure, but he also tends to err on the side of paranoia."

"Is it really paranoia, or just caution?"

Kazo didn't quite stop his scoff, but managed to smile. "Look. We know people are worried, especially these days. However, being scared of the dark isn't going to help anyone." He didn't let the reporter cut in, talking over him, "Since the public is now so concerned, we want to do our best to lay those concerns to rest. There will be an independent investigation into the cause. If there was any sabotage, we'll find it."

"Independent investigation, huh?" I smiled as the next segment started.

Sherlock half-grinned. Five minutes later, the phone rang.

"Mr. Kazo. I just saw your interview," Sherlock answered over the speaker. "Did Andrea pick that tie?"

"... yes."

"It's her favorite color."

"... how do you know what my wife's favorite color is?"

"Wife? Congratulations. She has a tattoo that glows green, and the first time I saw her she wore a matching dress, it wasn't too far of a leap to think she might be fond of the color. I presume you're calling to ask me to investigate the power outage?"

Kazo laughed a little, possibly wondering why he had

called a madman, "Yeah."

Sherlock was loving it. "Excellent. Where and when shall we meet you?"

"The scene of the crime, detective," Kazo drawled. "City Grid Control Center on 35th and Electric, asap."

Kazo stood in front of the massive grey block of a building with a man in a workman's uniform. He was scowling at whatever Kazo was telling him. Kazo saw us coming and waved.

"Gentlemen. Thank you for coming on such short notice."

"As you asked us to meet at the Control Center, I presume mechanical malfunction is not the sole cause of the blackout?" Sherlock said.

Kazo smiled a little, and gestured to the man next to him. "This is Mr. Wrasse, the man in charge during this... crisis."

"What happened, Mr. Wrasse?"

Mr. Wrasse frowned, and sighed. "What happened is that we've got too few people and an outdated system, sir. Late night shifts are run by a skeleton staff, and if someone doesn't come into work, it leaves a big hole in the schedule. The door doesn't always close completely on its own. There's a fault in the lock that we've logged before, but never had fixed, because we simply don't have time and the people who'd have to pay for it don't want to." He glared at Kazo as he said this.

Kazo was unfazed. "I already told you I'd take care of things. There's no reason for the state of this control center to be so desperate."

"I appreciate the words, sir, but I can't help but feel there's something of a disconnect between you and what actually happens down here on the ground."

"As much as I would love to listen to the critique of a system of corporate oversight," Sherlock interrupted, "I do have to ask what exactly went wrong?"

"I left the control room is what went wrong," Wrasse said. "I was the only one on duty at the time, and… well, sometimes you gotta go. Came back, the door was open, and all hell had broken loose. Someone had flipped all the wrong switches, like they'd just sat on the control board a few times."

"Security footage?"

Wrasse scowled.

Sherlock looked to Kazo for an explanation. Kazo sighed. "I'm afraid there isn't much of a mystery, after all. Come on in, take a look. See what you think."

The control center consisted of a main observation room with a couple offices adjacent. The observation room was filled with monitors displaying different portions of the City's electrical grid in real time, every red flash of trouble countered with a green flash from another portion of the map, the system's automation compensating for every hiccup. Wrasse led us into an office, and turned on the computer on the desk.

"Here's the security footage," he said, narrating as we watched. "Everything's normal. I leave the room. Something comes in the door… here."

A figure crawling on the ground came into view. It was moving fast, paused, turned, then moved toward the controls in front of the monitors. 'Figure' is the best description I can give for it, because it was indistinct. It was indistinct, because it was glowing green.

"What the hell?" I muttered.

We could only see a head and torso from the camera's angle, the legs out of view until it propped itself up on the front half of the controls, grabbed an object sitting next to it with its teeth, and dragged it across the control panel, triggering chaos.

"That object?" Sherlock asked.

"Lunchbox," Wrasse grumbled.

Sherlock half-grinned. We watched the animal, as it was now obvious the glowing thing was, run into a corner. Wrasse came back on-screen, hurried over to examine the controls and start trying to reset everything.

"Took me ten damn minutes," he grumbled again, "like rewiring an ecosystem that's had a hole shot through it."

"I'm not certain that metaphor made sense, but I understand your sentiment," Sherlock didn't laugh, but was clearly tempted to. He turned to Mr. Kazo. "Why am I here?"

"Once I got the full, accurate if somewhat embarrassing story from Mr. Wrasse, I realized I didn't need you, but thought you might want to find out who's breeding glowing dogs and setting them loose around town."

Sherlock studied the Corporate man carefully. "Are you doing me a favor, Mr. Kazo?" The way he said the word 'favor' suggested he thought it anything but.

"You helped me out once," Kazo's smile was dark, "and I really don't like Corporate Security's new Chief."

Sherlock frowned. "What makes you think this animal has any connection to Corporate Security?"

"It's got a BioTech lab collar. BioTech—"

"—has a contract with Corporate Security to create genetically modified watchdogs," Sherlock nodded, "of course."

Kazo paled. "How the hell do you know that?"

It was Sherlock's turn to smile, cold and calculating. "It is my business to know things others don't."

"… Right. Well. If you want to use the opportunity I'm handing to you on a platter, then we'll spin it however you want, as long as Dynamo doesn't suffer from it in the end. If not, then Dynamo claims mechanical malfunction, and no information about the dog comes out."

"It would be rather awkward to explain to shareholders how a dog managed to shut down nearly an entire sector of the City," Sherlock stated, deadpan.

"Precisely."

"Why bring me into this at all?"

"I told you, I didn't know the cause was a dog when I called you. I knew it sure as hell wasn't a mechanical malfunction, but Wrasse did a hell of a job covering his ass. No one knew what happened except him, and he wasn't telling until the minute before I saw you on the street. By then I figured it was too late. What were you going to do, just turn around and leave?"

"I would have expected an explanation," Sherlock acceded.

"And would 'never mind, a runaway dog did it' have satisfied you?"

"I may have wanted more details, but yes."

Kazo scoffed, "No, it wouldn't have."

"Mr. Kazo, do not make the mistake of assuming I think and act like you do. Your concern for reputation is touching when applied to your family, but utterly annoying when applied to your company. Dynamo can simply hope everyone will forget any rumor of sabotage, or you can tell the truth, that a faulty security measure let in a runaway Corporate Security dog. The public will have a laugh, and then move on. If you think for a moment that using me to blackmail Chief Cole into silence is an option, you are horribly mistaken."

Mr. Wrasse made an impressed sound. "Man's got standards," he muttered.

I smiled.

Kazo sighed. "Alright. We'll release the footage with a statement, I'll think of something clever."

"Where's the dog now?" I asked.

"In here," Wrasse said, walking to the other office door.

The dog dozing inside was a brown and white long haired lop-eared mutt. A muted blue-green glow could be seen through his fur. Its eyes opened a moment, its head jerked up to stare at us, short tail thumping once behind it.

"Why is it glowing?" Sherlock asked.

"Lots of biotech companies use bioluminescence to track genetic changes in organisms," I said. "He's a prototype for… whatever trait they were trying to isolate. Something didn't quite work right, obviously, since he shouldn't be glowing all the time."

"And the intensity has significantly faded."

"A stress trigger? Who knows."

"I'll let BioTech know we found their dog," Kazo said,

"and I'll give you gentlemen a ride home."

Kazo made his announcement through a press conference early the next morning.

"I want to take the opportunity to thank Corporate Security for alerting us to the hole in our own security measures. Control centers are designed with humans in mind; it never occurred to us that a dog might engage in sabotage."

The reporters laughed. The media brought it up a few times through the next hour, eventually managing to get a comment from one of the personal victims of Chief Cole's criticisms.

The picture shifted to a very tired looking Red outside Police Headquarters, obviously on her way into work and obviously severely under-caffeinated.

"Detective Murphy!" reporters chimed, "Do you have anything to say about the cause of the recent power outage?"

"The only thing I've got to say is that the police may have to ask for outside help now and then, but at least our dogs are well trained."

We could hear Ghost laughing from upstairs. She later informed us that Corporate Dog Training was now an Internet sensation. Cole couldn't be found for any sort of comment, by any media outlet.

"Well, if he wasn't angry before, he is now," I said as I got ready for my appointments.

"Mr. Cole will either keep his head down for a time, or attempt to lash back in anger as soon as he can string together a coherent sentence," Sherlock muttered as he filled his pipe. "I sincerely hope it's the former. I'm getting tired of listening to that man talk."

"Unfortunately, Corporate Sector hasn't gotten tired of him, yet." I slipped on my jacket over my pistols and grabbed my bag.

"Will you be long?"

"I'll be home in time for supper," I smirked. "Think you can find something to do all day?"

"Yes, I've an idea. There's a matter requiring my attention."

"Good," I said, amused at the intentional vagueness. "See you later."

I came home to a surprise.

"Sherlock. Why is that dog on our sofa?"

He glanced up from his book. "I'm sorry, Watts, I didn't even consider you might be allergic."

"I'm not."

"Good, neither is Miss Ghost, or any of the Irregulars for that matter." He went back to reading.

"Sherlock. What is that dog doing on our sofa?"

"Sleeping."

"Sherlock. *This* was the matter requiring your attention you mentioned before I left?"

He sighed and closed the book, a finger keeping his place. "Would you rather he be in a Corporate laboratory, the failed prototype taken apart and examined to see what went wrong?"

"… no. But why does he have to stay here?"

"Part of the time he'll be with the Irregulars. They're already working out a schedule."

"Of course they are."

"He responds to Toby."

"Of course he does," I sighed, and put away my things. I didn't really object to the dog staying, every now and then, I just wasn't thrilled by the idea of a pet in general. At least the Irregulars would be doing most of the work, hopefully, and a watchdog might be a good thing for the Hideout anyway.

I returned to the kitchen and started preparing supper. The dog's head instantly perked up. He stretched, leaped off the sofa and trotted over to sit down at the edge of the kitchen tile.

"If you think begging is going to get you anywhere, you're sorely mistaken," I said. "The pushover is sitting in the armchair." Sherlock unsuccessfully covered a sudden laugh. I looked back at him to glare, but couldn't stop from smiling when I saw him watching, a fond expression on his face. "Don't think I'm forgiving you for getting a pet without asking my opinion first."

An eyebrow rose. "I didn't think you would mind."

"That's not the point."

"Very well, I apologize. All domestic decisions will be made jointly from now on."

"Good."

Ghost came down, "What's cooking, Doc?"

"From the state of the fridge, breakfast for supper."

"That'll do."

"So glad you approve," I joked. I was secretly ecstatic she was taking an active interest in food.

She stuck her tongue out at me, and turned to Sherlock. "Cole's got something solid on you."

Sherlock cocked his head, confused. "He what?"

"He figured out that the Crusaders were part of the crew that took down Sangrave's people after you pushed her out a window," she explained. "He's claiming that if you, and the cops, worked with them back then…"

"Then I am secretly working with them now," Sherlock glared.

"And to top it off, there was an attack on the Corporate Security headquarters today. I mean, it was just a propaganda bomb, leaflets proclaiming Cole to be a liar flew everywhere, but—"

Sherlock leaped to his feet. "Show me," he ordered, and followed her up the stairs.

If my hands hadn't been covered in egg at exactly that point, I would have followed him. Instead, I cleaned off, contemplated how long I could afford to leave bacon on a pan without it burning, and decided he'd fill me in on the details as soon as he came down.

Someone knocked on the door, and the dog ran over to it and started barking.

"This is one reason I never wanted to own a dog," I muttered as I walked to the door. "Hush, Toby."

He positioned himself directly between me and the door, and growled at me. Then he turned back to the door and barked. I froze, the growl worrying me. I didn't think he was going to hurt me, per se, but something was definitely wrong. Toby started pushing against my legs, as if he wanted me to move backward. He leaped up, front paws on my chest when I didn't move.

"Whoa! Down, boy, what—?"

Sherlock screamed my name as he bolted down the stairs.

The bomb left in front of the door exploded.

"Sherlock?"

"You're safe, Watts. You're in an ambulance."

I opened my eyes all the way. He was by my left side in the cramped space, my hand in his. Whatever painkillers I was on, they were good. "Damn it. Toby?"

"Ghost is taking him to Maddie Murphy's veterinary clinic."

"… driving?"

"Captain was on watch, he can drive."

"Legally?"

"No, but he's perfectly capable. He warned me over the communicator that someone had left a package on the porch and ran. I tried to warn you, but it was too late."

"Damn dog saved my life, huh?"

"Very likely."

"Hell. Guess we'll have to keep him, then."

He smiled.

"Alright, that's enough talking now," a vaguely familiar voice said to my right. I turned my head and saw a woman with her strawberry hair in twisted braids smiling down at me. It had been over two years since I'd seen her last, in a bar after one of Sherlock's cases.

"… Kiera?"

"Hey, Watts," she smiled. "Fate's brought the ol' team back together again."

I groaned.

"Don't sound so thrilled!" she chuckled. "You rest now, we've got things well in hand. Oh, before you go back to sleep, tell your boyfriend to let me check him over, will you?"

"Sherlock."

"I'm not your boyfriend."

"We're not arguing semantics in an ambulance. Let Kiera make sure you aren't injured."

He sighed. "Very well. I take it you worked with Watts on the emergency medical team?"

"Sure did. Open your shirt please, I want to check your ribs. So, you aren't sleeping with him, then."

"No."

"But you seem really close."

"Is sex required for two people to become close?"

Keira shrugged, "Guess not, people don't have to be close to have sex so… whoa."

"Is that a response to my scars, or my physique?"

Kiera laughed, "Oh, I like you. Hold still."

The scene faded as I fell asleep, smiling.

I woke up in a hospital bed, Sherlock asleep in the chair next to me. The door slowly opened, a nurse peeking inside. He smiled, and gestured to whoever was behind him that they could come in.

Red softly laughed, "Evening."

"What's funny?"

"Nothing. Just relieved he's here instead of hunting someone down."

"If I knew who I should be hunting, I might have," Sherlock muttered, covering a yawn.

"Really?" I asked.

The slightest grin pulled at the corner of his mouth. "No," his voice was quiet as he took my hand. "After all, this time I knew for certain you would wake up."

I couldn't figure out what I wanted to say. Red saved me the trouble, and cleared her throat, "Maddie wanted me to tell you the dog's going to make it. He's beat up, going to need a lot of care for a month or so, but he's going to be ok."

Sherlock smiled. "Good. Give her our gratitude. What do we owe—"

"Shut up, she'll bill you for supplies if they need them. You two are weirdly friends of the family, so." Red shrugged, "Maddie will let you know when she needs something."

Sherlock's expression shifted, small tender surprise and pleased humility. "Tell her I expect to hear from her. I won't have debts between us."

Red chuckled, "Sure. So, any idea who wanted you dead?" Sherlock opened his mouth, and she cut him off, "I mean who would try to kill you by putting a bomb on your porch? And not a very big bomb either, all things considered. There's a big hole where the front door used to be, but the rest of the building was pretty much unharmed."

"Someone who didn't have time to see if I was home first."

"Security?" I asked.

"Possible, though until now Mr. Cole did not seem the sort capable of murder."

"Just framing and trying to utterly ruin you."

He half grinned, "There is a difference." He sighed, "Anyone I think of would want proof of my death, especially after my coming back from the dead. They wouldn't just drop off a bomb when I'm not home and hope for the best. Ever since the Crusaders disbanded, my street has been bereft of regular spies… ah."

"Crusaders," I said.

He nodded. "Joshua Hall's extremists, in particular."

"Hell."

Red swore. "Them again. But why now? You saved their tails from Sangrave."

"I'm still a demon, by their estimation. And I was involved in the case that saw them framed, even if I was not responsible. I also recently made some headway spreading the word about alternative welfare services and condemning their violent members, causing a slight dip in their numbers."

Red shook her head, "Still hardly justifies blowing up your front door. You were a lot more of a pain in their ass before you died, and they never attacked you at home."

"Maybe it's Cole after all," I said, "though I don't know what he hoped to achieve."

Sherlock sighed, frustrated. "There's no way to be certain who it was, yet."

"I'll see if we can get some officers to keep an eye on your place while repairs are happening, just in case they want to try again, whoever they are. You're both welcome to stay at my place until the work's done."

"Honestly, Red, you do enough for us as it is," Sherlock smiled, "and besides, I can't put you and your family in danger. If my unknown foe has resorted to explosives, then no place I stay will be without risk."

"You still need someplace to stay."

"I've thought of a possibility. Watts, the doctors have given permission for you leave, if you feel up to it."

"Hell yes, let's get out of here," I said, "I hate hospitals."

"I'll give you both a ride," Red grinned, "wherever you want to go."

None of us quite anticipated the number of reporters that would be waiting for us. Apparently, word of someone trying to blow up Sherlock's home had spread, as had the hospital we were staying at. I idly wondered if Kiera had told anyone, but decided it didn't matter. All it took was one orderly with a fondness for gossip.

"Sherlock!" voices called out from the mass of people, "Who attacked you? Do you think the recent attacks had anything to do with your criticism of Security? Do you have any response to Cole's accusations of your involvement with terrorists?"

Sherlock stopped to speak, giving Red and I a chance to slip to the car. "I will say this only once, so listen well. The Crusaders, as led by Joshua Hall, have always considered me to be a demon, and always will. Mr. Cole's assertion that I am currently facilitating their actions is nothing but a continuation of his classist paranoia. I do not know for certain who blew up my front door. I don't think I've raised Mr. Cole's ire quite enough for him to attempt murder, yet. It isn't the first time someone's tried to kill me, though it is the first they've struck so close to home. I will not run from a fight... but I must also consider the safety of those I care about. We are going someplace safe until our wounds are healed and our home repaired. I will remain in communication with the Police to keep abreast of the situation. Once things quiet down, we will return."

The press hounded him to the car, backing off as Red revved the engine. As soon as he was inside, we were off.

"Sounded like you're planning on leaving town," Red said.

"That was my idea, yes."

"You think that's necessary?" I asked.

"I can't risk you, Watts," he gripped my hand, "I won't. Besides, none of my bolt-holes are equipped for a comfortable recovery."

"Home to pack, and then the airport?" asked Red.

"No. Home to pack, yes, but I want it to be exceedingly difficult to find us, which really only leaves one option."

Red and I were both confused. "Where?" I asked.

"The Roaming Wolves happen to be in town. I may as well take advantage of them."

"Wait," Red said as I sighed, "your plan is to travel with Drifters?"

"I just need them to give us a ride. They're better equipped for off-road travel, and I doubt even you would be generous enough to take us all the way to the Colony."

"A Colony?"

Sherlock nodded, a bit of chagrined humor on his face. "It's the safest place I can think of. My mother will be shocked to see me, I'm sure."

From the Author

As always, I must thank my family and friends for their continued support and interest, but most of all I must thank you, dear reader, for taking a chance.

Katie Magnusson lives with her husband and son in Milwaukee, WI. Her short stories can be found in the anthologies *Sherlock Holmes: Adventures in the Realms of H.G. Wells*, *Holmes Away From Home: Adventures from the Great Hiatus*, *An Improbable Truth: The Paranormal Adventures of Sherlock Holmes*, and *Curious Incidents: More Improbable Adventures*. You can find her reblogging whatever strikes her fancy at kaelma.tumblr.com

Visit www.wattsandsherlock.com for bonus materials and news about upcoming books. You can also follow The Adventures of Watts and Sherlock on Facebook at facebook.com/WattsandSherlock

Made in the USA
Middletown, DE
09 April 2018